KINGDOM OF
SCABA

KINGDOM OF SCABA

M.K ALSULAIMANI

Order this book online at www.trafford.com
or email orders@trafford.com

Most Trafford titles are also available at major online book retailers.

Printed in the United States of America.

ISBN: 978-1-4907-2260-3 (sc)
ISBN: 978-1-4907-2262-7 (hc)
ISBN: 978-1-4907-2261-0 (e)

Library of Congress Control Number: 2013923681

Trafford rev. 12/29/2014

 www.trafford.com

North America & international
toll-free: 1 888 232 4444 (USA & Canada)
fax: 812 355 4082

CONTENTS

DEDICATION

"To my sons Jamal and Noah and to the Children
who are the hope for the future"

THE DREAM

For the last three nights, Lillian hadn't been able to stop a recurring dream. It was always the same: a group of people in formal eveningwear—long gowns and tuxes—were having fun, chatting, and laughing. The gathering looked familiar to her, but she was unable to recognize any of the people. They looked pale and bloodless, and their eyes were intensely yellow. She herself wasn't present in the dream. She couldn't see herself near the gathering but was able to see her twin brother, Jamal, who didn't look happy. Though he was giggling loudly, he looked panicked amid the gathering.

The attendees' clothes kept changing during the dream, but her brother's remained the same. He winked at her and nodded his head, telling her to run away; but she remained, immobilized and transfixed by the event. The music playing in the background was grim and scary. It started slowly and then accelerated. After a while, it returned to a slower pace.

Two of the partygoers approached Jamal and lifted him over their heads while still laughing. It looked as if they were playing with him, but he grew more panicked and started to laugh hysterically. He shouted at them to put him down, but they didn't. Lillian wanted to help him, but she wasn't there. She felt her existence but not her presence. She wanted to scream and order them to leave him alone, but she couldn't. Her voice, muted in her throat, could be heard only by her. It was shaky and supplicatory.

"Leave my brother alone. He's only ten years old. Please."

All the partygoers were watching what was happening to Jamal, but they looked indifferent to his plight. They even started to laugh joyfully. After a while, the two who had lifted Jamal threw him to the ground heavily, and a big thud was heard along with a painful scream.

Lillian woke up from her sleep with her small heart beating fast. She looked around her, breathless. Darkness was sweeping over the whole room. She turned the lights on as she tried to control her panic and was relieved to discover that it had been just a dream. She went back to sleep, leaving all lights lit.

The same thing happened to her twin brother, Jamal, that night, as it had the two nights before. He had had the same dream as his sister, with the same details. Only he was watching, and Lillian was the one who was lifted up and thrown on the stiff ground. He shouted at the two men who lifted her, but his voice was dumb and stuck in his throat, exactly the same as his sister in her dream. He heard only the echo of his voice telling the two men to leave his sister alone, and then he woke in a state that resembled Lillian's. He went back to sleep, leaving all lights on.

The next morning, all family members gathered for breakfast: Lillian, Jamal, and their father and mother. All were in a good mood, and it seemed as if Jamal and Lillian had recovered from the trauma of their dreams of the last three nights.

Their father hurried Lillian and Jamal to school. They all kissed their mother, who was standing at the door of the house to bid them farewell.

"You are my priciest pearls in this life," she told them after they expressed their love to her.

At school, Jamal used to boast that he was ten minutes older than his sister. Despite being disgruntled by this, Lillian grudgingly offered no retaliation because she knew how obstinate Jamal was and knew he would have gone too far in teasing her as usual.

Despite being twins, the two were extremely competitive with each other, whether in sports or in their schooling; but when united, they were an unbeatable team. They felt each other's joy and sorrow, even when they were apart.

In geography class, which they both liked, the teacher was explaining a point when the twins heard, although they were seated apart from each other, the voices of a group of people who reminded them of the dream they had had.

The voices whispered to them, "Come to the party."

A chill ran through their bodies, and they exchanged looks, asking if the other had heard the voice. They nodded their heads at one another, and their eyes widened out of fear.

After the end of the geography class, which had seemed to carry on forever, Jamal approached his sister and took her by the hand, leading her to where nobody could hear them.

He asked her, "Did you hear that?"

She replied, "Yes."

They wondered if the other students in the class heard what they had heard but thought it very unlikely. No one else had reacted the way they did. Jamal told Lillian about the dream he had had the previous three nights and discovered that she had had exactly the same dream. Lillian asked him, "Shall we tell Mom and Dad?"

Jamal shook his head and said, "No."

He explained to her that they wouldn't believe them and would, as usual, accuse them of having twins' illusions. Jamal embraced his sister and promised to protect her from the voices because, as he put it, he was the elder brother.

She looked angrily at him and said, "You are only ten minutes older than me, and I will tell Mom and Dad."

When they arrived at home, they saw a man talking to their mother in the doorway. They couldn't see who he was because his face was turned away from them, but he was a tall man with short hair, and on his neck was a tattoo composed of two straight lines tilted in the same direction. Jamal was curious to know what the symbol behind the tattoo meant, but he was even more curious to know who the man was. They got out of their dad's car and ran to the doorway. The man turned, and his eyes met with theirs. He seemed vaguely familiar to them, but they still couldn't recognize him. He acknowledged them with a nod of his head.

Lillian whispered to her brother, "What a weird guy!"

Their mother said to her husband, who arrived a little later than his kids and was busy shaking hands with the stranger, "This is our new neighbor."

She then said that he had come to tell her that he wanted to celebrate moving into the new house by throwing a party and was apologizing in advance for any noise the party may cause. Her husband appreciated the new neighbor's consideration, but Jamal and Lillian exchanged concerned looks and hurried upstairs where they sat down in Lillian's room to talk.

Jamal asked his sister, "Are you thinking what I'm thinking?"

Lillian replied hesitantly, "You mean the party?"

"Yes, the party and the new neighbor who looked strangely familiar."

They tried to recall if they had seen the neighbor before but failed to remember anything.

Lillian said firmly, "We should go to his party."

"What? You want us to sneak into our neighbor's party?"

"Yes, it is the only way to silence these voices and dreams."

Jamal looked at her. "So you think that this neighbor has something to do with our dreams and the voices that we heard?"

"We must discover that for ourselves, brother."

Jamal smiled and asked her sarcastically, "Remember what you said at school about telling Mom and Dad?"

Lillian felt teased and said, "Okay, I'll tell Mom and Dad."

She made to go, but Jamal grabbed her hand and said, "I was just kidding with you. Let's just do it without telling them."

They agreed to tiptoe out of their house at night and sneak into the party to investigate the matter for themselves in order to discover the secret of that party.

That afternoon, their mother took them to the equestrian club to ride horses, something they both enjoyed doing. Lillian raced her brother and managed to outrun him. He didn't like the idea of losing and nudged his horse to go faster. While racing, however, they both heard the voice again, saying, "Come to the party."

The horses bolted as if they had seen a ghost and started to run wildly. The kids tried to control the horses, but it was difficult. Jamal shouted at his sister, "Be careful, Lillian."

Their mother saw what was happening and sank with fear. She ran to help in any way possible. Jamal fell off the horse onto the ground but was not hurt. He stood up very quickly to see his sister still trying to control her violent horse by pulling firmly on the reins. She even succeeded in patting his neck, and after a short while, the horse cooled down. She was happy and said to him, "You are just a marvelous horse." She dismounted and ran to hug her mom, who asked them about what had happened. Jamal winked at his sister not to tell.

Their mother said angrily, "This must have happened because you raced each other." Jamal and Lillian exchanged looks, and Jamal whispered to his sister.

"It is the voices again," Lillian replied.

"The horses must have heard them this time."

"We must go to the party to understand what is going on."

 # THE PARTY

T hat night, Jamal and Lillian waited until their parents were deeply asleep and then tiptoed out of the house through the kitchen door that overlooked the backyard, which was closest to their new neighbor's house. They were in their pajamas, and no sooner had they left the kitchen than they heard the partygoers chatting and laughing. The two looked at each other, and Lillian whispered, "It is exactly the same as in the dream."

They weren't able to see the party because the walls were too high, so Jamal helped his sister climb it, and then he used her hand to pull himself up gracefully. They jumped down on the other side and hid themselves behind the beautiful bushes in the garden.

The voices became clearer, but they were unable to see any of the partiers. Nobody was there at all, but the voices and sounds were strong and clear, as if the attendees were all invisible. A chill of fear crept down their spines. They exchanged panicked looks, and all of a sudden, people popped up from nowhere in their elegant suits and dresses. Some of them were laughing, some were eating, and some were busy listening to music. It was the same funereal music that Jamal and Lillian had heard in their dreams. People appeared as if they had been there for a long time, and the twins' hearts started to beat very fast. Lillian wanted to say something.

"Jamal."

The moment she uttered that, all the people there looked directly at the source of the sound as if they saw or heard the troubled twins. Lillian zipped her mouth, and the people went back to what they were doing. The twins were too afraid to breathe for fear of being heard. After a while, the guests disappeared, but their voices remained. Jamal and Lillian were about to run back to the safety of their own home when their neighbor came out of the house and, walking slowly to the middle of the garden, welcomed his invisible guests.

The neighbor smiled at his guests as if he could see them, and at that moment, the guests appeared again. Jamal grabbed his sister tightly to calm her down, but his looks betrayed him this time. He was gazing at her lifelessly because of fear and perplexity. Both realized that they had put themselves into a fearful deadlock.

Suddenly the neighbor looked to where they were both hiding and said, "Come on out of your hiding place. We know you are there."

Lillian wept, and Jamal was unable to breathe. They started shaking with panic, and Jamal said to his sister in a shaky voice, "When I count to three, we run away."

Lillian nodded her head.

He counted, "One . . . two . . . three . . ."

They stood up to flee, but to their surprise, everybody appeared again. They surrounded the little twins, gazing at them with yellowish pale scary eyes. The twins couldn't withstand their fear, and both fainted instantly. The neighbor laughed while looking at them. He bent forward, patting them on their heads very slowly, and said, "These two will remain in the palace."

Then he rose while still looking at them and said to himself, "I feel that these two will be very special." He looked around, and then he nodded his head. The attendants carried the twins and stood in a queue behind the neighbor, who looked up at the sky and raised both his hands. Then he lowered his hands and bowed his head. When he did so, a whirlpool of mirrors suddenly came from underground and started to swivel in midair while rising, generating a current of strong air that shook the trees of the neighbor's garden. Suddenly, the wind stopped, and a high-rising wall of crystal clear mirrors formed immediately in front of the neighbor. He looked back and, with a gesture of his head, ordered the guests to follow him. The neighbor walked directly through the mirror wall. They all followed him, carrying Jamal and Lillian. A descending glass ladder then appeared at the other side of the mirror wall. The neighbor went down the ladder, followed by all the guests. Seconds later, the mirrors and the glass ladder disappeared.

The neighbor and the guests went up from another spot, which was a small hill. They threw Jamal and Lillian onto the grassy ground, waking the twins up to find themselves in another world, one that was unfamiliar to them. The grass was blue, and it felt like feathers. The sky above them was green and seemed very close to the hill. They felt as if they could touch it if they lifted their hands. The place was full of dwarf ponies no bigger than cats. They were beautiful, colorful, and fluffy; and they were galloping, neighing, and laughing in a way that resembled the laughter of human children. One of the small ponies approached Jamal and Lillian and asked what their names were. Before they replied, they heard a hoarse voice ordering them to stand up. They looked in the direction of the voice and almost fainted at the sight they beheld.

There was a scary creature standing among hundreds of other similar ones. They had human bodies and cobras' heads with three horns, two on each side and one on the top. They also had big ears and legs with tails attached to them. The two tails were spirals that moved continuously. Their eyes were pale yellow, and their noses had two nostrils that puffed smoke whenever they breathed. Their tongues poked in and out of their mouths like snakes, and they wore uniforms that looked like an army's. They were covered in wooden shields but carried no weapons.

The twins thought they were still dreaming a stupid dream that they would return to normal after a while; but when the creatures grabbed them fiercely and forced them to stand up, they realized that it wasn't a dream and that they were in a strange, unfamiliar, and fearful world. They noticed the presence of their neighbor among the creatures. He looked at them and smiled strangely. Then he told the creatures to take the twins to the king's palace. He then went down the hill. The twins looked down to see where he was going. He was walking quietly down the very steep hill as if he were tied to a rope. When he reached the bottom, he started walking on sands of a strange rainbow-colored desert. They also saw magnificent tents in the desert that looked like palaces. Orange elephants with cochleae trunks were standing in front of the tents. Their neighbor went into one of the big tents.

The kids were astonished by what they had seen. They were still standing near these scary creatures when a magic carpet came down from the sky bearing one of the creatures. He drove the carpet immediately in front of the kids. The carpet didn't touch the ground but was hovering at the level of the kids' knees. The carpet had pairs of holes in it. The scary creature shouted at them, "Come on. It's time to go."

The other creatures pushed them toward the carpet. The two kids didn't know how to ride the carpet, but the creatures told them to put their feet into the holes. When they did that, the carpet went up a little till it forced them to sit, and their feet went down into the holes of the carpet. The driver's seating area was higher than theirs, and the carpet gradually began to rise. The two kids hugged each other as they went up while their legs hung loosely in the air. The sky appeared to be farther away than they expected. The carpet continued to rise slowly, eventually coming to hover over the rainbow desert. The kids were very afraid of falling, but that didn't prevent them from watching a strange formation of amphitheaters that were being built within a huge construction site. It looked like preparation for a festival.

After that, they saw the strangest city imaginable. It was unlike anything they had heard or read about. The city was full of those scary creatures, along with others that looked less scary and fierce, but as big as other creatures. They had lion heads and human bodies with only one tail. Among that bizarre mixture of creatures were thousands of human children from different parts of the world, all of whom looked miserable, sad, and broken. Some of them were cleaning the streets, which were huge wooden logs that stretched horizontally. Other streets stretched up vertically between the buildings, reaching as high as the sky and ending above the clouds. Colorful elephants and zebras were the main means of transport in the city, certain of which were tagged with the word "taxi" on their backs and driven by children. Even the traffic controllers were children. Zebras and elephants moved horizontally on the horizontal roads and vertically on the vertical ones. Gravity didn't exist. The twins saw some of the half-lion, half-human creatures lying on beds carried by human children. They also noticed that each of these creatures was taken care of by a group of children who carried their heavy bags and cleaned their belongings for them. Jamal and Lillian exchanged looks of fear and confusion.

The buildings were very high, and their colors changed every second. Pictures of one of the creatures with the lion head were everywhere on the signboards, in different colors and costumes. In every picture, the creature had a different expression. Jamal couldn't fail to notice that the eyes of the creatures in the pictures followed them wherever they went. The two kids saw craters like those of volcanoes with holes and cavities on their sides. There were also winged animals that looked like striped tigers but bigger, which were puffing fire from their mouths into the volcanic holes to keep the fire blazing. These tigers were tied to each other with thick ropes that wouldn't let them move freely. Craters spread around the city, and the same thing happened with these animals on each of the craters. The twins saw some children dragging the corpse of one of these tigers under the command and presence of the fearful creatures.

The magic carpet started slowly to land in a piazza in the middle of the city surrounded on all sides by buildings. Their feet touched the ground softly, and then the carpet stopped and descended down their legs till it hit the ground.

The driver ordered them to move away from the carpet, and they obeyed without hesitation. The carpet then rose and disappeared while some of the creatures with snakeheads approached. Nearby, some boys were cleaning the piazza. Jamal was eager to get the attention of any of these children to ask them about the weird place, and one of the children, pretending he was mopping the area in order to get closer to them, came within whispering distance.

Jamal asked him in a low voice, "Where are we?"

The ten-year-old replied, "You are in the kingdom of Scaba."

"What is the kingdom of Scaba? And what are these creatures?" Lillian asked.

"The kingdom of Scaba is a kingdom that lies beneath the human world," the boy answered while mopping the ground.

"Under the ground?" Jamal and Lillian wondered simultaneously.

The boy nodded then added, "The fearful creatures are called the Makash, and they are dominant here. The other ones are called Shakam, and they are lazy creatures that rely on children to serve them."

"Are they going to eat us?" Jamal asked hurriedly.

The boy was about to reply when one of the guards pushed him forcefully and ordered him to go back to work. Then a big red elephant arrived with a boy sitting on its head. The elephant kneeled down in front of them, and the boy sitting on the elephant said, "Next station is the palace."

Guards ordered the two kids onto the elephant. The twins climbed on cautiously, and the elephant started to walk. The guards rode zebras as they escorted the elephant on his journey to the palace. The kids couldn't help noticing the strange mix of that peculiar world. Everybody seemed to know what they were supposed to do, and the children were running around, trying to satisfy the Shakams they served.

They tried to talk to the kid who was taking them to the palace, but he ignored them. They eventually arrived at a colossal palace on the outskirts of the city. The palace had hundreds of gates guarded by Makashans. The elephant stopped at one of these gates, following the orders of one of the guards. Two guards then came closer and started to look at the twins in an interrogative manner. One of the Makashans, who had come along with the kids, told the guards that they had only brought two kids that day.

Someone ordered the guards to open the gate. The elephant and the zebras went inside, where they had to pass through two more gates to reach the entrance of the palace. The two kids were ordered to climb down and were taken inside the palace through a long narrow corridor that looked endless. Other Makashans received the kids at the end of the corridor and took them into the white shining marble hall of the majestic palace. Pictures of the Shakam creature hung on the walls. They were then led to a bigger hall, in the center of which was the throne.

The ladder that led up to the throne was made of gold, and around it were two more majestic chairs. A woman of the Shakam was sitting on one of the two chairs. She was beautiful and wore a tall dress that changed colors every now and then. She smiled gracefully at them, and it was only at that point that their fear began to subside. One of the Makashans was sitting on the other chair. He was bigger than the others, with a hair-raising face, horrible muscles, and many different costumes. One of his hands grabbed a silver shaft. He frowned at them and pushed his tongue out, making a hissing sound like that of a snake. The twins were terrified anew and started to look around. It was at this point that they saw a huge picture of the same Shakam creature occupying the whole wall behind the throne.

Seconds later, the same Shakam creature, whose picture was everywhere, went inside the hall. He looked a little different from the other Shakams, Lillian thought. He wore a jeweled crown on his head, and a cobra rested and twisted on his right hand. All Shakam and Makash stood with respect for him, and they bowed their heads. He walked toward the throne without looking at the two scared children. He sat on the throne, and then the Makashan creature and the female Shakam sat. A child with fluffy hair came into the hall carrying tools for drawing and headed toward a corner in the hall where there was an incomplete drawing of the king and started working on it. Later, a musical band, composed of children, came forth, headed by a fat child with a saxophone. They took their positions in the hall, and the fat boy closed his eyes and started playing. His performance was so good that it made Jamal and Lillian forget where they were; and a short while later, the band started playing with him, following his lead.

Another group of children came forth, led by a nine-year-old girl. These started dancing, following the musical rhythms with their bodies. The little girl's dancing amazed the twins.

The king and his company enjoyed this. After that, the dancers went out, and three children in clown costumes came into the hall and started to act out funny scenes for the king and his retinue. The twins couldn't help themselves from laughing; it seemed to them that everyone was the best in what they were doing.

The king ordered the clowns and the musical band out and, looking at the twins, asked the Makashan, "Are these two the only catch of today?"

"Yes, Your Majesty," the Makashan commander answered shyly and hesitantly.

"They are enough for this year, Your Majesty," the female Shakam said.

The king said angrily, "It is me who decides what enough is." The snake also got angry and started hissing and looking at the princess.

The princess said firmly, "You know, Your Majesty, that I am against bringing children to serve us."

The king got angrier and replied, "Never put yourself into that, Princess Filda, and never make me angry. Leave now!"

Princess Filda frowned and went out. The Makashan commander asked the king, "Why don't we put her in jail, Your Majesty?"

The king committed himself to silence for a few seconds, and then he ordered the child artist to go out.

"She even sympathizes with the runaways, Your Majesty," the commander said. The king remained silent but frowned at the words of the commander. Then he ordered that the two kids be sent out of the hall and said to the commander, "Never discuss our internal matters in front of human children."

The commander bowed in humility, and then the king explained to him that he would keep her to one day use as a bargaining chip in return of the runaways.

"She doesn't know that, and she thinks that I take care for her because I promised her father that I would do so. She knows also that, if she worked against me, I would deprive her of her only child, Dashan."

The commander collected what was left of his boldness and said, "But, Your Majesty, you promised that we would get rid of all Shakams."

The king looked at him while rubbing the head of his snake and said, "I will keep my promise, but we have to get rid of the runaway mutineers outside the borders of the crystal ball first."

The commander told the king that he had sent another reconnaissance team that contained the most powerful knights, which was by all means better than the first team that failed to capture the runaways. But the king was nonchalant and mocked the new team, saying that nobody could capture the convicts except himself.

"The king had to do everything in Scaba," he said.

The commander praised the king and affirmed the idea by saying that he was the king that all Makashans and Shakams were subdued to.

The king looked at him unbelievingly and said, "Solar told me that these two kids are special."

The commander said, "So they are the ones that we need. It is difficult to find humans who are gifted in more than one way."

The king agreed and said, almost as if in soliloquy, "Humans, perhaps, aren't gifted at all."

The commander couldn't hear him properly. "Pardon, Your Majesty, I didn't hear what you said." "They will replace the adolescent and the fat boy in grand contests."

The commander agreed and told the king that he was wondering how Kameel was getting fatter when he wasn't eating more than the other kids and how he had changed from an active boy into a lazy one.

"It is the genes, General Falca. Humans vary in height, weight, and inclination to fatness or slimness," the king replied. He then told the general to prepare the palace team for the grand contests and explained, "I want the upcoming contests to be bloodier and more violent than ever. I enjoy watching these children hurting each other."

"Sure, Your Majesty, everything will be as you wish," the general said, bowing to the king.

The twins were taken to a small room in one of the palace's corners and told to stand in front of a strange camera. Pictures were taken of each of them, and then they were taken to a huge dining hall in which there were hundreds of children eating their lunch. The children all wore the same uniform, with the girls in red and the boys in orange, but the twins were still in their pajamas.

One of the kids told the perplexed twins to go ahead and take food. The cooks were all children wearing blue uniforms. Jamal and Lillian took their plates to fill them with food, and the cooks glared at them in a hostile and uncompromising way. They ordered Jamal and Lillian to select their food as quickly as possible.

When the two had done so, they started looking for a place to sit. All the other children in the big hall were gazing at them. They saw the children of the musical band who played in front of the king, and when they got nearer to sit next to them, the children told them not to. They were also able to recognize the young dancers and tried to sit next to them but were warded off. Then the clowns, teasingly, drove them back. After that, they noticed some unoccupied chairs next to an adolescent who was sitting in the middle of a group of younger children. Jamal and Lillian were about to head for the chairs when a nine-year-old girl, the leader of the dancing team, told them not to. They felt embarrassed, disappointed, and desperate, not knowing where to sit; but the same girl laughed and told them to come back and sit.

They said hello to other children and sat down. All other children welcomed them except the adolescent, who looked deeply depressed. The girl smiled at them and introduced herself, "My name is Samar, and this is Kameel."

Kameel was the leader of the musical band. He was the fat boy sitting next to them. He barely lifted his head and welcomed them sluggishly. Then she pointed at another boy sitting on the opposite side of the table and said, "And this is Shaun." Shaun waved his hand happily and welcomed them by saying, "You are most welcome here. You will be very pleased here, as we have many activities to do."

"Yes, like mopping and cleaning the toilet. That's your favorite, Shaun, isn't it?" Samar interrupted.

"Yes, there is lots of water to play with," Shaun replied happily, as usual.

The twins were baffled by what they heard but preferred to remain silent. Samar pointed at the adolescent boy and said, "That's Dany. He is sad because after a month he will be sent back to the human world."

Then she told them about the others who were divided according to their talents. The ones who were good at dancing joined the dancing group, and the ones who were good at playing music joined the musical band, and she added that she and the other boys sitting at the table had come to the kingdom of Scaba on the same day.

Jamal introduced himself and his sister by saying, "I am Jamal, and this is my sister, Lillian."

Shaun asked Jamal about his age, and Jamal replied that he was ten. Samar asked Lillian, "What about you, Lillian? How old are you?"

"I am ten years old too."

At that point, Jamal interrupted her by saying, "But I am ten minutes older."

"How come you are both ten years old? Who is your mother? Are you stepsiblings?" Shaun inquired.

Samar laughed and said, "Obviously they are twins, stupid!"

"But how could it be that they are twins when they are a boy and a girl?" Shaun asked again.

"There are different types of twins: a boy and a boy, a boy and a girl, a girl and a girl," Lillian explained.

Shaun focused, trying to figure that out. Eventually, he opened his mouth, saying, "Aha!"

Samar asked Lillian to ignore Shaun because he needed more than a single day to understand that. All laughed happily, except the adolescent boy, Kameel, who laughed lazily as if forced to do so. The child artist approached the table and was introduced to Jamal and Lillian. "This is Wang, the artist."

Wang welcomed them and said, "It seems that King Bermuda isn't in a good mood today."

Then he told them what had happened to him at the royal hall, when the king ordered him to be dismissed after Princess Filda had objected to bringing more human children to the kingdom.

"They ordered me out even before the king saw what I had drawn, as he used to."

"We heard that hateful Makashan saying that the princess sympathizes with the runaways. Are there any runaway children?" Lillian enquired.

"I wish it were so, but nobody can escape from this unbearable place. It is inescapable," the adolescent boy explained.

"But you are sad, I hear, because they are taking you back into the human world?" Jamal asked.

Some tears gushed out of the boy's eyes, and he hastily left the hall. Lillian looked angrily at Jamal, blaming him for hurting his feelings. Jamal looked around, searching for anyone to relieve him of the blame. Shaun explained to him that Dany didn't want to go back home because his parents didn't want him anymore. But Samar interrupted him, saying, "No, idiot, it is not like that."

Wang explained that children who came to kingdom of Scaba wouldn't be allowed to stay when they were eighteen years old. Lillian asked curiously, "But why?"

Samar said that nobody knew the reason, but whoever went back to earthly life wouldn't remain sane and wouldn't recognize his past life before Scaba, and the creatures would leave them in deserted mountainous areas, and the chances of finding and saving them would be almost nothing.

Shaun said, "Aha, now I got it."

Lillian expressed her deep sympathy with Dany and asked if there was any way to help, but they all agreed that nothing could be done. Jamal thought for a while and said that there had to be something to help them all get out of that dreadful place.

Kameel looked at him slowly and asked him not to try anything like that because the consequences would be horrible. He said that he had been there in Scaba for three years, and some other children had been there five or ten years, like Dany, but could change nothing. Then he added, "Never try to be a hero here."

The smile vanished off Samar's lips. She looked at Jamal and said, "We are just helpless kids."

Lillian said persistently, "Who are the escapees, then?"

"The runaways are . . . ah, there are no runaway children here. We told you that," Shaun explained.

Kameel shook his head pathetically and said, "The runaways are the aids of the former king, Princess Filda's father." Then he went on, explaining to them that those runaways, who were all from the Shakam, objected to the way the new king ruled the kingdom and ran away to outside the borders of the crystal ball and that nobody knew where they were. He also told them that the runaways demolished whatever King Bermuda had built outside the borders of the crystal ball, thus disabling him from expanding the borders of kingdom of Scaba.

Thousands of questions lingered in Jamal's and Lillian's minds, demanding answers. This new world was pregnant with secrets. It looked dreadful but in a strange way also beautiful at the same time—marvelous buildings, majestic palaces, dreadful creatures, enslaved and exhausted children. Outside the palace, children wore the same uniform, as if belonging to a certain school or party. Boys wore green uniforms, whereas girls wore yellow ones. Children of the palace, however, had different colors. Talented children weren't allowed to socialize with ordinary ones. Jamal and Lillian couldn't understand why the helpless children had to do all the work while the strong creatures only rested lazily. They weren't even sure of the other children's feelings and intentions, and whether they were really upset about leaving the human world, and so Jamal told his sister not to trust anyone.

Nevertheless, they didn't stop asking. They wanted to know everything, and they discovered that the king owned a big crystal magic ball that would tell him the location of any child within the borders of the kingdom. That's why there were no guards inside the palace, except for some of the Makash who were working as photographers. Photography was a redline job for the children. Some of the Makashan guarded the king himself and his suite, but the crystal ball did everything other than that both inside and outside the palace. Anyone who left the palace would immediately be noticed by the ball, and the king would be informed within seconds. Jamal asked the other children about the volcano craters into which the winged tigers spilt their fire, and they explained to him that those creatures were called enar. They were untamable wild animals that were brought from places outside the borders of the crystal ball and tied to the craters to warm the city and provide it with energy. When they died, they were eaten by another fierce type of animal called the azoufa, which could blow stones from its mouth. None of the children had seen one before, but it was said that it was very huge and fierce.

PRINCESS FILDA

Lillian wanted to know more about Princess Filda, so Samar
told the twin her story:

Princess Filda was the daughter of the late kindhearted
king who had ruled the kingdom of Scaba for several centuries. She
was married to her beloved, courageous knight and army leader,
Commander Medan. Their wedding party was magnificent and
was attended by all types: the Makashans and the Shakams, and
even the human black magicians and the zodiac tribe. All came
to congratulate the loving couple and enjoy the celebrations. The
zodiac tribe showered the princess with many gifts. One of them
was a group of butterflies made of pearls that were as big as eagles.
They were transparent and could radiate dazzling colors whenever
they flew. At that time, as they didn't have human children in
their service, the Mobacks would sing and dance for everyone,
and the elephants and zebras participated in the dancing as well.
The princess's wedding dress had been woven by silk caterpillars,
and the wedding lasted for a month. For the entire month, the
flying carpet dropped fresh red roses on Scaba every night and day.
All inhabitants of Scaba celebrated the event, each in their own
way. The couple spent the honeymoon in the dreamland, and then
they visited the astrology signs one by one. They also visited the
moon, Neptune, and Uranus; and then they went back to earth.
Commander Medan treated his wife with love and respect. It was
a customary where they came from to grant wishes to human
beings during their honeymoon, and that was easy for them, as
human beings' wishes were easily granted. The princess felt happier

whenever she helped realize people's dreams, which she thought were very simple. When they went back to their world, the king received them with a shower of gifts, which included a beautiful palace in which to live.

When Princess Filda recalled such sweet memories, she wished to return to the past and never come back again. Everything happened very fast, like a curse. She still remembered her father's journey to the human world when he entrusted the affairs of the kingdom to his deputy, Commander Medan. He told her that his journey would take only a few days and that he was going to have a little adventure and come back. She remembered telling him not to do anything reckless, and then he laughed and looked at her fondly and told her not to worry. He was healthy at that time.

He went to the human world and came back after a few days but with a mysterious, untreatable disease. He was dying. She was sitting in the palace when he came forth, carrying a small box along with the *Doom's Book*. It was as if he was evading and running away from something. He couldn't say much and fell in the middle of the royal hall. She ran to him, put his head in her lap, and started crying, "Father, Father, what happened to you?"

Her husband rushed to her side and told her to calm down in order to hear what the king was trying to say. She controlled herself for a moment with difficulty, and the king looked at them and said to Medan, "Protect my daughter from him and never trust him." Commander Medan asked him who he meant, and the king gathered what remained of his strength and said, "He couldn't know anything . . . I didn't tell him everything, but he—"

Before he finished his sentence, someone shot him with a wouf (a ray). It was neither Shakam, nor Makashan wouf, but it was fatal. Her husband saw the killer, and she remembered him saying to him, "I will kill you!" She couldn't hear the rest of his sentence because she herself was shot with a wouf that put her in a coma for seven months.

When she woke up, everything was changed. She was in her father's palace, fatigued and head aching. She looked at herself to find that she had a big stomach and realized that she was pregnant.

She called for help, and a human child came forth. She was surprised to see a human child in her world and thought it was just a dream or that someone had taken her into the human world. The child said to her, "Thank God, you are well now. I will go to carry the good news to the king."

The princess asked her who she was and if the world she was in was the human world or the kingdom of Scaba. The girl reassured her that she was still in Scaba and told her that she had been brought from the human world to serve her. Filda was astonished to hear that and told the girl to take her to the king. She prayed that the king was still her father and repeated to herself several times, *Please, God, let the king be my father, please, please.*

The young girl looked at her curiously, and the princess watched with incredulity the posters of Bermuda occupying the walls of the palace. These gave her a bad feeling, but she tried her best to drive it away. They arrived at the royal court where children were singing and dancing in front of the new king. King Bermuda saw her and ordered the musical band to stop playing. His smiles couldn't diminish her shock, especially when she saw General Falca sitting next to him. She was frightened, but Bermuda called to her and said, "Princess Filda, don't be afraid. Come closer."

Before that, Bermuda had been an insignificant personage in the palace. He appeared from nowhere, and when she asked her father about who he was, he told her that a close friend had recommended him and that he was a loyal and honest Makashan. Thereafter, he did his best to get closer to the king.

She looked with fear at the Makashan commander, who smiled at her gloatingly. The king said, "Don't be afraid of General Falca. He is one of us now. Things have changed since you fell into your coma, dear." She remained silent, trying to understand what was going on. The king ordered the children out of the court and then said to her, "You must be very curious to know what has happened. It is better that you sit because what I want to tell you will fill you with shock and surprise."

She told him that she was fine and did not need to sit. He exchanged smiles with General Falca and then approached her and said, "You must sit. It is very bad news." She sat grudgingly, waiting impatiently to hear the news. The king told her that her father and husband had been killed. She was unable to control the tears that gushed from her eyes.

She then asked the king, "How did my husband die? He was fine last time I was with him."

The king turned his back to her, to avoid meeting her eyes, and said, "Your husband was a traitor. He killed your father."

She couldn't believe this and said angrily, "This is impossible! You are lying—you are the traitor."

General Falca tried to attack her, but the king grabbed him by the hand and said, "She is not to blame. She is still intoxicated." Then he asked her, "What is the last thing that you remember?"

She thought for a moment and said to him, "I remember that someone shot my father with a wouf. My husband saw him and threatened him with death."

The king told her that the story was true but that it had later been discovered that it was only a conspiracy between the two and that they tried to kill her after she had fainted, but the guards saved her and killed them both. She couldn't believe the story and cried, "This is impossible. It is all a lie."

The king told her that, had the guards who killed them been alive, he would have summoned them for testimony. "But what is General Falca doing here?" she asked suspiciously.

"I told you that many things have changed since you fell into the coma," the king replied. He explained to her that war had broken out after the death of her father and that the kingdom, having been drowned in chaos, ended up with the victory and dominance of the Makash. Bermuda told her that he had convinced the kingdom to unite into one great society to get rid of the specter of war that had shadowed the place for centuries, and that was what had made the inhabitants of Scaba accept him as king.

She found the story difficult to digest, but having no way to oppose the king, she grudgingly accepted it. The king then said to her, "I know that you will ask me about the children." She looked at him approvingly, and he told her that on the first day of his ascension to the throne he had promised to provide the people of Scaba with all ecstasies of life and to make human beings servants to them. "I wanted to see my people as affluent and happy as possible."

She didn't look convinced with that and asked, "But why didn't the wouf kill me as it did my father?"

The king laughed and said, "We normally feel sorry for losing life. It is the first time I see someone who feels sad for survival." She told him that she was very confused about the incident. The king explained then, "Maybe the killer failed to shoot you in the head or heart, or maybe it was because you were pregnant. You know that pregnant Shakam women have extraordinary immunity."

She thought a little while and then asked the king, "But what happened to the *Doom's Book* and darzar's box?"

"The book is in the royal safe, but the darzar's box had been smuggled away by your husband's aides." He looked at her to see if she believed him, but she was lost between what she heard and her intuition, which told her to disbelieve the whole story.

"By the way, congratulations on your pregnancy," he added awkwardly after a moment of silence. The princess put her hand on her abdomen, reminding herself of her pregnancy.

But why have none of the children tried to run away before? Jamal wondered.

They tried to find out more about the runaways and their demands, but nobody could help them with that or with why the crystal ball was unable to tell their places.

A very fat boy from the Shakam entered the hall escorted by a Moback, the small fluffy ponies. He headed for the table at which Jamal and Lillian were sitting. Samar saw him and said to them, "This is Prince Dushan, and he will be your responsibility."

Jamal and Lillian exchanged a quick surprised look, and Jamal asked, "What do you mean?"

"You will be his servants, and the first thing to do for him is to change his diapers."

Jamal and Lillian felt bitter and sick and shouted at once, "What?"

All other children giggled, and Prince Dushan looked innocently at them and said, "My diapers need to be changed."

Then he dashed outside the hall. Samar told them to run after him. Once they were out of the hall, everybody burst into uproarious laughter. While chasing the young prince, Jamal promised Lillian that he would get them both out of that despicable place. The young prince ran toward the suite of his mother, Princess Filda, and the two kids ran after him. The princess hugged her child with passion and love, and after seconds, the twins came forth. She smiled at them, as she could guess what they were running after him for. She asked them if the child had told them that he needed to have his diapers changed, and the two nodded their heads. She laughed, together with Prince Dushan, and explained to them that they had been just fooled by Samar, who did the same thing with all newcomers.

The First Attempt

Kameel approached the twins lazily and asked them to follow him. He walked slowly and didn't look back. He looked indifferent to what was happening around him. Jamal and Lillian observed every inch of the palace carefully as they followed Kameel. The windows of the palace were very big, and the kids were able to see the backyards outside the palace. They whispered to each other whenever they passed a window. They stopped near one of the windows and looked to gauge its height. It was low, and one wouldn't even need to jump to reach the other side. Kameel stopped when he discovered that they weren't following him. He said nothing but waited for a while, and then they went on. He took them to a room full of clean new clothes that were put on roofs. He asked them about their measurements and then fetched the best-fitting uniforms and said, "These are the uniforms that you should wear inside the palace."

Jamal examined the clothes and asked, "I don't like the color orange. Can I have another color please?"

Kameel looked at Lillian as if asking her to help Jamal understand the options and rules of the palace. Finally, he said, "Can you see any other options? Girls wear red, and boys orange."

"What shall we do with our clothes?" Lillian asked him.

"You give them to me, and I will burn them, and in this way you get rid of all sentimental connection with the human world."

On their first night in the kingdom of Scaba, Jamal and Lillian had decided to run away. They didn't believe that running away was impossible. Jamal said to Lillian that the children had never tried running away, not even once. "It seems that they are convinced of the impossibility of running away," Lillian said.

"No," replied Jamal firmly, "they are afraid."

"So what is your plan?" Lillian asked.

"When everyone goes to sleep, we will sneak out of the palace and go back home."

After the twins had put on the new uniforms, Kameel asked them to go to Prince Dushan and do their best to serve him and play with him. The two went to Prince Dushan's room. He was sleeping at that time. They didn't know what to do, but seconds later, Dushan farted, and the two had to suppress a big laugh. Soon, though, they had to hold their breath too because of the bad smell that overshadowed the place. "I am really happy we won't have to change his diapers," Lillian said. Jamal agreed and laughed but refused to wake him up, as suggested by his sister, explaining to her that it was better for them if he remained asleep.

They examined the room around them and were about to rest for a while when Dushan woke up and called, "Sisimi, Sisimi." The twins were alerted but unaware of what they should do. Seconds later Sisimi, a Moback, came into the room. When Sisimi saw them, he asked, "Are you the new friends of Prince Dushan?" When they answered in the affirmative, Sisimi jumped swiftly onto the bed and said to Dushan, "Come on, wake up. Here are you new friends. Let's play together."

Dushan smiled at them and asked, "Are you my new friends?"

Jamal answered quickly, "Yes."

Dushan said happily, "So let's play together."

Sisimi suggested that they play a game of hide-and-seek, and Dushan got excited and started clapping his hands. Sisimi jumped off the bed and asked them their names. When they introduced themselves to him, he said to Jamal, "We will hide, and you will try to find us." Jamal agreed and closed his eyes. Sisimi hid himself under the bed while Lillian searched for a place to hide herself. Dushan remained immobilized; Lillian eventually hid herself behind the curtains and watched Dushan, who didn't move from where he was. When Jamal finished counting, he opened his eyes to see that the prince was still lying on his bed with his eyes closed.

"I got you, Prince Dushan," Jamal said, but the prince shook his head as if saying that he wasn't Prince Dushan. Jamal said, "I found you. You are still in your bed."

Dushan started crying, and Sisimi had to go out of his hiding to whisper to Jamal, "You shouldn't have found him."

"But he didn't even hide himself," Jamal explained.

Sisimi came closer to Jamal and told him to kneel so that he could tell him a secret. When Jamal did that, Sisimi whispered in his ear, "He thinks that you didn't see him because he believes that he had made himself invisible by closing his eyes."

Jamal looked at his sister strangely but then decided to pretend it was true. Sisimi jumped on the bed again and tried to placate Dushan. He even told him that Jamal didn't find him but guessed his place. Then they decided to go back to play again.

Jamal counted again, Sisimi hid himself under the bed, and Lillian hid herself behind the curtains. When Jamal finished counting, he opened his eyes and started searching, pretending not to see Dushan, who was closing his eyes and standing in the middle of the room. Jamal found Lillian behind the curtains and said, "I found you, Lillian." Then he went on. "But where are Prince Dushan and Sisimi? Where are they?" he said sarcastically. He looked under the bed and found Sisimi and asked again, "Where is Prince Dushan?"

Dushan opened his eyes and said, "Here I am, stupid," and then started laughing. Jamal looked at his sister, who was smiling, and Sisimi winked at them.

They played again and again. It was monotonous and tiring for all of them except Dushan, who didn't feel seem to be bored or tired. They kept playing the whole day.

At bedtime, Samar came to Dushan's room and told the two kids to follow her to the sleeping ward. They heaved a gasp of relief at that, but Dushan started crying, asking for more games. Samar ignored him and told Sisimi to take care of him. The twins thanked Samar for helping, and she explained to them that punctuality was very important in the palace and should be observed. Otherwise, the king would get angry and punish them.

They arrived at the sleeping ward to discover a long queue of children outside it. They asked Samar for an explanation. "All these kids will play hide-and-seek with Prince Dushan and his Shakam friends. We will also play ourselves when our turn comes," Samar explained. The twins felt desperate and disappointed.

"Oh my god, not again," Lillian said.

Samar laughed and said to them, "I am just kidding. There is no more playing, don't worry." Then she explained to them that the children who were about to go to sleep had to wish the king a good night's sleep. Jamal wondered how the king could come to the children's ward every night, but Samar told him that it was only the king's picture that was there and that the children had to wish the picture a good night's sleep. The two kids were amazed by that but decided that they had seen more bizarre and weird things in the palace.

When it was Lillian's turn, she gazed at the king's picture and wished him a good night, just as she had seen Samar doing before her. But when it came to Jamal's turn, he said nothing and just looked angrily at the picture. He said to his sister, "We will pretend that we are asleep."

After a while, when everybody had fallen asleep, they tiptoed outside the ward. Kameel woke up and saw them sneaking out but pretended not to see them. They walked toward the clothes room.

"I don't see any crystal ball watching us," Jamal whispered to his sister as they went out of the low window. Jamal said to Lillian, "You see how easy it was!"

"But where can we go now?" Lillian asked, looking in all directions. Jamal looked around and told her to follow him until they found a way out. They walked very close to the walls until they reached a big yard in which some children were taking food from a wagon pulled by a green zebra.

Jamal said to Lillian, "This will be our means of transport outside." When the children had finished emptying the wagon, they went back to the palace, and the tall boy seated himself in the front of the wagon and whipped the zebra that started to move slowly. Jamal and Lillian ran and hid themselves under the wagon, where they hung by its axle. At one point Lillian almost fell, but her brother grabbed her by the hand. It was very difficult to hang on while the wagon moved. Lillian almost wept, but Jamal told her not to worry. They passed the first gate, where the wagon was checked by the Makashan guards. Jamal smiled; and when the wagon reached the second gate, the guards looked all around it, and one of the guards asked the tall boy, "You are not smuggling illegal items, are you?"

The boy said in a terrified voice, "No, sir."

The guard said, "Good. You know that the palace's food is for the palace, and the city's food remains in the city."

"Yes, sir." Jamal and Lillian had by now become very happy because they knew that there was only one gate left. The wagon waited at the third gate while it was inspected by the guards. Then it was allowed to move on. The kids' hearts beat quickly, and the guards were about to close the gate when one of the guards of the second gate came running and shouting at them to stop the wagon.

The wagon stopped, and the guard said, "There are two kids hiding under that wagon."

When Jamal heard this, he told his sister to run, but both failed because the guards had seen them hanging by the rods of the wagon. Jamal smiled at the guards and said, "Hello." The two kids were taken back to the palace where the king and General Falca where waiting for them. The king looked at them and said, "You think you can run away from my world?"

"We don't want your world. We want to go back to our parents," Jamal replied.

The king laughed and said to them, "There will be no going back. You will stay with us until you are eighteen years old."

"Please, sir, send us back where we belong," Lillian begged.

The king ignored her and said to General Falca, "Take them to the big theater and wake up all the other children to witness their punishment."

General Falca bowed his head. The king added, "I want you to punish them in your usual harsh manner so that they become a lesson for all who think of running away."

General Falca, with the help of one of the guards, dragged the kids who tried to resist but in vain. The king then said to his snake, "These evil kids will not go home. I hate them. They will never return, and I will break the hearts of their parents." He added, "When you kidnap children, their families can't lead a normal life anymore, and their life will turn into hell. Families will break up, and with this we will remain safe and prevail. Nobody can attain access to *Doom's Book* in this way."

Some Makashan guards went into the children's sleeping ward and started to wake them up harshly. The children were terrified, as it was the first time they had been woken up after midnight. They were ordered to assemble in the theater hall, where Jamal and Lillian were tied to a big wooden board. They were barefooted, and the board was grabbed at either end by Makashan guards. The children couldn't understand what was going on and thought it was a play. Some of the children from the musical band said, "Not these dumb kids." It was a weird timing for a play, however.

General Falca went up to the stage with a bat in his hand and looked at the children while pointing at Jamal and Lillian. "These naughty kids tried to run away tonight."

Kameel slapped his forehead sorrowfully, and General Falca added, "So they have to be punished." He looked around to see that his message was clear. It appeared that he was enjoying what he was about to do. He said, "The king wanted you to see the punishment so that you will never think of doing such a stupid deed."

Dushan and Sisimi sneaked into the theater hall to see what was going on. Filda herself came to and watched the scene with pain and fear. General Falca hit the kids' bare feet savagely and harshly, and they screamed with agony. The scene moved the hearts of the children, and Princess Filda was surprised to see punishment taking place for the first time in Scaba. She went up the stage to prevent the commander, but the guards warded her off. She blazed the guards with her woufs, beating them back one by one. Then she was left face-to-face with General Falca. They had at each other with woufs for some time, but she was eventually fatigued and defeated by the commander, who managed to force her to her knees in pain. General Falca ordered the guards to take here away, and at that moment, he felt something grabbing his legs. When he looked down, he saw Dushan, with his eyes closed, crying, "Leave my mother and friends alone."

General Falca kicked Dushan away. Sisimi didn't know what to do, but he approached the agonized Dushan and tried to stop his crying. General Falca ordered the guards to take him away along with his mother, and then he completed the flogging of the kids. All attendant children, including dancers and singers, started weeping in sympathy with Jamal and Lillian. The torture was so painful that the twins weren't able to tolerate it and eventually fainted. Despite that, the commander didn't stop. He appeared to be enjoying the occasion, especially because he knew for sure that the king was watching the scene with joy in the crystal ball.

When he finished, he looked at the children and smiled hatefully at them; and before leaving, he said to the other children, "Come and untie your friends and take them to the sleeping ward."

When the commander went out, Wang, Samar, Shaun, and Kameel sprang to their feet and untied the twins, who were still unconscious. Their feet were bleeding. Wang asked the other children to help carry them, and they took them to their beds and treated them with bandages and warm water. Princess Filda was prevented from approaching the royal suite that night.

Jamal and Lillian were so weak in the coming three days that they couldn't walk. Even so, Jamal promised his sister that they wouldn't remain there for long, and Lillian couldn't agree more. Other children visited them whenever they had the chance to. Wang told them that what they did was a very big mistake because even if they managed to get out of the palace, they wouldn't succeed in going back to human world. The only way to get to Hill Gate was by the magic carpet. Samar and Shaun begged them not to try escape again. Jamal told everybody that there must be a way out of that place. Dushan and Sisimi visited them, and they enjoyed a sweet song by Sisimi.

The City's Teenagers

Dana

O n her fifteenth birthday, Dana wanted more than anything else to drive her father's new dream car. He had just bought it with lifetime savings. She always asked him if she could drive the sports car, which could accommodate two people only; but her father never let her, always saying, "I will never allow you to do that." Then, he would explain to her that she was still too young to drive, especially his dream car. Dana insisted that she, besides being a fan of gymnastics, was very skillful at driving and was one of the most outstanding go-cart drivers.

Everyone was having a lovely time at her birthday party except her. She was preoccupied with getting the keys of her father's car. She pretended that she was enjoying herself by laughing from time to time and showing some of her gymnastic skills to convince everyone that she was into it. She watched her father as he came into the house carrying some items needed for the birthday party. She saw him putting the items in the kitchen, and then she saw him putting the keys of the car on a table. This was something he had never done before. Her eyes widened, and she smiled naughtily, knowing that such a chance would not present itself to her again as it did now, with her father busy arranging things for the party. Dana ran to the kitchen and put the keys in her pockets and then came back, waiting for the chance to sneak out of the house and seize the car. Her heart beat very fast, and she tried her best to control her breathing so that she wouldn't be discovered by anyone.

Two minutes later, she managed to sneak out of the house without being noticed by anyone. She headed quickly to her father's car and opened it. Her heart was beating fast, and because of this disturbance, she dropped the keys on the car floor. She picked them up again quickly, started the engine, and pressed the accelerator carefully; but the car didn't move. She thought for a moment, and discovered that she hadn't put the gear on drive. When she did so, the car moved slowly and cautiously. She smiled happily, achieving a lifetime dream. She searched for a CD to listen to while driving. She didn't want to drive far; she just wanted to try driving for a short distance and get back home before her parents even discovered that she had gone. No sooner had she found a music CD and lifted her head to put it into the slot than she crossed an intersection without looking out for traffic. Out of the blue, another car came flying into her. She screamed at the top of her voice and looked around, trying to assess the situation. She climbed out of the vehicle. The owner of the other car rushed up to her to check if she was okay, asking, "Are you fine?"

Dana was shaking with fear and looking back at her house. She couldn't hear what the other driver was asking her. Her parents and some guests who had come to attend the party had heard the crash. They rushed out to see Dana involved in an accident and her father's car wrecked. They all ran toward her.

She could clearly see the dismay on her father's face and felt very ashamed. She ran away from her father, and all of them started shouting after her to stop and come back but in vain. Filled with remorse and sorrow, she kept running aimlessly through the alleys; and after getting too tired, she sat in one of these alleys and started crying. She couldn't imagine how she would face her father. The only solution she could think of was to run away forever and never come back. She wished she had never taken the car. While she was in that state, the driver of the other car involved in the accident appeared in front of her. He was a tall man with a weird smile on his face. When she saw him, she tried to run away again, but he said, "Don't be afraid, my dear. I am here to help you."

She was relieved to hear that but rose to her feet, determined to run away. He told her affectionately that he didn't care about his vehicle and that he had arranged with her father to get it repaired and convinced him not to punish her. She was pleased to hear that. He told her to go into his house, which happened to be only a few meters away from where they were. He told her that he was throwing a party to celebrate his new house, and it was a good chance for her to attend that party in order to calm down and gain some time during which her father would regain temper and reason. She agreed but told him to tell her father where she was, and he agreed in turn.

His house was neat and beautiful, and she could hear voices of attendants coming from the backyard, although she could hear nothing while she was outside the house. The man ushered her inside, and when she was in the middle of the living room, she felt that something was not right, and so she asked him again to call her father. The man just told her to relax and said, "It seems that you don't trust me. Or maybe you are scared."

It was Dana's Achilles' heel to be described as a coward, and she thus obstinately always tried to prove the opposite. "I am not afraid, and you can even call my dad later," she said defiantly.

She then followed him through the glass door that led to the backyard and was relieved to see some attendants in their elegant suits and dresses. Once she stepped out of the glass door, one of the guests closed it behind her quickly. Dana looked back with fear and suspicion to see a man with yellowish eyes. She was filled with panic but decided to move ahead. She smiled at him, but his eyes were like glass balls. He kept looking at her with those lifeless, frigid looks. Dana walked cautiously between guests, who paid no attention to her. All of a sudden, all of them disappeared, as if the ground had swallowed them. Dana was plunged in fear, and her heart almost stopped with panic. She looked around, trying to figure out what was going on and searching for the owner of the house, but she couldn't find him. What scared her most was hearing the voices despite the disappearance of their owners. Then, they appeared again suddenly, almost sending her insane. She could hear her legs shaking. She looked at the guests' lifeless faces. Despite their eeriness, they were smiling at her. They ignored her for a while, but then they surrounded her and started looking at her silently. She screamed at them, "What do you want of me?"

Nobody replied, and the host came toward her with his weird smile, and suddenly the attendants' eyes turned a pale yellowish color. They closed in on her in a circle. She fainted immediately.

When she woke up, she was on a hill in the kingdom of Scaba. She looked around to see four other teenagers, two girls and two boys, who were waking up from similar comas. She tried to remember what had happened to her. Everything around her looked unreal, as if she were inside a painting. She touched the feathery grass and looked at the nearby sky. She heard one Makashan ordering a child to stand still. She looked at the source of the sound and almost fainted again when she saw the ugly fearful Makashans with their scary snake heads. The Makashan, with his horrible sound, ordered them to assemble. All children stood up, except a little girl who fell into a coma with fear.

Dana, along with another girl, tried to help, but the Makashans prevented them. The two girls' eyes met in shock, wondering where they were. The Makashan ordered one of the boys to carry the unconscious girl and take care of her, and then they forced all the teens to their feet. A boy asked the Snakehead about the place, but he scolded him severely, telling him that it was not time for questions and that they would know everything at the right time. Suddenly, a magic carpet came down from the sky with three Makashans on board, and the children were ordered onto it. They were seated in rows, as if on a bus or an airplane. When they put their feet in the carpet's holes, the carpet raised a little, forcing them to sit. The other girl sat next to Dana silently. Dana looked around, searching for a seatbelt or something alike. When the last child put his feet in the holes, the carpet started to go up slowly. All the kids panicked. Dana kept looking around nervously, and the other girl asked her what she was looking for. Dana told her about the seatbelt. "It seems that this world is totally different from ours," the other girl commented.

Dana drew a pathetic smile and introduced herself, "I am Dana."

"And I am Nora," the other girl replied.

All children were on board the magic carpet. The boy who had asked the Makashan about the place had refused to ride in the beginning, but he was pushed on by one of the Makashans. His eyes met Dana's, who sympathized with him. Nora asked Dana about the reason that made these creatures treat them in that harsh way, but Dana replied to her, as if she hadn't heard the question, "Don't be afraid. We are just in a dream and will wake up soon."

The carpet flew over the rainbow desert; and they were able to see the elephants, the tents, and the amphitheater. "Look! Nothing here is real. We are in a dream," Dana said to Nora.

"But whose dream is it: mine or yours?" Nora asked innocently.

Dana couldn't answer the question and remained silent. When they flew over the city and saw the vertical streets and how creatures walked on them, as if gravity was absent, they sank deep into perplexity and stupefaction. They looked at one other in bewilderment. They could see the miserable state of the children in that world. One of the Moback animals that were riding with them said to the five children, "They brought you here to serve them."

The children looked at the Moback in amazement, and Dana said to Nora, "I can't believe that this animal can talk."

A Makashan looked angrily at the Moback, who stuck to the fainted girl in fear. The carpet landed in front of a weird building that looked like a combination between a tent and a traditional house. The door was triangular, and the building itself was cubic. Once the carpet landed and their feet touched the ground, the door guards ordered them off the carpet and go inside the building. Dana noticed that all Makashans had left the carpet in front of the building, so she asked Nora, "Can you run fast?"

Nora looked at her wondering what she meant, and Dana explained, "Can't you see? There is nobody on the carpet."

She explained to her that they had to run as fast as possible to pass through the Makashans and grab the carpet to fly back to their own world. Nora couldn't agree more strongly, and once the children began entering the building, Dana ran as fast as she could. Relying on her skills in gymnastics, she ran up the wall and somersaulted over to maneuver herself through the guards, overcoming some hurdles in the way. Nora also ran fast, and because she was a skillful dancer, she was able to overcome the guards by slipping herself between their legs.

The scene drove Sikwel, the Makashan commander, insane as he saw with shock what was happening. He ordered more guards to watch over the kids and ordered the rest of the Makashans to chase the two girls.

The girls, after overcoming the guards and the hurdles, met at the carpet and quickly sat on it. Nora asked Dana if she had any idea of how to make the carpet fly, but Dana looked at her reproachfully and said, "This is my first day here, and I haven't got an aviation license yet."

They wondered how to make the carpet fly. "But why did you make us run away if you didn't have a plan in the first place?" Nora said nervously.

"I had a plan, but it doesn't work," Dana replied.

They tried to recall what the Makashans did to make the carpet fly but in vain. Nora said, "There must be a password."

Dana clapped her hands once and then twice, but it didn't work. Nora asked her what she was doing.

"I am trying and trying. Do something instead of asking questions," Dana shouted.

Nora thought for a moment while looking at the guards who were approaching and then said, "Open sesame." She waited to see the effect of the words, but Dana looked at her in amazement and said, "Open sesame? Really, really, who do you think you are, Ali Baba?"

The Makashans were approaching them, and Commander Sikwel smiled gloatingly as he came toward them with his tall vestment that covered his two tails. The two girls surrendered to the guards and climbed off the carpet. They were captured and pushed toward the leader, who looked at them with the same smile still resting on his thick lips. "The first lesson that you have to learn is that the carpet of Misfar can't be flown by humans," he said.

He looked at the two girls for a while and said, "I admire your courage, but I am disappointed by your stupidity." Then he asked them, "Did you think that we are so stupid as to leave the carpet unmanned if humans can fly it?"

Dana looked at Nora and said, "Open sesame, huh?"

Nora shook her head and said, "Did you have a better idea?"

Sikwel explained to them that the carpet flew only with Makash or Shakam, the other creatures that they saw while they were on their way to the building. He ordered the guards to take the two girls inside the building and watch them closely.

So they went back to join the other kids. The girl who had been in a coma regained consciousness and, when she saw the creatures, felt very scared. The Moback animal tried to entertain her. They took the two girls to a hall where they took photos of each of them. Dana wrinkled her face in front of the camera. Then they were taken to the clothes store, where they received their uniforms. Boys wore blue uniforms, and girls wore pink ones. Then the guards segregated them. Dana was taken to a Shakam family to begin serving them.

It was a small family that consisted of parents and two daughters. The family members looked beautiful compared to other Makashans despite the fact that they were very obese.

The family welcomed Dana, but the guards told the family to beware of her. When the guards left, the father also warned his family members of her. She felt indifferent about this, and she replied to their question regarding her name. Then she asked them who they were and what they wanted of her. They explained to her that they were from the Shakam and she was there to serve them. She nodded her head, only one thought occupying her head: *running away*. Minutes later, the wife told her to go to the kitchen and cook food for them. Dana said that she didn't know how to cook. The wife explained to her that cooking in the Shakam's world is different from that at the human world. She took her to the kitchen, which contained a big store full of paper rolls that looked like cigarettes. She took one roll and opened a wall that double-functioned as a wall and an oven. It was a giant, deep, and very cold oven like a freezer. The Shakam wife put the roll into the oven and closed the wall. She told Dana to wait until the oven told her that the food was ready. Then she had to pick it up and serve it. Dana nodded her head unbelievingly and said to herself, *All these fat creatures going to share this little roll. Ha, I will wait to see the end of this comedy.*

Minutes later, she heard a whistling sound coming from inside the oven. She opened it to see a huge amount of strange food. She couldn't figure out how a tiny roll was able to generate such a huge quantity of food—enough to feed the whole population of that world. It looked delicious, and although it was put in a cold place, smoke was coming out of it. She was tempted to try a piece, so she cautiously took a small bite. She was surprised by how soft it was. She tasted it, but it was so bitter that she immediately started coughing and trying to spit what was left of the tiny piece. She realized that the Shakam food couldn't be eaten by humans. The family heard her coughing and came to the kitchen and started laughing. The husband said to her, "Never taste our foods. It will kill you."

"It is simply inedible for humans," the wife elaborated.

They ordered her to put the food on the table. Dana looked at the great heap of food and said, "Sure, I'll do that."

No sooner had the family gone out of the kitchen than Dana started searching for an exit from the house. She tried to open the windows, but they were all closed. She sneaked out of the kitchen while the family was sitting lazily in the living room. Though the house had a second floor it had no staircase. She remembered seeing the Makashans, Shakams, and the children of the city walking vertically up and down things; so she decided to try that herself. She stretched one leg on the wall, and surprisingly, amazingly, it worked. She walked upward with a big smile on her face. The family didn't notice her. She entered one of the rooms and searched for any opened door or window. Finally she found a small door that led to the roof. She went out of it up to the roof of the house. It was too high to jump from. She decided to walk downward this time. She closed her eyes and took the first step down. When she floated and didn't fall, she took another step and started walking down the house vertically.

She felt good to walk that way and smiled happily. Once she touched the ground with her feet, she ran away.

The city was weird, and so was its population. None of the children were alarmed by her walking among them in the streets. They were too busy serving the Shakam. She hung around for a while, but then she remembered her family, and tears formed in her eyes. She felt very sorry for everything and wished she could have gone back home to apologize to her parents for being reckless and irresponsible. When she felt tired, she sat on the sidewalk to rest and watch what was happening around her. She saw some Makashan security guards walking around checking and inspecting security. She walked by them cautiously. She asked many kids there about the hill where she regained consciousness, but nobody helped her with an answer. She wanted only to go back home to her previous world. The children of the city looked miserable and lifeless and worked like machines. When she felt exhausted, she went into a corner between the high buildings to take a little rest and think what to do next. Minutes later, three Makashan guards came and arrested her, saying, "Come with us, Dana."

She was surprised to be caught that easily. She also was baffled that they could know her by name. She tried to run away but in vain.

STEVEN

At his new school, Steven hated to be recognized by his classmates as a diligent student. He preferred, rather, to be known as naughty so that he could befriend the famous and popular students at the school. He had learned from his previous school that diligent students were always discriminated against and bullied by student gangsters and always had to struggle in fighting back. Now he was sixteen, and he decided not to play the role of defender of the bullied students anymore. Biology was his favorite subject, and he always dreamed of becoming a famous biologist, a scientist in animal behaviors. He always dreamed of dissecting animals. The frog that the biology teacher dissected before the class wasn't enough for him. He tried many times when he was seven to capture his mother's cat and dissect it but failed to do so because either it usually ran away or his mother came in on time to stop. When he was thirteen, he found a dead mouse in the garden of their house. He hid it in his room to dissect it the next day, but he was supposed to join his parents and little brother on an outing to a nearby park to spend the day. The dead mouse occupied Steven's mind all that day. He planned to turn his room into an operating theater when he got back home and imagined how beautiful it would be to practice anatomy on the small animal, removing its organs and then putting them back in their place. Because of this, he wasn't in the mood to play with his father and little brother.

When it was time to go back home, Steven helped the family by cleaning the area in which they had been with an enthusiasm that surprised his parents. They all sang on their way home, and once they opened the door, they were overwhelmed by the bad smell coming from inside the house. They all wondered what the smell could be. The stench became stronger as they went upstairs. Steven knew the source of the smell, but despite that, he helped the family with their search. His mother asked him if it was a dead animal he was planning to dissect causing the bad smell, but he denied this. Steven's father went upstairs to search for the smell inside the rooms. Steven felt worried seeing his father going upstairs. He tried to convince him that he could do it instead, but his father didn't listen to him. He went up, sniffing around and following the smell. When he approached Steven's room, the smell became so strong that he had to cover his mouth with his hand. He shouted at Steven in a high nervous voice, telling him to come immediately to remove the source of the bad smell. Steven went upstairs while the sharp looks of his mother were dressing him down. He took the dead mouse from under the bed and headed to the garden of the house where he buried it. Then he came back shyly and full of worry about what he would face inside.

His mother didn't talk to him about it, but his father started scolding him. He called him stupid and irresponsible, accusing him of never thinking about the consequences of his work. His father was so angry that he called him a loser and that such action was not to be expected by a boy of his age, especially with his eccentric hobbies. He then told him that he wished to see him achieve success and advised him to play a certain sport so that he could forget these weird activities. He also compared him to his little brother, saying that his little brother was more popular at school because of his excellence at basketball. Steven's father had always reminded his son that he wanted him to become a famous athlete and that he hated to see his son idling about without practicing a sport like other kids. So his father decided to not buy a pet dog for Steven for a year until he changed his behavior. Steven decided to change and put aside his love for biology and dissection to focus on his schooling and sports. Moving to a new school was a chance for him to try new things. He excelled in ping-pong and trained to take part in the state's championship, and to win it to please his father. His love of animals and biology hadn't altered a bit, but he didn't try to dissect any more animals until one day when he had to stay behind at school to train with another student for the championship, which was expected to start in a month's time. Steven was excited by the approach of the championship, through which he could realize the dream of his father. After he finished training and bathing, while he was in the changing room, he saw a Moback outside the room. It looked very strange, so he dressed up and ran outside the room and tried to get closer to it by calling it, but it ran away. He chased it while it kept playing a chasing game with him to urge him to run farther. He followed it outside the walls of the school. Steven wanted so eagerly to catch the Moback that he forgot any other commitments. The Moback went into a nearby forest, and Steven was on its heels. In the middle of that forest, Steven heard voices, and when he looked around, he saw a group of people in elegant dresses and suits gathered as in a party. The Moback animal went through the gathering. All the attendants looked at him as if they were trained to do so. Steven was afraid, but the Moback occupied his mind. He smiled to them and said hello, and when nobody replied he added, "These are beautiful animals. Which species are they?"

He waited for an answer, but they disappeared all at once. He was completely terrified. He turned back to run away, but they were there standing behind him. They were not looking at him, as if he didn't exist. He became more frightened and remained silent. He wanted to run away from the other side, but Solar was there standing in front of him, saying, "Welcome to the party." Steven fainted immediately.

When he woke up, he saw a lot of Moback animals surrounding him. He forgot what he had just gone through and tried to catch them, but a hoarse voice ordering him to stand still froze him. When he looked at the source of the sound, he was shocked by the terrifying shape of the creatures that were talking to him. He didn't move an inch and tried to understand what was happening around him. There was a group of children there, a boy and three girls, who were all as terrified as him. One of the girls fainted again. The other boy asked them where they were, but they scolded him and ordered him to remain silent. Steven understood then that it was unwise to ask them anything. They were ordered onto the carpet, but the other boy refused to do so, and they started beating and kicking him. At that point, Steven realized that these creatures were totally serious. He was ordered to take care of the unconscious girl. One of the Moback animals joined them to help the girl regain consciousness as well. Steven's curiosity toward the Moback turned into hatred. He wished he could kill them and dissect them, but he promised himself that he would do so later. He put the feet of the unconscious girl into the holes of the carpet, and then he put his, though. When the carpet started flying, he felt afraid and disturbed. The higher the carpet was, the more terrified Steven became. His heart was beating very fast while the carpet was passing over the strange world. He was even more perplexed to hear the Moback talking, explaining to the kids where they were. He couldn't believe that animals could talk and became even more resolved to dissect these animals to know the secret behind it. He looked around searching for a landmark that would reveal the identity of that place, but there was nothing in that world of any similarity to his. Posters depicting another type of creature were spread everywhere. He tried to recognize him, but he was unlike any other thing he had ever seen. However, Steven felt safe and relieved when the carpet landed and his feet touched the ground. He carried the unconscious girl and immediately tried to step off the carpet. The Makash ordered him to slow down and stay in line with the other kids. He heard the Makash giving their orders. After a while, the little girl woke up and felt somehow relieved to see Steven carrying her, but she was shocked to see the Makash. Steven reassured her by telling her that she wasn't alone.

The girl he was taking care of wanted to ask Steven what was going on and where they were, but Dana's and Nora's attempt to flee put the whole place in chaos and she couldn't ask anything. The guards were too alerted, and Steven, admiring the girl's attempt to run away, decided to do the same.

But it was almost impossible because of the heavy guard's presence. Suddenly, the other boy grabbed one of the guards by the hand and called Steven for help. Steven jumped on the guard, but the guard, with the help of his colleague, easily defeated them both. Steven and the other boy started to yell, urging the two girls to run away. They told them about the posts of the Makashan guards but were soon disappointed as the two girls were arrested.

The group of children was then taken for photography and uniforms, and later Steven was taken to a public transport facility. They explained to him that his work would be to carry the Comfort Bed, which is what they called the bed he was told to carry along with nine other boys. One of the Shakam would seat himself on the bed, and the children had to carry it around following the Shakam's wish. He remembered seeing some pathetic children doing the same thing while he was on the magic carpet.

He felt sad for them but didn't know that he would have the same hard job. He decided to run away at the nearest possible chance. Minutes later, someone called him for his first assignment in Scaba. He was ordered to follow one of the Makash toward the bed. There, he saw a noticeably obese Shakam. He was as heavy as a small car. Steven was shocked. He studied the Shakam for a while, trying to figure out how much he weighed. Steven was pushed by the guards to join nine other children who were waiting for him to carry the heavy creature. They lifted the bed painstakingly and started walking. Steven tried to chat with the other children, but they ignored him. Once they were out in the streets of the city, Steven left them without the least feeling of remorse. One of the children called him back and said, "What do you think you are doing?"

"Aha, you are not dumb then?" Steven shouted.

"Come back. In Scaba there is no escape. They will find you easily," the boy replied.

But Steven wished them good luck in finding him as he ran. He ran as far away as possible from that spot, and the boy who was talking to him said, as if he were talking to himself, Newcomers!" Steven was taken by the city of Scaba, and he thought to himself that no way anybody could find him in such a big city. Then he hung around in the streets and watched the different lifestyle there. He saw some Shakam kids eating ice cream and snatched one from one of the children, running away, leaving the child crying at the top of his voice. Steven put the ice cream in his mouth to discover that it was extremely bitter. Little did he know he could have been killed because of that horrible taste. He threw it away immediately.

After walking for a considerable time, he felt exhausted and sat down on a corner where nobody could see him. Seconds later, he was surrounded by three Makashan guards. They called him by name, telling him to come with them, which he did that without any resistance.

NORA

Nora believed that she was different from all other girls of her age. She didn't care about fashion, unlike other sixteen-year-old girls. She didn't try to catch up with the latest makeup trends. All what she cared for was dancing. She adored hip-hop and always spent a considerable amount of time learning new techniques. Her parents wanted her to improve her dancing skills, but they believed that studying came first. They often blamed her for the loud music in her room. She would often sneak out of the house at night to join other dancing maniacs for a party. There, they would compete until late at night; and she would get home before dawn, exhausted.

She would hardly have snuck back into the house and be sleeping deeply before her mother would wake her up with difficulty to prepare herself for school. She would go to school and barely manage to open her eyes in classes. Things were arranged upside down for Nora. She put dancing before all other things in her life. She couldn't help being tired all the time in school, but once she was invited to attend a dancing session, she would become alert and happy. Everybody knew that she was very good at dancing and always enthusiastic to learn new dance movements, but at school, her academic record was bad.

She used to skip many classes, which forced the administration of the school to warn her, but she didn't change her attitude. This forced the school to suspend her. She was not allowed to come back to school without the attendance of her guardian. She didn't care much about this, though, and didn't tell her parents; she saw it as an opportunity for her to officially skip school and do what she liked most instead. She would fill her school bag with her baggy clothes instead of schoolbooks, and when her mother dropped her at school, she would pretend to walk toward the school until her mother went away. Then, she would go away from the school and change her clothes to join her friends, who would hang around competing with other hip-hop dancers in the city. Nora would enjoy it to the full when she and her friends beat other street bands.

Later, things developed, and Nora and her friends started to occupy certain places and street corners to dance in front of passersby and collect money from them.

One day, a naughty troublemaker asked to join their band. He was an amazingly skillful dancer, and that's why they agreed at once. They took him to their usual spot, and when they finished their dancing, he suggested that they go to a nearby restaurant to celebrate the money they had collected that day. They liked the idea and selected a restaurant well-known for serving delicious meals. The new member of the band told them about his previous adventures and how enjoyable he felt undergoing them had been. He asked each of them about their adventures, but their answers were disappointing to the new member, as they were related only to hip-hop dancing. He told them sarcastically that dancing was only a pastime and couldn't be considered an adventure, explaining that real adventures should involve an element of fear, which should be overcome by courage.

He asked them if they wanted to try an adventure with him, and they agreed. So he asked them to get closer, and he whispered, "Let's run away from this restaurant without paying the bill."

They all looked at each other, but he didn't give them time to think and hurriedly said, "Forget it. It seems that you are good at nothing but dancing."

"Come on! We will run away with you. We are no lesser adventurers," Nora said encouragingly.

The boy was pleased to hear this, looked at them, and said, "Now!"

They all stood up and start running out of the restaurant at once, but one of the waiters ran after them. He was young and athletic. The new boy suggested that each of them go in a different direction. The waiter, disturbed for a few seconds, decided to chase Nora. Nora ran as fast as she could, looking back from time to time to see that the waiter was still enthusiastically catching up on her. Nora went into one of the alleys to hide, but he was still running after her; and when she felt that he was about to discover her hideout, she ran away once again. She reached the outskirts of the town and was still running when she saw a house that she has never seen before with an open door. She could hear voices and the sound of music coming from inside of the house and concluded that there was a party going on. So she decided to go into the house very quickly to hide herself among the partygoers. There were many guests at the party chatting and laughing together, but the music was funereal. A tall man with a scary smile came closer to her and said, "Are you here for the party?"

She nodded her head shyly.

"So please come in and don't feel shy," he added.

Nora walked toward the partiers, and there she discovered their scary shapes, but she was still more scared of the waiter who was still chasing her. Suddenly, all the partiers vanished for a moment before appearing again. Nora was very frightened, and her heart almost stopped beating, but she thought that it was only imagination. She rubbed her eyes, and the tall man came toward her. He asked her if she had been enjoying the party, or if she wanted to get the music track changed. She agreed with a nod of her head without being able to speak. The tall man looked around, as if searching for an assistant to change the music for him; and all of a sudden, all people in the house disappeared again. Nora was filled with shock and fear and started shivering. The tall man came back to her and looked at her with his terrifying eyes. She tried to run away, but as she tried to do so, all the attendants surrounded her with their yellow eyes, and she collapsed.

When she woke up, she found herself on a strange hill. Then she realized that she was into an extreme trouble. She was terrified when she saw the Makash. She remained silent, trying to figure out what was going on; and when she tried, along with Dana, to help the unconscious girl and saw the Makash's reaction, she realized that she simply had to obey the orders until she found a chance to flee.

She had never imagined being on a magic carpet. When she was high in the sky with her feet hanging in the air, she wished her friends were with her to come up with a new dance.

She started rubbing her ears when she heard the Moback speaking. She didn't know how to react to Dana's remark when she said that she couldn't believe that there was a speaking animal. She remained silent, although she wanted to say to her, "And you can believe that there is a flying carpet?"

All the time on board the carpet, Nora could think of nothing but running away, and when she saw everyone in that world walking both vertically and horizontally, she thought maybe she could fly. If that world was this bizarre and surrealistic, everything seemed to be possible.

When Dana proposed a plan for running away, Nora couldn't agree more and thought enthusiastically about the teenager who had joined her dancing group and kept showing off, talking about his adventures. She said to herself, *Wait until I come back and tell you about my adventures, which will for sure dwarf yours. This will make them look like bedtime stories.*

She ran as fast as she could to outrun the Makash, aided by her natural agility and dancing skills. Despite the fact that the plan ended in failure, she enjoyed the attempt. She hated Sikwel very much—that arrogant, disgusting creature—and wished she could punch him.

They took her to an old Shakam woman in a flat on the seventieth floor. She was a very old woman and could barely walk. The old woman welcomed her, saying, "I only want you to sit here next to me and tell me about your life."

Nora nodded her head, but she was still thinking of running away and reaching the hill where she regained consciousness to go back to her normal world and life.

Nora got permission from the old woman to look around the flat, and she headed toward the main door to discover that it was not locked. She was surprised when it opened easily. So she left happily and went down to the streets where she hung around. She enjoyed walking up and down vertically whenever she wished and still couldn't believe herself able to do it. She walked up and even danced up as well. Then she started searching everywhere to find the hill but failed. She took refuge in one of the alleys to have a rest and hide from the passersby, but seconds later, she was arrested and, knowing the harshness and strength of the guards, didn't resist and went away with them.

ADAM

Adam was a great fan of his father, the famous boxing champion in their small city. His father had encouraged him to practice boxing since he was very young. He liked the sport, as his father had loved it before him, and he wished he could realize the dream of his father and became the world champion. After his father had retired from boxing, he started training his son in his newly opened private boxing club. Adam was a fast learner, driven by the urge to make his father proud of him. At the age of eight, he became the club champion in his age category. He remained champion for the next few years until he turned sixteen years old. When the city championship approached, his father told him to double his training sessions, but Adam was overconfident of his abilities. He was sure that he would obtain the title easily, thanks to his long experience and glorious history. Also, he was the son of the undefeatable hero. His father always urged him to have discipline and to respect others and warned him of arrogance by saying, "Arrogance speeds up the defeat of champions."

Adam tried to follow his father's advice, but he couldn't help behaving arrogantly at school; and because he was a champion, he was always received with respect and amiability. Other students tried always to satisfy him. He considered his physical superiority as one of the axioms, or unchanged facts of life, and he thus fell into the arrogance that his father warned him of.

On the day of under-sixteen boxing championship, Adam believed he was more than ready for the match. He entered the ring looking arrogantly at his opponent. He even didn't hear his father's instructions before the match. He was totally confident that he would knock down his opponent easily, especially since he had beaten him before, in the under-fourteen championship. The bell rang for the first round, and the match started with Adam's attempted blow to his opponent, who managed to evade it skillfully and retaliate with another blow that dropped Adam to the canvas. Adam was shocked and thought, *This is impossible. This can't happen to me.*

The referee pushed Adam's opponent back and started counting. Adam couldn't see or hear anything except his father, who was urging him to stand up. On the count of five, Adam stood up again, but this time he lost all thoughts of underestimation. He frowned and decided to take revenge. He attacked his opponent harshly, but his jabs and punches lost their way and ended up in thin air. His opponent, meanwhile, looked calm and confident. He fended off Adam's combinations and retaliated with calculated ones. The first round ended in a draw, and both took their corners to prepare for the second round. Adam said to his father, "I can't believe this is happening. I defeated him easily two years ago."

His father looked at him and said, "And that is exactly what drove him to improve himself." Then he continued, saying, "You just have to stop underestimating him. You are forgetting what I taught you and only thinking of what happened two years ago. Don't think of that, and go back to your normal style, and you will beat him."

The bell announced the start of the second round. Adam decided to follow his father's instructions. He managed to evade his opponent's punches swiftly and then knocked him out with a powerful blow. The referee counted to ten, and when the opponent failed to rise, he announced Adam the winner. His father rushed into the ring excitedly and carried him on his shoulders with pride. After the match, Adam's father took his son to a restaurant to celebrate the title. He was so proud that he took every possible chance, when speaking to acquaintances and passersby on the street, to allude to the match and to the happy news that his son had won the city boxing championship. Adam had never been happier. He wanted to tell everyone about his achievement. When they arrived at the restaurant, his father noticed a frailty in his son's behavior. When a waiter came to serve them and saluted them,

Adam didn't reply. He told the waiter to bring the selected dishes quickly without even looking at him.

His father was upset with this behavior and decided to teach him a lesson. After a short while, he said, "You know, son, in this world you have to respect and be nice to others so you can make real friends."

Adam seemed not to be convinced by this and replied by saying, "I don't need others. They need me, Dad. I'm the champ. Everybody wants to be a friend with the strong guy." Adam thought that, with his strength, he didn't need anybody. When they finished their dinner, instead of going home, Adam's father took his son to the gym. Adam didn't understand why, but his father told him to get out of the car and follow him. His father took him to where the cleaning and bleaching tools were stored and told him to clean the whole facility. Adam felt very embarrassed and disturbed and couldn't find a reason for what his father was doing. He asked why.

His father ignored the question and told him to do what he was told to do. Then he left him alone and went to his small office in the gym after telling his son that he wouldn't go home without finishing cleaning. Adam, full of rage and resentment, started cleaning the place. He tried to find an explanation for what happened but couldn't. He concluded that his father was jealous of his achievements and of his becoming a champion at the age of sixteen while he himself couldn't make it before the age of twenty-five.

He mopped the ground for a little time, but as soon as his father went inside his office, he went outside the gym. He had no idea where to go, but he didn't want to stay with his father. He passed a house where he heard music and chatter. He concluded that there was a party going on inside the place. He wished he had been inside to celebrate the title with them. Suddenly, he heard a voice saying to him, "Come to the party."

Adam looked around to see who was speaking, but there was nobody there. He walked away, but a tall man with a weird smile approached him and said, "Are you Adam the champion?"

Adam replied yes, and he felt happy to be recognized only hours after attaining the title. The man said, "So join our party. I am sure you will like it."

Adam hesitated for a moment, but then he followed the tall man inside the house where the attendants were gathering. The tall man addressed the guests, "I would like to introduce Adam, the champion, to you."

The clutter stopped, and all guests looked at the young newcomer, who felt scared. A chill rippled down her spine, but despite that he smiled at them. Suddenly, all the attendants vanished, except for the tall man. Adam panicked and looked at the tall man begging for an explanation for what had happened, but the tall man only smiled in a weird way. All of a sudden, the guests appeared again. Adam was so terrified that he couldn't swallow his saliva; and when all of them disappeared again, including the tall man, Adam ran toward the main door. There, however, he found the guests, who appeared from nowhere with their yellowish eyes, waiting for him and blocking his way. Adam couldn't control his fear and fainted.

When he woke up, he was upset that he had faced the situation in a cowardly way and surprised to see that everything was changed. He was now in a totally different world. When he heard the Makash scolding Steven and telling him to stand still, he turned his head to see who was speaking, but he was filled with shock and fear when he saw the Makash. He managed to control himself with difficulty and looked around to see a group of other children. He felt rest a little assured to know that he wasn't alone in whatever it was he had gotten himself into. He was ordered to queue with some other children but couldn't remain silent anymore and asked, "Where are we? And what is this place?"

The guard didn't reply and reprimanded him instead. He told him that it wasn't the suitable time to ask questions. Adam held his tongue grudgingly and promised himself to run away. When he flew on board the magic carpet and heard the Moback animals talk, he realized that his martial art skills would not be enough and that he should change his ways, as it became clear to him that he wouldn't be able to beat this new world with his young fists and punches.

He examined the city carefully as if he were examining an opponent before a boxing match. He tried to memorize the streets so that he could use the same routes back to the hill and get back to his world. When the carpet landed and the two girls tried to run away, he tried to help by attacking one of the guards and asking the other boy to help. The two boys tried to control the guard and almost defeated him, but other guards thwarted their little project and arrested the two girls.

After he was given his uniform and sat for photographs, Adam was taken to a clothes factory. He was seated in front of one of the machines, and the Makash sent a ten-year-old girl to train him on how to use the machine. He asked her, after the guards had left, "Where is the exit?"

She didn't reply and kept on explaining how to use the machine, but he repeated the question many times. She said to him, looking around in fear, "It is there," and moved her eyes toward the exit.

He smiled to her and said, "Is this the only exit?"

She replied, "There is a window that leads to the street in the boss's office." Adam was very surprised to discover that the person in charge was a fifteen-year-old child.

Adam listened to the girl's instructions on how to operate the machine while watching the child in charge carefully. When Adam saw him enter the office, he followed him inside and said to him, "I am leaving this place, and you will help me."

The other child looked at the newcomer with surprise and said sarcastically, "And where do you want to run away to?"

"It is none of your business," Adam replied.

The child in charge felt angry and said, "How did you know that I would help you?"

Adam looked back to him and laughed. "Because I will beat you mercilessly if you don't."

Adam went to the window, and when the child in charge tried to prevent him, he received a powerful punch that dropped him to the ground. Adam ran out of the window, and the other boy stood up and yelled at him with his torso protruding from the window, "You will not go far because they will catch you. There is no way out of Scaba."

Adam ignored that and started running. The factory was situated in the outskirts of the city. He could see the city's high-rising towers from where he was, and so he headed toward them. He saw a group of Makash passing by and hid himself behind the trees and watched them carefully. They dismounted their zebras to catch one of the enars that had fallen into their nets. The enars resisted them and screamed whenever they got near to it. The commander of the Makash group threw a wouf at the enar, which took away its legs and dropped it to the ground. The Makash then attacked it, tied it up, and carried it on the back of one of the elephants. Adam waited until they had left and then completed his trip to the city.

Like other children, Adam ended his trip exhausted, walking and walking in circles. He couldn't find the hill that they had landed on, and so he hid himself in one of the corners between the buildings to have a rest. He pondered over what had happened to him and realized that being a champion would not help him there. He needed someone to talk to, and being alone only made things worse. Moments later, the Makashan guards came forth and captured him. He resisted them and even punched a guard in the face, but it didn't work, so he gave up and surrendered to them.

SARA

Every time Sara fought with her younger sister, she would wonder about how her life would have been without the grumpiness and selfishness of her sister. She would resort to her violin, playing and playing to forget what she was going through. Despite being fourteen years old, her sister, who was ten, still considered her a rival. Their rivalry upset her mother, who often advised her to take care of her sister rather than fighting with her.

Sara was jealous of her sister because of the special treatment she received from the parents. She also felt that her sister was more beautiful than her and that the rug had been pulled from under her feet. She hated to be regarded as the second best in everything. When she had been the only child of her parents, life was more beautiful for her. Her parents cared only for her, and she still remembered how happy her mother had been when she saw her play the violin for the first time. She was very proud of her. At that time, her mother was her best friend, and the violin was her second best. Now she felt lonely and that her mother had let her down to befriend and take care of her younger sister. The violin was the only friend left to her, and although her parents often encouraged her to play the violin and stood by her in everything, the feeling of jealousy toward her sister prevailed and grew stronger day by day. Her parents didn't ignore her incessant urge to take part in musical competitions, and they attended all of them, where she always won one of the first places. Despite that, her feeling of her parents' favoritism toward her younger sister broke her heart.

She hated to see her mother prepare her sister for the beauty pageant competition that was organized by her younger sister's school. Sara was filled with resentment because of it. Her mother noticed her permanent mental distress and her inclination to play sad music of late. One day her mother, hearing her play sad music, entered her room to ask her about the cause of her sadness. Sara, however, was totally immersed in her playing, and her eyes were closed, so she didn't notice the arrival of her mother. Her mother deeply felt the melodies coming from the violin talking to her and rippling through her entire body. She waited for her to finish playing and clapped her hands warmly. Sara smiled to her mother and felt happy to see her mother around. She ran to her and embraced her saying, "Oh, Mom, I miss you."

"But I am here with you, darling. I didn't go away from you anywhere," her mother replied while smiling at her amiably. Then she looked at her while she was still smiling and asked her about what had made her depressed and sad and why she secluded herself from them.

Sara refused to reveal her feelings, and her mother understood because she knew how tender and sensitive her daughter was. She didn't want to see her sad and embraced her and told her that she loved her very much and she was proud of her. Then she told her that she was confident that she would become well-known and eminent when she grew up. She advised her to keep on practicing and have faith in her talents. Sara happily agreed with her mother.

Her mother turned to leave the room but then turned back as if she had remembered something and asked Sara to help her prepare her sister's dress for the competition. She said while looking at her in the eyes, "I wish your sister had a talent like yours. She would have won easily."

Sara thanked God that her sister didn't have such a talent and said to herself, *Her beauty is enough for her.* Then she resorted again to her violin but this time played a funny melody.

On the day of the beauty competition, while everyone was taking their breakfast, Sara sneaked into her sister's room and took her sister's dress from the box. She ruined it by cutting parts out of it. Then she put it back into the box and went down to take her breakfast as if she had done nothing. She soon felt guilty for what she had done, especially when she saw how excited her sister was about taking part in the competition. She wished she hadn't done that and thought of confessing, but it was too late because all of them were in the car heading for the school competition by then. Sara felt bitterly sad and started weeping silently. When they arrived at the school, her mother and sister headed to the coulisse, and she and her father seated themselves in the front row. She was filled with remorse and sorrow for what she had done and couldn't tolerate it when she saw her father preparing the camera happily. She told him that she needed to go to the toilet, but instead she went outside the school, running away from that horrible scene. She ran aimlessly until she reached one of the houses where she could hear the clamor of a party inside. She paused outside the house, drawn by the sound of the violin, and forgot herself. A tall man came out of the house with a scary smile and interrupted her joyful moments by asking, "Are you lost, dear?"

Sara was startled, but she replied with a yes.

He asked her kindly to come inside and use the telephone to call her parents to come and fetch her and added, "You can wait for them inside and enjoy listening to the violin meanwhile."

Sara accepted the man's offer and followed him inside the house. She had a strange feeling while passing through the hall of the main house, and a chill rippled down her spine. She kept looking around while following the tall man until she arrived at the place where the guests where. They were enjoying their time, and that calmed her down a little. She felt lost among the guests, as nobody paid her any attention. She tried to talk to the tall man, but she couldn't find him. She started searching for him everywhere when, all of a sudden, the attendants vanished, as if they had never been there. Even the sound of the violin stopped suddenly. Sara was terrified; her vision blurred, and she started shivering severely. Then she collapsed to the ground, unconscious.

Sara woke up on the hill, unaware where she was or what time it was. She saw the beautiful Moback animals smiling to her. She returned the smile. She heard a very harsh sound, and when she looked around and saw the Makash, she fainted again. She woke up after a while to find herself, along with a group of children, in a strange place. One of the children carrying her told her not to panic. She felt good, but her fear of those terrifying creatures remained. She couldn't believe all she was seeing was real and felt confident that it was some kind of a nightmare. When the two girls tried to run away and the boys attacked the fearful creatures, she wished she had her violin with her to play a melody that could change her mood. That was the first time Sara had been apart from her family. She said to herself, after closing her eyes, *God, please send me back home, and I promise I will never feel jealous of my sister again.*

She was sure that what was happening to her was a kind of heavenly punishment for what she had done to her younger sister. She noticed that one of the small beautiful Moback animals remained by her side wherever she went. They took her to the photography room, and then they gave her the new uniform, but she fainted again when they took her away from the other children once again.

She woke up this time to find herself in one of the Shakam households. There was a family that consisted of four children and two parents. All of them were surrounding her bed, and when she woke up and saw them around her and that small beautiful animal sleeping by her side, she fainted again.

City Jail

Dana, Nora, Adam, and Steven met at the prison into which the guards had thrown them. They felt a little safer seeing each other once again. This time, they had the leisure to introduce themselves. Nora asked about Sara's whereabouts, but Dana concluded, "It seems that she didn't run away."

"What I can't figure out is how they found me. I was hiding in a safe hideout," Adam wondered.

Dana looked into their faces and said, "Everything in this world is perplexing."

None of them were able to decipher the secrets of Scaba. Adam said to them, "If we don't run away from this world, we will stay here for a very long time. Maybe we will end up spending our entire lives here."

"But how can we run away when they are so much stronger than us?" Steven asked.

Dana said, "There must be a way."

"They are much stronger than we are; I punched one in the face, but he wasn't hurt at all," Adam explained. "I saw one of these evil creatures shoot a ray from his hand at a trapped animal and hurt it."

Nora said, "They have a flying carpet, they shoot rays, and their animals talk. Where are we?"

They held their peace, as they didn't know the answer. Dana looked at them. "It is not important where we are. More important is how to get out of here and go back to the human world." They talked in detail about what they had seen and noticed in Scaba so far; and suddenly, the door of the jail opened, and Sikwel came in, wearing a smile filled with gloating. He didn't speak for seconds and then said, "It seems that you are going to give me a lot of trouble."

Dana wanted to say something, but he silenced her with a gesture from his hand and said, "No. No. Before you say anything, I want you to know that Scaba is inescapable."

Then he explained to them that, wherever they went, the faultless crystal ball would find them, and so there was no use in futile attempts to run away.

"But we don't want to stay here. We want to go back to our world," Dana said resiliently.

Sikwel laughed out loud and said to them, "Whoever comes to Scaba can never go back to the human world in one piece. He will go there without sanity."

Then, in a threatening tone, he warned them about trying to run away again, saying there would be very bad consequences if they tried again. He told them that they would spend some time in jail and then go back to their jobs. He left the kids puzzled without answering any of the hundreds of questions lingering in their minds. Their perplexity even doubled when he told them that whoever goes back to the human world would lose his brain. Also, they were puzzled when they heard about the crystal ball that could find them wherever they went.

The kids discussed that point in particular without arriving at a conclusion, but they agreed on one thing: They should keep trying to run away from that place and never surrender, no matter the circumstances. Dana said to them all, "We shouldn't allow that hateful creatures frighten us."

The four kids tried running away again many times later. Every time they were sent back to their jobs, they ran away. Reuniting at the jail became a normal occurrence for them. They even tried to run away when the Makash changed their jobs and places, but they were always captured. Despite that, they didn't give up. They planned to keep on doing the same until the Makash got weary of them and sent them back home. At least, that was what Dana came up with. But that didn't happen, and after their fifth attempt to flee, Sikwel came to them maddened by the repeated attempts and swore he would torture them. He took them out of jail and lined them up in front of him. He said to them, "You put me in an embarrassing situation in front of my commander, General Falca."

The children suppressed a laugh at that moment, watching Sikwel in such a state. "Finally I have received orders that I have been waiting for a long time, to punish you." Then he explained to them that they would receive a new style of punishment, invented by General Falca. "I hope you will like it," he said.

Then he ordered his assistants to bring the tools of punishment: a long wooden piece of wood and cudgels. Two of the Makash held it horizontally; and other guards forced the children to lie on their backs, remove their shoes, and tie their feet to the piece of wood.

The kids looked at each other in shock, and Sikwel took a cudgel and started beating their bare little feet mercilessly. The kids screamed in pain, but he didn't stop beating them until their feet started to bleed. Then he ordered the guards to untie them and throw them back in jail.

They remained in jail in that state of pain and suffering for two days. On the third day, they were sent an old Shakam physician called Wajdbeer to treat them. He felt sorry for them and served them with some herbal treatment. The pain, surprisingly, vanished in just seconds. They thanked him for that, and once he was gone, Sikwel came in and said, "I hope that you learned a lesson from this punishment."

They remained silent and didn't reply, so he added, "This punishment is just a taste of what is to come. If you run away again, you will be sent to the Higher Court. General Falca himself will prosecute you then."

He smiled after a few seconds of silence and added sarcastically, "You should be assured that he will not treat you mercifully."

Despite that strict warning, which filled them with horror, they decided not to stop their attempts to run away.

FILDA AND BERMUDA

For the three days that the twins spent in bed recovering from their wounds, Princess Filda tried to meet the king to protest her objection to the punishment that had taken place, and on the third day, she was able to meet him and talk to him face-to-face. She raised her voice when she was telling the king that she was even against bringing human children to the kingdom of Scaba.

This was not the first time she had expressed her objection to bringing children into their world.

The first time she woke up from her coma, she didn't like seeing human children in their service. So she decided to do something in that regard. She took some children with her on board the carpet and flew with them toward the hill that led to the human world. She was very close to the hill and had almost succeeded, but General Falca was watching her closely. He followed her with a group of tough guards and intercepted the flight, forcing her to go back to Scaba. The king decreed that she shouldn't go aboard the carpet unaccompanied again. He didn't punish her but only scolded her for doing what she had done. This, however, increased General Falca's resentment and hatred toward her.

But this time, the king got angrier, and even his snake got her tongue out with anger too, trying to attack princess Filda. The king said to her angrily, "I told you many times not to interfere in this."

"But this is unfair," she explained indignantly.

He told her that it was none of her business and he would forgive her that time but that it would be the last, and he advised her not to test his patience anymore because he would punish her severely the next time. Then he added, "Never believe that I will not hurt you just because I promised your father to take care of you."

General Falca smiled when he heard that, but Princess Filda got angry and said defiantly, "I will not turn a blind eye to your bad deeds toward your people and these children anymore!"

The king gnashed his teeth in anger, and his snake tried to release itself from his hands to attack the princess. He said to her, "Are you challenging me, Filda?"

"You forced me to do that," she replied.

At that point, he released the snake to attack her, but the princess shot it with a wouf and wounded it. When the king saw his disabled snake, he threw a wouf at Filda, but she managed to evade it. She moved to attack the king, but General Falca turned around her and seized her with his powerful hands. The general waited for the orders of the king, who told him to throw her in jail, adding, "Also deprive her of her son."

She looked angrily at the king and said to him in a threatening tone, "A day will come when you will be beaten by someone."

The king laughed sarcastically, and General Falca took her with the help of some guards out of the royal hall. They took her to the jail of the Shakam and Makash, which was not a building in any normal sense of the word. It was, rather, a group of metal rods fixed to the ground in a circular shape. They weren't connected to each other, and the space between each was large enough to allow a child to pass through easily. The Shakam and Makash prisoners enter it through a small wooden door in the roof. The guards took her to one of the alleys in the palace. Then they mounted a ladder. She knew where they were taking her because she knew every inch of the palace in which she was raised. At the top, they opened a small wooden door, and a wooden staircase opened automatically. They ordered her to descend the staircase to the bottom, and she did so. She was put in jail, and then they pulled the staircase up again, leaving her down.

General Falca

General Falca hailed from a family of leaders and senior officials in the kingdom of Scaba. He was still a loyal follower of Queen Nafarit, the founder of the first kingdom of the Makash. He believed that she was good and always rejected what others said of her. He always defended her when others spoke of her in a bad way. He never loved the Shakam and always considered them oppressors who had stolen the legitimate rights of the Makash. He hated the Shakam's sense of superiority over the Makash but managed to get the support of thousands of Makash around him. His main dream was to take revenge on the Shakam and retrieve the rule of the kingdom from them. He had been a leader of a Shakam brigade under the command of General Commander Medan when the army of Uranus invaded Scaba. He fought courageously and was awarded a courage medal, which had remained hung on his bosom ever since. He befriended Solar the Magician after he noticed his emotional inclination toward the Makash. They became intimate friends, each disclosing his secrets and daydreams to the other. Falca revealed his ambitions to rule the kingdom to his magician friend, who promised to help him realize that dream someday.

One day Solar visited him and told him that he wanted to talk to him about an important matter. He looked hesitant, and Falca inferred that it was a very important matter. He gave him all his attention. After moments of hesitation and fumbling, Solar told him that he had found a way that he could rule the kingdom. Falca received the news with surprise and happiness and told Solar to reveal it to him very quickly. Solar looked around and whispered, "Kill the king treacherously."

Falca couldn't comprehend what he had heard from Solar because the laws of Scaba wouldn't accept the unstated and unannounced killing of the Shakam by the Makash. Also, war should be declared before such a deed was done because killing without war was very illegitimate in their doctrines. So he inquired, "Do you mean that I declare war against him?"

Solar looked at him and said to him, "Treachery, dear . . . treachery. You should kill him without declaring war."

Then Solar clarified the matter for him and told him that such a deed would disturb the whole country and put it into a state of chaos, as it would have happened for the first time ever, and he could use that to declare himself king. Falca thought it over but couldn't digest the horrible idea, so he said to Solar, "We can't kill others in that treacherous way. It is forbidden in our norms and customs. Besides, the Makash themselves will disown and renounce me and consider me villainous."

Solar insisted on the plan, telling him that it was the only way to get rid of the king and gain control over the Shakam. Then he told him that the Makash would soon forget all the laws of Scaba when they retrieve the throne. The magician gave his friend some days to think about it. Falca was left perplexed, but he started to think of that plan from all directions. The idea of becoming king was more than a dream for him and pushed him hard to accept the plan. After three days of daydreaming and thinking, he decided that he was convinced and went to Solar asking for details of how to carry out the plan. Solar was happy with Falca's decision, so he gave him the details of the plan to kill the king.

The plan stated that Falca gather his supporters and loyal adherents and put them in readiness for a big event. Solar warned him against telling his group his real intentions, and told him that, when he killed the king, he should order his followers to arrest all people of any importance in the kingdom and put them in jail, the first among which would be Commander Medan.

Falca did what he was told and gathered his followers for the big day. On that day, Falca entered the royal hall to meet with the king, who had just finished a meeting with some Shakam senior officials. The king welcomed him with a smile and told him to come and sit next to him. Falca walked slowly toward the king with his heart beating fast. His two tails were moving awkwardly. The king looked at him suspiciously but continued smiling. Falca stopped in the middle of the hall, and at that moment, Commander Medan entered the hall, but Falca didn't notice due to his excitement. Falca suddenly shot a wouf at the king who managed to evade it, miraculously considering the fact that he wasn't expecting it at all. He couldn't imagine that Falca would do that to him. The king was shouting "Why? Why?" when Falca tried to throw another wouf at him. But at that point, Commander Medan screamed in the shrill anesthetizing voice that paralyzes the Makash, and Falca fell down in pain. Medan threw a wouf at him that left him unconscious. The king approached Falca and asked Commander Medan, "What was that?"

Medan couldn't believe what had happened and said to the king, "It seems that he was trying to kill you treacherously, sir."

He was taken and put in jail while still unconscious. He stayed there for a while until his followers entered the jail secretly and took him out with the help of Solar, whose role in that plot remained a secret. Falca hadn't revealed Solar's role in the plot to anybody, not even to his adherent followers. Falca hated the Shakam furiously and had waged a number of wars against them but lost them all, and he could thus do nothing but give up and wait for that day in which he could defeat the Shakam and retrieve the rule from them, but this time he has turned into nothing more than a pathetic exiled outcast living away from the kingdom.

Falca then lived outside the kingdom for years with his followers, who chose to join him rather than live under the rule of the Shakam. One night, which Falca would remember for years to come, a Shakam came to him on the back of a yellow zebra. The guards stopped him, but he told them confidently, "I would like to meet your leader. I have a message for him from Solar."

Falca was at that moment sitting with Sikwel and some of his close followers. He looked as desperate as usual when the guards came forth to tell him of the Shakam guest's desire to meet him.

"What an insolent, shameless Shakam! I swear I will kill him no matter what he wants."

He told them to bring him forth quickly. The Shakam came forth with confidence and said to him, "My name is Bermuda, and I have a message to you from your friend, Solar."

"My friend vanished after he sent me into oblivion," Falca replied bitterly.

The man, however, told him that Solar was very sad about what had happened and that he would never break his promise to him. Falca looked at him and said, "He had better stop his lies. He can do nothing."

He then ordered the guards to arrest Bermuda, but when they approached him to do that, Bermuda took a piece of metal out of his cloak. The weapon, which was called darzar, was shining in the darkness. The guards were very afraid, as was even Falca himself, and they kneeled down asking the guest for mercy. Bermuda said to them, "Now you know what type of power I have. Can we talk now about what I came for? I came here carrying with me the means of your victory over the Shakam," he added.

"But you are a Shakam!" Falca pointed out grudgingly.

Bermuda explained to him that neither he nor Solar liked Scaba anymore, and that they had decided to take the human world for themselves, as it was bigger and more exciting for them. They had even agreed between them how to rule it. Then he added, "I own one of the two dazars. I will need the other one to control both Scaba and the human world." He paused briefly and then said, "We will leave Scaba for you, and Solar and I will rule the human world."

The ideas of ruling Scaba mesmerized Falca once again, and he asked Bermuda, "What can I do in that regard?"

Bermuda looked at him and said that the other darzar was with the runaways who had kept it with them after the killing of the king and that he needed to get it back to help him rule.

He confessed to Falca that he needed his help to seize the throne temporarily and promised that he would give it to him afterward, but during the interregnum, he said he would give all important ranks in the government to the Makash. He told him to declare war after two days, and he would help him win over the Shakam who lost their king and their leader. Falca wondered about how the war would be run and how he would defeat the Shakam while they still had their unbeatable weapon, their deafening voices.

"I have a gift for you that Solar brought from the human world. It will help you defeat your enemy," Bermuda said confidently.

Then he asked for a box that was still on the zebra's back to be brought to him. Falca ordered the guards to bring the box. They did so, and Bermuda opened it. Falca looked inside it to see a huge piece of cork.

"What is that?" Falca wondered curiously.

Bermuda cut two small pieces out of the huge cork to demonstrate. He asked Falca to put them into his ears. Falca took them cautiously and put them into his ears. Bermuda screamed at him, but he didn't hear him. Other Makashans put their fingers into their ears because of the high voice. Falca was amazed to see all followers put their fingers to their ears while he felt no need to. Bermuda then told him to remove the two pieces and said to him, "You can sometimes defeat the most powerful weapons in the whole world with trivial things." They smiled together. "Now you don't have to worry, you will be able after getting used of the cork in your ears to hear everything but Shakams' deafening voices," Bermuda added.

That gift was the most valuable Falca ever received in his life. He rejoiced and celebrated as he had never done before. The Makash celebrated that night in their unique way. They played their music and sang the songs that were related to the shining history of the Makash and Nafarit. They danced their famous Makashan dance, rejoicing hopes of victory and retrieving Scaba from their enemies. Falca danced and danced that night until he fell deeply asleep.

HOMELESS KIDS

When the kids met in the jail for the sixth time, they realized that their punishment would be very harsh, but despite that they were very happy that they had kept their promises and tried to run away. They even agreed to run away no matter how harsh the punishment was. They were left in jail for a week without being told of their destiny. A week later, some guards came and put them in a wooden carriage that looked like a cage pulled by an elephant and took them to another bigger building. While passing through streets of the city guarded by some guards, everybody looked at them with fear, as if they knew what they were about to face. Scaba was like ordinary cities in the human world: there were shops that were full of Shakam and some Makashan shoppers. There were shops for shoes, clothes, and tools. Everything looked usable by human beings, but the truth was that nothing could be used by people. The streets were crowded all over, and human children were wondering around with their masters following a stern order that they couldn't violate, except those four who broke the roles, and henceforth they decided to punish them.

They arrived at the court building and were ushered into a courtroom that was furnished with seats. There was a raised platform that was occupied by one big chair; it was the judge's seat. The kids were put inside another wooden cage inside the courtroom. The courtroom was crowded with Makash and Shakam, and the kids managed to see Sikwel among the attendants. He was sitting in a seat that was separated from others by a small wooden partition. Sikwel looked at them with his threatening smile. After a while, General Falca entered the courtroom from a door behind the raised platform. All attendants rose to their feet and didn't sit down again until he sat himself on the big chair. The kids exchanged looks. Falca looked around the courtroom and looked at the children; then he looked at Sikwel and waved his hand, ordering him to start his pleading.

Sikwel stood up and said, "These four human children have violated the roles of Scaba."

Voices of condemnation rose in the courtroom, and General Falca knocked on the small table in front of him with a small wooden gavel to silence the voices. When all of them were quiet, Sikwel went on. "We gave them the chance to think rationally, but they insisted on repeating their mistake. So we punished them with the Falca punishment, but it didn't work, as they did it again and ran away many times."

He approached the wooden cage and looked at Dana and said, "They decided to run away and insisted on violating our rules from the very first moment they arrived here. We tried our best to rehabilitate them but in vain."

General Falca moved his head many times as an indication of disapproval and said to the children, "You left us with no other choice. We have to inflict upon you the most extreme punishment for humans in Scaba."

Murmurs filled the courtroom, and General Falca used his gavel once again. When the room was quiet, he said to the shocked children, "You have to know that you are the first human children who receive such a punishment." He spluttered and added, "We decided to stamp you with the 'homeless kids' stamp."

Voices rose again in the room, and General Falca had to use the gavel again, this time strongly, but voices didn't stop. All attendants looked sympathetically at the children who were unaware of the punishment, and they looked at each other with sarcasm. Sikwel approached them and said, "You will die of hunger, dear. You will creep toward us begging for forgiveness."

Then he explained to them the details of the punishment. Homeless-kids punishment meant that they would be stamped with a certain stamp that couldn't be hidden or covered by any means. No matter how hard they tried, they would not succeed in hiding the stamp because it was like light; if they used their hands or anything to hide it, the stamp would appear on it. After being stamped, they would be left in streets, free to go wherever they wanted, as they would be monitored by the crystal ball. The stamp also meant that no Makash or Shakam was allowed to feed or harbor them, which meant slow death of hunger. Also, it meant that the Makash and Shakam were allowed to shoot them with woufs.

At that moment, the children's faces turned yellow with fear and shock. None of the Shakam or Makash had shot them with a wouf before, and they knew that woufs meant death.

Sikwel added that if they decided to repent and come back to their reason and become good citizens in Scaba, they could go to him and declare their repentance and sorrow.

Despite being afraid, Dana said to him, "We prefer death to repentance."

Sikwel laughed and said to her, "You will soon die of hunger."

Then he looked at them and said, "By the way, if you still think that you can reach the hill of the gate that you arrived at to Scaba, I advise you to forget that. To reach that place, you will need a carpet; and even if you manage to get on board one, which is impossible, you will never manage to fly it."

It was true: the kids had discovered that reaching the Rainbow Desert and the hill of the gate was impossible without the help of the flying carpet.

After the trial, the kids were taken to another hall, and they tried to resist the Makash but failed. The Makash stamped their foreheads with a strange luminous material. They wrote "Homeless Kids" in the Makashan symbols: "#*#*#."

Then they were led out the building. They looked at each other, and Nora asked, "What is the next step now?"

Adam said, "We will die of hunger."

"There is nothing edible in this world," Steven said.

Dana said, "No, you are mistaken. There are edible things."

They looked at her hoping for an explanation. She said to them, "We can eat the food that is served to human children."

"But that food is only available at food courts, which are heavily guarded," Nora replied.

Dana smiled and said, "We will find a way to steal it."

Steven said, "But this time they will not tolerate us with mercy! They have a license to kill us."

Dana told them not to be discouraged and said, "We have to bear what we decided to go through with our own well from the beginning."

She explained to them that they could have been like all the other kids who lived and worked as slaves in the kingdom of Scaba, but since they had chosen freedom, they had to fight for it to the end. Then she reminded them of their skills and talents that they could use to realize their dreams. Their morale was raised when they heard this, and they agreed with her.

They formulated a plan to get the food and distributed the tasks among themselves. Dana, who had appeared to become leader of the group without any discussion, explained the task for each one.

They were divided into two teams. One team consisted of Dana and Adam, whose mission was to discover the borders of the city and locate the direction of the hill. The other team consisted of Nora and Steven, and their mission was to locate the food courts and see if they could locate any weak points they could take advantage of.

Adam and Dana managed to locate the borders of the city and realized that it was impossible to cross those borders because of heavy guarding. There were foot patrols and other flying ones along the borders, so they failed to locate the direction of the hill. The other team hung around and managed to locate the food courts, but they also noticed that everybody was trying to avoid any contact with them. Life sentence would be the punishment for any Makashan or Shakam dealing with or helping them, and as for other children, the punishment for the first time would be flogging.

If it were repeated, the punishment would be joining them to die of hunger.

With the advent of night, they gathered under the big tree in the outskirts of the city where they had planned. They shared information they gathered, and since they were very tired and hungry, they decided to sleep under the tree.

On the other day of their trial, they decided to break into one of the food courts. Steven and Nora put a sketch on the ground of the food court they decided to break into using branches from the big tree after breaking it into small pieces; the drawing also included the possible routes of escape and the number of guards at the door of the food court.

They planned to send Steven to hijack two taxi zebras and put them near the food court so that when they went out with the food that they stole Steven would be waiting for them. They headed for the city. Everyone was looking at the stamp on their foreheads, but they didn't care about that. Steven saw a number of zebras standing at a transport station waiting for passengers with some driver children who were taking care of them and chatting together. He got as close as possible from the station. Adam and Dana were supposed, according to the plan, to attack one of the two guards at the door of the food court; and when the other guard shot the wouf at them, they would evade it, and it would hit the other guard. Then Nora would run inside the hall to bring the food.

Adam took a thick branch from the big tree with him and approached the two guards along with Dana, cautiously nodding their heads so that the guards wouldn't recognize the stamp on their foreheads. The guards stopped them and one of them said, "Go back from where you came. This hall is not your designated one, and it is full."

They ignored what they heard and kept walking. When they were very close, Dana attacked one of the guards, and Adam ran toward the other guard but slowly. When he saw that Dana had reached the other guard, he stopped. Dana attacked the guard but was careful only to direct her back at him. He grabbed both her hands and twisted them back. She pretended that she was resisting him and shouted at the other guard, "Please don't shoot me with your wouf. Please don't kill me."

The other guard ignored her plea and shot her with the wouf. She jumped gracefully at exactly the right moment by pushing her back against the guard and pushing her feet against the ground to lift herself up high and flip in the air, doing so at exactly the right moment so that the guard received the wouf instead and fell down. The other guard was disturbed to see that; and when it was Adam's turn to get involved in the fight, he pushed the guard hard on his big ear and hit him with the branch that was in his hands, putting him into deep sleep.

Meanwhile Nora had gone inside the big food court, which was full of children sitting in order taking their meals. When she entered, children stopped eating, and murmurs swept over the whole hall. Nora told them not to worry because she hadn't come to hurt any of them, and all she wanted was some food.

She headed for the kitchen and told the cooks, who were human teenagers, to fill some plastic containers with food. The cooks did so with fear; and while Nora was looking around the place, she noticed that Sara was there among the children with the same Moback animal who was with them on the carpet, sitting in her lap, so she approached her after she had taken the food containers. Pretending that she was taking some food off her plate to eat, she whisper to Sara, "Meet me tomorrow at the big western tree outside the city."

Dana joined Nora and took more food, and then they rushed outside quickly. Adam was waiting for them outside. They all looked around, searching for Steven, who was nearby waving to them, and there were some Shakams and human kids who stopped to see what was going on. Steven, then, took two zebras and ran toward his friends with the two drivers running after him, but he managed to reach his companions who stood in the face of the two drivers and forced them to retreat. Dana and Sara mounted a zebra, and Steven and Adam mounted the other. They went off away from the city feeling very happy at having captured that much food. They hid themselves in a cave and started eating their meal avariciously. "We did it!" Dana said joyfully.

"We will live this way until we find the hill," Steven commented.

"We can't reach the hill without the help of the flying carpet," Sara said.

Adam added, "And the carpet will not take us up without one of the Makash or Shakam on board."

Dana ended the argument by saying, "We will succeed in reaching the mountain as we did in capturing the food."

She advised them to be patient and to watch everything going on in Scaba very closely. No sooner had they eaten half of their food than they heard the footsteps of a Makashan group of guards who had come to arrest them. They ran away without thinking immediately, leaving food and zebras behind. When the guards entered the cave, they couldn't find the kids, who had now run toward the city and hidden themselves among the crowds with their heads bowed low to hide the stamps. They reached one of the main streets that was full of buildings and hid themselves in one that happened to be the same building in which the old Shakam woman which Nora served for a very short time before running away.

They sneaked into her flat and hid themselves inside, but Dana was worried about the old woman, so she asked Nora in a very low voice, "Are you confident that the old Shakam woman can't hurt us?"

Nora said, "Yes. She is very old, and we can hide here for sure until tomorrow."

"But how do they manage to find us every time we run away?" Adam whispered.

"It is the crystal ball that finds us every time. It is inescapable," Steven explained.

"We must take turns watching over the place so that we can manage to run away every time before they reach us," Dana said.

"But in this way our life will be very difficult," Nora complained sadly.

Dana nodded but said, "It is true, but we will live it this way or that way."

Meanwhile a group of guards had followed them to the building, but they stood outside unaware of where to search. They stood by the entrance studying the place carefully. Two of the guards went inside through the big main gate and looked inside for some time, but soon they went out to join the group that had decided to resume search in another place.

The next day, the kids woke up at sunrise, before the old woman, and left the flat without being noticed by her. They left the building and headed for the big tree, hoping to meet Sara as Nora had explained to them that she had told Sara to meet at the big tree. She justified the thinking behind this by saying that they might need her to help them since she was the only one who was eager to help them, and she wasn't stamped as they were, so nobody would suspect her.

They couldn't agree more and headed quickly toward the big tree, but Sara didn't show up in time and was very late. This made them feel very uneasy, and they started to lose hope.

"It seems that our kind friend isn't coming today," Steven said.

"I think we should leave because she might tell the Makash about our place," Adam suspected.

"Okay, guys, let's go away," Dana said.

But Nora objected to that and said, "Let's give her some time. I am sure she will come."

Steven asked her what made her believe that Sara would come, and she told him that it was just a hunch. Her hunch came true because moments later Sara came along with the Moback animal.

The group welcomed her wholeheartedly, and she smiled to them and said, "Your news are everywhere; everyone in the city is talking about you."

The Moback animal said, "It is very risky to meet you and talk to you."

Sara apologized and introduced her friend to the group, "This is my friend Kilsha. I believe you have met her before."

They all nodded and thanked Sara for coming; meanwhile, Steven was looking at Kilsha with one desire lingering in his mind: to dissect her. They asked Sara if she was doing well, and she told them that she had been sent to serve a very good Shakam family who looked so frightening in the first week that their horrible shapes made her faint many times. After a week she got used to them, and her panic vanished, especially with their kind treatment and light chores that she was supposed to carry out. They didn't tell her to do anything for them; on the contrary, they asked her about her wishes and desires, and she asked them to bring her a violin so that she could play it, and they did. Once she got the violin, she started to play on it every day and travel with its melodies too faraway worlds; at the same time, they enjoyed her playing. Sara told her friends in detail about that kind family, especially the head of the family who served in the army of the former tyrant king Bermuda, whom he didn't like or agree with.

"Do you know who Bermuda is?" she asked them.

They all answered that they did not, and so she went on, "He is the hateful creature that you can see everywhere on the pictures and posters around the city."

She then told them that the head of the family had told her once that Bermuda hadn't only expelled all Shakam from the army service but also prevented them all from using the flying carpets and restricted them to the Makash only, which made many, including him, hate Bermuda very much.

They asked her to help them, and she promised that she would bring food for them every day, so they thanked her and Dana said to her, "We want you to ask the family you are staying with about the location of the hill of the gate."

"It is near the Rainbow Desert, but you will never be able to reach there without the flying carpet," Kilsha explained instantly.

"What do you mean? Is it very far?" Nora asked.

"On the contrary, it is very near but can't be accessed without the flying carpet," Kilsha replied.

The group was dismayed and disappointed to hear that, and after moments of silence, Dana tried to boost their morale by asking, "And how can we get that carpet?"

Kilsha explained to them that, as far as she knew, there was a huge store off those carpets at the building where Sikwel's office was situated.

"You mean the Makash headquarters where they put us in jail?" Steven interrupted her.

Kilsha said it was true and added that Sikwel had all the keys to that store where he kept them in a secret place in his office. They all started wondering where that secret place could be, but Kilsha told them that Sikwel kept the key to the carpet store in the locker that contained the files of all the children. He had a copy of all files of the city's children. She told them then that the key of that locker was hidden in one of the legs of his office's table.

"So we will never leave this place," Steven murmured.

"And how do you know all that, Kilsha?" Dana asked while looking angrily at Steven with reproach.

Kilsha looked at her and said, "There is nothing in Scaba that the Moback don't know, and believe me when I tell you that the Moback are very talkative too."

"So it would be a very difficult mission to capture one of those magic carpets," Nora said.

"Even suicidal!" Adam commented, "We not only have to open the locker but break into Sikwel's office, and this is simply suicide."

They were quiet for a minute, feeling desperate, so Dana tried to raise their spirits again. "Nothing is impossible in this world. You just recall all that we've been through in this strange world pregnant with secrets and surprises."

She paused a little and then looked at Kilsha and Sara and said, "We will break into Sikwel's office to take the key, and then we will steal the carpet and fly it to the hill of the gate in order to go back to our world."

"But how can we tell the place of the key of the carpet store inside the locker? I mean, if we succeed in breaking into the office and finding the key of the locker," Sara asked spontaneously.

The children exchanged looks of bewilderment, but Dana smiled again and said, "Don't worry about that, guys. We will figure it out. It won't be that difficult."

Adam looked at her angrily and said, "Who do you think you are fooling? It is like a mission impossible, and you are nothing but a foolish, stubborn daydreamer. Since we have decided to follow you, we have gone from one deadlock to another."

Then he left them and walked away, heading toward the city. Nora called him back, and Steven tried to make him turn back as well, but he insisted on going away. Dana felt bad about what she had heard and said sadly, "Yes, I am stupid and stubborn! And my stupidity and stubbornness were the reasons behind me being here in this world." Then she looked at them and said, "Do you think I am happy being here? I feel very sorry for the foolish things that I have done. I am sorry I dragged you into all that trouble. Go back and give up to enjoy the quiet life other kids are leading. But for myself, I will fight, even if it is the last moment of my life, until I go back to my human world and apologize to my father for what I did to him."

"But I don't see you as stupid," Nora said. "You might be obstinate but not foolish, and I will be by your side no matter how hard life will be."

"I have many reasons that make me fight to death in order to go back to my parents and apologize to them for my recklessness and carelessness," she added.

"I hope we can go home so that I can love my sister as I should do and desist from my stupid jealousy of her," Sara said.

"I have to go back to prove to my parents that I became the normal kid they always wanted me to be," Steven said.

They were all filled with enthusiasm and said one by one, "I am with you, Dana." They hugged each other.

Sara came back to the city, and the group sat under the tree to try to come up with a plan to break into Sikwel's office.

Adam had not gone very far by then. He was angry, walking slowly and wishing to go back to his world to prove to his father that he didn't need anybody. He was sure that he would—one way or another—be able to get back by himself.

All of a sudden a big net covered all his body, and in seconds he was surrounded by Makash guards. He tried to set himself free but failed. The guards put him in a wooden carriage while he shouted and called to them to leave him. At that moment, he realized that he wasn't as strong as he had always thought. The guards took him with them. He wished that his friends were with him and prayed to God to give him another chance so that he could go back and apologize to his father and treat people with modesty and kindness. The rest of the kids heard Adam crying and ran toward him, but the Makash were surrounding him, and he was as helpless as a lamb inside the wooden cage. There were five guards: two in the front, riding zebras; one in the middle, riding the elephant that was pulling the carriage; and another two on zebras at the back.

The kids decided to help their friend, so they waited until the carriage started moving, and then Dana and Nora jumped on the two guards in the back and knocked them to the ground. They then mounted the zebras. Meanwhile, Steven ran quickly toward the wooden carriage and opened its door to release Adam. They both jumped swiftly behind Nora and Dana. The guards were too slow to realize what was going on, and by the time they had, the kids had already gone too far.

"I am sorry for what I said," Adam said.

"No worries," Dana replied with a big victorious smile.

THE PALACE

The twins started recovering after the third day of the punishment, and they went for a short walk. They found it very painful, but they insisted on walking. Escorted by Samar, Wang, and Shaun, Jamal and Lillian went to visit Princess Filda so that they could thank her for what she had done for them and beg her to help them go back to their world where they belonged; but first they wanted to understand what Scaba is and ask her lots of questions.

She was lonely and desperate behind the bars. She was aware that she could do nothing alone and would never manage to defeat King Bermuda. When they arrived there, she was sitting in the middle of her space gazing at nothingness. The twins were bewildered to see the bizarre design of the jail. Samar explained to them that the Shakam and the Makash feel afraid of iron because it can burn them, sometimes even fatally.

The twins realized that the more time they spent in Scaba, the more mystified they would get. The princess welcomed them and invited them in. Samar, Shaun, and Wang went in, whereas Jamal and Lillian hesitated for a moment to go through the iron bars but were encouraged to do so by Samar's cheering and inviting looks. The princess felt happy to see the kids again and asked them how they were feeling.

They thanked her for her feelings and for her sacrifice when she faced General Falca to defend them. Filda wished that she had the power to stop him and added that he was a relentless, merciless

Makashan. Lillian asked her about the endless secrets and mystery of the kingdom of Scaba, and she asked if the princess could clarify things for them. Filda told them that it was a long story, but to make things clear for them, she decided to reveal it.

HISTORY OF SCABA

The story of the kingdom of Scaba starts with two sisters, Nafarit and Biarit, who were among the ordinary creatures living in Scaba at a time in the past. Scaba was full of these creatures who resembled human beings in their shapes and who didn't have tails at that time. Their heads and faces were as beautiful as those of gazelles and deer, and their physical competencies much outsmarted those of human beings. The two sisters decided one day to travel to the human world and live there, encouraged by the exciting and adventurous possibility of a romantic life up there. They went into a deliberate kind of metamorphosis to make themselves look exactly like ordinary human beings. Nafarit was so astoundingly beautiful that even when she assumed human shape, she remained much more beautiful than her sister Biarit. Men on earth were fascinated by her bewitching beauty, and all wished for a glance from her stunning eyes; but the only one who occupied her mind, soul, and heart was the hero Achilles, the son of Peleus, king of Myrmidons, and the nymph Thetis. Nafarit liked nobody else, although men were ready to do anything to please her. Achilles was too busy with wars and fighting, so he didn't pay her much attention, but she kept trying to gain his heart by following him around and pretending she had run into him by coincidence. After some time, he came to like her and married her after she had deceived him by hiding the truth and pretending that she was a human being. Her marriage was based on deception, unlike that of her sister Biarit, who fell in love with Hercules, son of Zeus, and confessed to him who she was and where she came from. Her honesty made him love her and respect her more deeply. Nafarit gave birth to the Makash, who inherited deception and evil from their mother, and obstinacy, love of war and mercilessness from their father, while Biarit gave birth to the Shakam, who inherited kindness and love from their mother and strength and tolerance from their father. Achilles discovered his wife's trickery, but it was too late, as he was already deeply in love with her, and so he forgave her for that.

The Makash and Shakam increased in number in the human world, but they were ruled by human beings. Nafarit resented this but was unable to do anything in that regard. Prometheus, who preferred human beings to all other creatures, gifted them with fire and restricted it to human use, forbidding Makash and Shakam from using or benefiting from it. He even ordered them to go back to their mothers' homeland. Biarit liked that, as she had always believed that her life would be better in her homeland, and so she asked her husband to allow her to go back, and he didn't mind. Nafarit, on the other hand, didn't want to go back but had to do so grudgingly. She wanted to stay in the human world. Prometheus gave another valuable present to the humans, which was two bars of iron called dazar, which were very powerful as they contained energy once released would help the one who owned them to rule over both the human kingdom and Scaba. Nafarit wanted to own the two dazar iron bars and revealed this to her husband, Achilles, telling him that she wanted to keep them with her so that nobody would come and enslave her children. Achilles was convinced by this argument, and he started wars, killing many people in order to get them and satisfy his wife. At the end he managed to put his hands on them and gave them to his wife as a gift. Nafarit had never been happier as she ruled over the two worlds, declaring herself empress of Scaba and Earth. She never treated her people fairly, not for a moment. Even her sister wasn't immune from her tyranny; she enslaved her and put her nephews and nieces at the service of her children. She prevented her sister's children from leading a normal life and forbade them from using their natural abilities while, on the other hand, she helped her sons to the highest ranks of the two emperors. Achilles knew all that but kept protecting her because she had put a spell on him and he became her puppet. Hercules was almost always travelling to other galaxies and planets and was unaware of all those changes, and after long years of travel, he went back home.

Achilles was killed by Paris, Hector's brother, in Troy, and Nafarit swore to take revenge for the death of her husband. She killed all inhabitants of Troy, not sparing a single soul.

Hercules came back to Scaba to see his wife and children enslaved by Nafarit, and that inflamed anger and ire in him, so he decided to take revenge on Nafarit and her children.

He wasn't alarmed by the power of the two dazar iron bars but didn't like to be reckless in attacking Nafarit and decided to adopt a wise plan for that. He waited for years for the right moment, using his time to train his sons in the martial arts and teaching them how to release their mental energy and how to utter the sounds that can paralyze the Makash and hurt them, which they had forgotten how to utter because Nafarit had forbidden them from using it.

One day, when Nafarit rushed to visit the human world, she forgot her two dazar iron bars back in her palace. Hercules was confident of this fact when he saw her show much hesitance in punishing someone who violated her rules, and so he sneaked into her palace in Scaba and captured the dazar, adding much power to his own. With that, he started with an army formed by his children against Nafarit and her children and managed to defeat her and release Scaba and the human world of her evil. He awarded the highest ranks to his sons, and then, with the help of magicians, he cast a spell on all inhabitants of Scaba to be burned and killed by iron if they dared touch it. The spell made both the Makash and Shakam fear iron to death. He put the dazar in an inexpugnable box along with all the secrets of Scaba, especially how to get rid of the iron spell and how the Makash can be killed. He put all that in a book, which he called the *Doom Book*, that nobody would manage to open except the two persons mentioned in the riddle, which said, "A couple of opposite genders unite into unconditional love. Through their veins runs amalgamated blood and possessing invaluable duo of pearls."

He put the book and the box in a safe place under heavy Shakam guard.

"The story of Scaba ends here," Princess Filda said to the children, who became even more curious to know more.

Shaun asked her promptly, "And who is that couple that the puzzle meant?"

She told him that the great-grandfathers of Shakam and Makash managed to solve that enigma and concluded that it referred to a human couple who loved each other and treated each other with absolute devotion and self-denial, but Shaun opened his mouth as if he were not convinced with the answer.

"Why didn't you look for that couple? There are many similar couples on earth, I think," Samar asked.

The princess told them that they had searched hard and failed to find them because they discovered that what bound husbands and wives on earth was conditional love; wives love their husbands as long as they took care of them and never looked at other women, and husbands were no different from that. What made it harder was that they couldn't find any couple who possessed an invaluable duo of pearls.

"Such a couple doesn't exist."

"Why you didn't search for a couple who owns a jewelry shop?" Shaun suggested spontaneously and then added, "You would definitely find your couple."

"I wish it was that simple, Shaun," said Princess Filda.

The two twins looked at each other, and Jamal said, "We think we know such a couple."

All the kids looked at him and said at once, "Really?"

"Where is that couple?" Filda asked.

"It's our parents," Lillian answered.

Princess Filda asked them if their parents possessed an invaluable duo of pearls, and Jamal asked her in reply, "Do you think Hercules meant pearls literally, or was it a figure of speech while he meant something else?"

The princess kept quiet, beginning to see where Jamal was going.

"Because my mother always called us her precious pearls," Lillian added.

"My ancestors were searching for the wrong pearls all these centuries. The real pearls are the children. They are invaluable for any parents."

"You know what this means?" Samar asked with excitement, and before anybody could answer her question, she added, "That your parents can open Hercules's book."

"And help us getting rid of tyrant Bermuda and his pack," Filda said to them.

Then she added that Bermuda was the first Shakam to rule with tyranny; he enslaved human children and brought the Makash closer to him and made them among the ruling elite.

Samar asked about the *Doom Book*, and Princess Filda told her that it was kept at King Bermuda's private suite and added that the palace is her father's and she knew all the pathways and secret passages in that palace where she was raised and that there was nobody else who knew about these secret passages. She even knew where Bermuda was hiding the *Doom Book*.

"But why did Bermuda bring us here? I mean, how does he benefit from enslaving the human children?" Jamal asked in a low voice as if he were talking to himself.

Princess Filda took some time to answer and said that she always asked herself the same question until she eventually arrived at the conclusion, especially when she saw what had happened to her son Dushan. The reason behind bringing children to the city, Filda believed, was to make the Shakam as reliant on others as possible and derail them from living a normal active life so that they wouldn't use their brains. She told them that, in Scaba as everywhere else, when someone didn't use their brain in thinking they would over time become sluggish and lethargic, and their minds would stop them from working. This was exactly what had happened to the Shakam, just as the king wanted.

She looked at them and said, "You know! My father once told me that we are superior to human beings in our ability in using our full mental potential, unlike human beings who use only 10 percent of theirs."

"Aha! Ten percent only," Shaun responded in his usual retarded manner.

"But this doesn't apply to you, Shaun. You use only 1 percent!" Samar said.

They all laughed, and for moments they forgot what they had been through. Wang looked around and asked, "How did you manage to build that jail with iron when you fear it?"

Princess Filda explained to them that the ones who built the jail were not the Shakam or Makash; it was the human magicians. After her husband put Falca in jail, which was made of wood, the Makash objected to that and called for his release because he was one of them and hailed from a big family. It was impossible to release him then because he had already been sentenced by the Higher Court on charges of treachery and deceit. The Makash weren't satisfied with that verdict, and rumors spread among them that it was a conspiracy from the king and Commander Medan to get rid of Falca. The one who spread the rumor wanted to convince the Makash that the king and Medan were against Falca and that they had made up a story that Falca was trying to kill the king. She added to them that, one winter night, a group of Makash attacked the king's followers and guards and liberated Falca.

Therefore, her father decided to build a prison that nobody could approach and started searching for ideas. Some human magicians offered their help as a giving back to the king who had saved their life once. "It is a big irony for me to be the first prisoner in this prison," she said with a sigh.

Jamal hesitated a little and then asked, "Can you help us escape and take the *Doom Book* with us, so we can help you in turn and free all the human kids?"

"Yes, we will give it to our parents to view it and save everybody here," Lillian said enthusiastically.

Princess Filda smiled and explained that it wasn't as simple as they imagined because reaching the king's private suite was impossible due to the heavy guarding. She added that the kids themselves weren't ready yet for that big day and promised to help in preparing them.

"I will train you on how to release your mental potential and how to use your brains optimally," she said.

"Does this mean that we will be able to fly?" Shaun asked.

"No, but I will teach you a lot of things. Maybe you will not be able to achieve it at the same level, but each will gain as far as his mental capacity can go," she explained.

Samar looked at Shaun and said, "If this is the case, then Shaun will learn nothing."

Shaun felt embarrassed because of Samar's comment, but Filda told them that it wasn't true and that all of them would learn something. She told them that when they became ready, she would inform them about the secret passages, especially the one that led to the king's suite. It was her father who had told the magician to build that secret passage with iron in order to enable the prospective husband and wife who would be allowed to open the book to pass through it in case it was impossible to go the normal way because of war, for example. This is if they managed to find that couple. Filda explained, "My father prepared himself for everything, except treachery, which is unpredictable."

They asked her about the crystal ball and how could it locate their places and hideouts, but she failed to answer as it was new to her, and she told them that only King Bermuda knew the secret.

When they were about to leave, Lillian said, "There is still one person who I want to ask you about."

"Who is that?" Filda asked.

Lillian asked her about their neighbor who had brought them to the kingdom of Scaba. Filda thought for a while, trying to figure out who he meant, and then she said, "Maybe you mean Solar?"

"We don't know his name, and all we know is that he was the one who brought us here and left us at a majestic tent in the Rainbow Desert," Jamal replied.

Princess Filda was sure at that moment that they were talking about Solar, the magician. She told them about his story and that he was a human magician who was trained by her father and that, since the death of her father, she hadn't met him but had only heard about him and his meetings with the king.

Then she told them to prepare themselves for the training because there was not much time left and they had to learn as quickly as possible. She also told them that every time they came to her, they had to pretend that they were doing their daily chores in order not to attract attention to their secret training matter, and that they had to practice as hard as they could for the Grand Competition so they wouldn't disappoint the king, and that they had to attend training for the competition so that they appeared loyal and obedient. In that case, they wouldn't be closely watched by the guards. She also told them to bring Sisami with them each time they came to her to ask him about how Dushan was doing.

On the following day, the children enthusiastically arrived to start learning, but she taught them nothing. She only told each of them to sit alone and meditate and contemplate for a while. She told them many times that focusing is the first way to release mental energy.

They came to her every day and learned the skill of concentration, and during the day they would pretend that they were doing their chores such as mopping and cleaning, but their minds were occupied with something else. Every now and then the princess would repeat to them that "focusing is the first step toward releasing mental energy."

After that they would go to the training hall where all children of the palace gathered to train for the competition day. During that time, Jamal was observing all the movements of King Bermuda. He wondered why the king was so keen on hanging pictures of himself everywhere, and to discover the secret of it, he would stand before those pictures every day, looking at them and studying them carefully trying to see anything unusual about them, but they were only normal drawings done by Wang. After a week, Filda told the five kids to try conducting telepathy among themselves because, in Scaba, telepathy was a normal means of communication. She explained to them that if they succeeded in that, they would be able to communicate telepathically with the animals of Scaba. The kids tried to achieve telepathy with each other, interrupted now and then by Shaun asking if any of them had said something to him through telepathy, and when they told him that it didn't happen, he would say, "I thought you telepathized with me."

But one time, Shaun was looking directly into Jamal eyes, and when Jamal asked him about it, he didn't reply; and all of a sudden, he slapped Jamal on the face. Jamal got mad and asked him why he had done that.

"Didn't you hear me asking you to put your hand on your cheeks because I was going to slap you on the face to see if you could hear me or not?"

The kids felt disappointed, and despite their incessant attempts and hard work, they couldn't make it, so Princess Filda told them, "It is fear and pain that hinder you from telepathizing with each other."

She explained to them that pain and fear spoil concentration and clarity of mind, so they had to learn how to control their fear and pain.

After persistence and lots of practice, the twins succeeded in telepathizing but only once. It was when Jamal sprang up from his place and looked at his sister, saying to her, "Yes."

Lillian was surprised and asked him, "Did you hear me call you?"

He told her that he did, and then he asked her to remain silent while he tried to transmit an idea to her. He looked at her deeply for a while but in vain because he failed to tell her what he wanted.

"Never mind, dear, we will try it again later," she said.

They ran to Filda and told her what had happened, and she smiled and told them to try to focus more. "Remember always that fear and pain will hinder you from doing that."

None of the children managed to do it, but they didn't stop trying.

After the passage of some days, the kids became more focused and prepared, and so Filda told them not to come to her as a group anymore but to come one at a time so that they wouldn't raise suspicions, especially when Kameel, the fat boy, started asking them where they went every day, and of course, they didn't tell him the truth. They wanted to keep it as confidential as possible because the fewer kids knew about it, the less likely their secret would be discovered by the king. They liked Kameel and trusted him, but since he was slow and lazy, they believed that it would be a waste of time to involve him in the matter.

Wang was the first to meet alone with Princess Filda. She asked him to focus on something that he loved the most, so he chose colors and drawing to focus on, and she told him that it didn't matter whether he closed or opened his eyes; what mattered, rather, was his ability to go deep into the colors and concentrate on them so that they would be turned into a powerful energy. He shouldn't be afraid of his colors; rather, he should have the yearning, more than ever, to aim the weapon of his colors at something without using his hand or tools. She approached him and asked him to try to aim the power of his colors into her, and when he told her that he couldn't understand, she explained to him that he would find his way by himself and that the power of his mind would lead him through. Wang started trying while thinking very deeply for a while, and during that time Princess Filda was encouraging him all the way through in a whispering voice and telling him not to give up. Suddenly, the princess started to feel something in her eyes, and the more Wang increased his concentration, the more pain she felt in her eyes until she lost her ability to see anything and instantly told him to stop it, but he went too far into concentration and lost control of himself. He went on for a while and then stopped when he felt very fatigued because he was consuming a great deal of bodily energy. His heart was beating fast, and he looked almost breathless. He came out of that state as if pushed by someone, and Filda regained her vision. She wasn't angry; rather, she smiled to him and said, while she was patting him on his shoulder, "You see? Your colors have been released."

It was difficult for Wang to understand what was going on, but he was happy with the miraculous results. The princess told him that training and concentration would help him realize his goals, and she told him not to tell the other members of the group unless they became disturbed by it. When he met with his friends at dinnertime, they asked him what he had learned, but following Filda's advice, he didn't reveal it to them. The next day, it was Samar's turn to visit the princess in order to learn how to release her mental power. She was a little afraid and confused, but Filda assured her that she wouldn't get hurt and all that she had to do was to concentrate on the dearest thing in her life. Samar—being very talkative, funny, and lighthearted—concentrated on the power of laughing and managed with great effort to paralyze the princess with the energy of her laughing; but she ended up, like Wang, very exhausted and tired. Despite that, she was happy and was fascinated by the idea that mere laughing could have such powers to paralyze others. Then, it was Shaun's turn. He was afraid of failure and very unconfident of his potential, and so he failed to make a success through his concentration. The princess told him not to give up and return to her after a few days to try it once again and even to try it while alone and he would surely achieve something.

Lillian selected her love for her parents as the focal point as that was the only thing occupying her mind. After a number of attempts, she managed to physically move the princess from her place. The princess felt that someone was moving her as they wished, and Lillian was very happy to see the power of her love toward her parents moving the princess.

When it was Jamal's turn, Shaun begged him to let him, Shaun, take his place and go back again that day. Jamal agreed, but Shaun again failed to release his mental energy and started to lose hope. Thus, he decided to desert his friends and to avoid any contact with them, but they stood by his side and encouraged him to try again and again and told him that he was indispensable for them and that they needed his help. He was egged on by that and decided to try it again.

Jamal, the other day, selected his great desire to protect his sister and friends as the focal point, and after some tries, he managed to build a transparent corona around his body that served as a shield that could defend him against woufs or other weapons that might be targeted at him. He liked it very much and told the princess that such a defense was all he needed to protect the group.

Shaun went back to Princess Filda filled with resilience and determination to release his powers. He selected physical strength to be his focal point, but minutes later he went for speed; then he went back to strength. While he was alternating between strength and speed, he managed to force the princess to sit down, and despite exhaustion, he danced and celebrated his victory.

Filda ordered the kids to continue practicing without attracting the attention of others and warned them of using their power against the Makash because it was not yet the right time. During that, Sisami attended the training sessions and spent long hours with the princess. The next stage was to steal the *Doom Book* from the king's suite and smuggle it into the human world to give it to the twins' parents in order that they could read it and learn how to defeat the Makash and King Bermuda.

They selected Lillian to go through the secret passage toward the king's private suite because of her ability to move things. The secret passage was situated in one of the halls near the food court. Filda told them that the seventh tile on the wall on the left side was movable and could be opened by pushing it aside. So the children set up a plan: they would pretend that they were mopping and cleaning near the seventh tile outside the food court, offering cover to Lillian to pass through the hidden passageway.

On the specified day, the five children went to the spot that the princess had described for them before going to the training hall and pretending that they were working. Jamal and Wang pretended they were cleaning the walls, whereas Shaun, Samar, and Lillian pretended that they were mopping the floor. At a certain moment, Lillian pushed the tile and crept inside into the secret passage. At the beginning she didn't know where the passage would take her, but after she walked a little, she found a ladder and climbed to find a tunnel at its top. She had to creep because the tunnel was not that high, and while on the way, she could see the royal hall down through the tiny halls in the tunnel. She passed over the theater hall before she arrived in the king's private suite. She was filled with horror as she saw the king sitting in front of the crystal ball. The king's snake somehow felt Lillian's presence and lifted her head up while oozing her tongue inside her mouth with fury. Lillian panicked but held herself together and started watching the king and the crystal ball carefully. It was bigger than any other ball that she had ever seen in her life, much bigger than what she had expected. She saw the images of all the children of the palace in a list on the right-hand side of the ball appearing one above another, and right in the middle of the ball it demonstrated image of only one child at a time, giving the king the time to watch them one by one. The crystal ball was showing where each particular kid was at that time and what he or she was doing.

Lillian realized that her picture was the third picture after Shaun's and Samar's, and she could see her brother Jamal displayed in the middle of the crystal ball cleaning the wall. She knew that at any moment her image would be displayed in the middle of the ball and would get discovered, and she decided to go back through the tunnel as quickly as possible. She crept back and climbed down the ladder quickly, almost falling down as she did so. A small piece of her clothing caught on the edge of the ladder, which put her into a state of horror and hysteria as she tried to pull it out. She started sweating and almost cried when she realized that she was taking too much time to release herself. Eventually she tore her clothes and ran back to where she came from.

The king selected Samar's picture, and he saw her cleaning the floor. Then he did the same with Shaun and saw him doing the same, but when he searched for Lillian, the ball couldn't locate her and started searching for her. But the king looked at his snake, which leaped to the ground exactly under the spot where Lillian was. The snake started oozing her tongue irritably inside her mouth while looking up, and the king looked up too; and at that particular moment, the crystal ball showed Lillian while she was pushing the tile to leave the tunnel, but the king didn't see that as he was busy looking up. When he turned back to watch the ball, he saw Lillian mopping the floor.

Later the kids visited the princess, and Lillian told them what she had seen.

"That confirms my suspicions," Jamal said.

Filda asked him what suspicions he was thinking of, and he explained to them that, after he had spent some time in Scaba, he started wondering about the secret behind the king's determination to distribute his pictures everywhere and his insistence on children standing before his picture every night to say good night before going to sleep.

"It is because he loves himself very much," Wang interrupted.

But Jamal said that this is what the king wanted his citizens to think, but the reality was a different matter. The picture, Jamal believed, was a kind of system that exhibited and monitored what the children were doing, and through that system the king could watch over everyone; and the crystal ball was a very advanced system that could identify faces, which was why the king insisted on taking photos for each newcomer to Scaba. He did that so that he could save it to the system.

"Well done, Jamal. This is why he can't locate the runaways: it is simply because his system doesn't cover places other than Scaba," the princess said while looking fondly at Jamal.

"But in what way would this be helpful to us? We knew before that he could locate our places," Shaun asked in a distressful way.

"Now we know how," Samar replied.

"Now we have to think of a way to overpower that system," the princess said.

"There are three times each day that we know for sure that he reviews our places and presence in them," Wang confirmed.

"In the early morning, at lunchtime, and when we sleep," Lillian explained.

"There is something else," Jamal said.

"What is that?" Lillian asked.

"I haven't wished him a good night from the first day I came here. I only gaze at the picture," Jamal replied.

Shaun asked him what the significance of that was, and he explained, "It means that he can't hear us. He can only see us."

The princess was happy to hear that and told them that such information was of great importance and that they had the advantage of knowing such strategic secrets that the king was willing to do anything to hide them. It was obvious that the princess had an idea lingering in her mind but didn't wish to reveal it to them at that time and preferred to think of it more deeply so that she wouldn't make any mistakes. All of them agreed at the end that Lillian would go back and try to steal the *Doom Book*.

When Lillian went to Kameel and asked him to give her new uniform because hers was torn, he looked at her suspiciously and wondered in his usual lazy way about how her clothes were torn, but she told him that while she was passing through one of the palace's doors, her clothes had become stuck in one of the doors and to release herself she had to tear them.

IMPORTANT MEETING

The city teenagers remained in that state of running away from one place to another and sleeping at the old woman's flat at night until a day came when the Makash broke into the flat to capture them. Chaos spread everywhere in the place, and the old woman woke up to see the Makash trying to capture the homeless kids, but she failed to understand what was going on. The homeless kids relied on their experience of facing the Makash every day at food courts, so they managed to elude them this time as well. The Makash started shooting woufs at them, and because of their agility, the woufs ended up injuring the Makash themselves, who were disturbed by the kids stepping on their tails and hurting them and slipping through their legs. The kids eventually managed to run away, but each pair went in a different direction, Dana and Steven from one side and Nora and Adam from another side, and they all met under the big tree as usual.

They realized that they had to change their plans every now and then because, with every coming day, the Makash would tighten the noose on them, and it would become easier for their places and hideouts to get discovered. They couldn't come up with many plans; the only viable plan that they had was to guard each other alternately and to change their places every night from buildings to alleys to caves and never surrender to the Makash.

They continued attacking the food courts, and Sara brought food to them every now and then by hiding it inside her violin; and while they ate the food, she entertained them with some sweet music playing with Kilsha singing from time to time. The news of the homeless kids spread everywhere in Scaba and became the main topic in many conversations and chats. The king himself heard the news and demanded an urgent meeting with Falca and his deputy Sikwel.

Sikwel was the first to arrive at the meeting room. He was filled with eeriness and dread while waiting for the advent of the king and sitting in the middle of the room watching the decorated walls full of pictures and drawings of King Bermuda. He imagined that the king was looking at him through the portrait, so he became more terrified because he had a hunch about the topic of the meeting. Therefore, he decided to promise the king that he would kill the kids once he captured them.

General Falca entered the meeting room, and Sikwel instantly stood up to salute him, but Falca responded with a nonchalant movement of his hand and ordered him to sit down. Seconds later, King Bermuda entered the room frowning, and they both stood to salute him, but he didn't respond and sat down while looking angrily at Sikwel.

"It doesn't matter to me if these insignificant kids stole some food, and you failed to capture them," the king said.

Sikwel, at that point, tried to say something, but Falca prevented him from doing so by a movement from his head. "What concerns me the most is that I don't want them to end up as heroes," the king added. He looked at his snake and smiled, and then he looked at Sikwel and said, "I want you to attract them to your side and put them under your service. These children, despite my hatred of them, proved that they have skills most Makashans do not. I want you to use them under your command, and after they come to trust you, we will annihilate them."

He said his last sentence with a gloating smile on his face, and then he said to Sikwel, "You can leave now to do what I told you." Sikwel was about to move, but the king added, "Train them and help them join the city team and take part in the Grand Competition Day. I will send Solar to evaluate them after you arrest them and convince them to take part in the competition."

Sikwel walked toward the door to go out, but the king stopped him and said, "I want to see more pictures of me hanging in the city and outside it and at the entrance of each building. I want citizens of Scaba to see me and feel my presence wherever they go or look."

Sikwel nodded his head in humiliation and then went out. The king said to General Falca, "I want you to fire him if he fails in this mission."

Falca nodded his head, showing as much obedience as possible.

RECONNAISSANCE TEAM

A reconnaissance team was sent by General Falca to locate the runaways' lair outside the scope of the crystal ball. They started their quest in untamed virgin jungles but couldn't trace any of the fugitives. Surprisingly, when they went through one of the wildest spots, the commander of the group noticed that the trees didn't attack them as the other trees did, as if they were tamed by somebody. Then, he saw some enar blowing fire in a hole in the ground, and he had to overlook that as he had strict orders from General Falca not to do anything other than locate the fugitives' place. They had even been instructed not to attack them because they were unaware of their number and power and could destroy the whole group by mistake. They were ordered to go back when they had located the enemies, and Falca would prepare his forces to attack them later. The commander of the reconnaissance team ordered his group to go back where they had come from because he felt that someone was watching them. It was true. There were a group who were closely watching them and were about to attack them, but the commander ordered his troops to withdraw at just the right moment.

They went back into the borders of the crystal ball, and their commander headed to see General Falca and to tell him about the fugitives' hideout.

The kids gathered again in the same spot in the corridor next to the seventh tile pretending that they were cleaning; they wanted to try and steal the book for the second time. The plan this time wouldn't involve Lillian alone. They all agreed that Samar, who was among the very few that could enter the king's private suite, go to the king's suite to clean it as usual; and when she made sure that there was nobody else except her in the place, she had to open the safe, which Filda had told them about, and taught them how to open and take the book and give it to Lillian who would be there waiting up in the tunnel along with Wang. Wang would wait in the middle way over the royal hall to watch the king, and Lillian would creep forward to reach the suite in order to take the book from Samar. In the meantime, Jamal and Shaun would wait in the aisle, which led to the tunnel.

They carried out the plan cautiously. Samar went into the royal suite after being searched by the guards. She was very afraid and confused; and when she reached the targeted spot, she stopped in the middle of the large room, looking around unsure of what to do next. But she then cooled herself down and turned a leg of the bed clockwise once, and once more anticlockwise. A safe in the middle of the wall opened instantly where Samar saw the book but was afraid to touch it. She waited for Lillian to arrive, and when she did, she crossed the tunnel cautiously and slowly toward the suite as planned. Wang remained in the middle of the tunnel to watch the king and General Falca underneath. Wang was able to see Falca showing the king a report that covered the latest incidents in Scaba. He heard him say to the king, "Tomorrow one of the children has to go back to the human's land. It is Dany, Your Majesty."

Wang remembered his friend Danny and felt very sad for him, but he had nothing to do for him in that regard, so he wished badly that they succeeded in finding the book as soon as possible so that they could get rid of the king and at the same time rescue Danny and all the other children in Scaba. Lillian reached the royal suite, and when she saw Samar inside, she went down very cautiously. There, she asked Samar about the book; and when Samar told her, she was reluctant to take it. Then, with a shaking hand, she took the book and read the hint written on its outside cover. There was nothing in the safe other than the book.

Meanwhile, conversation between Falca and the king went as normal as it should be.

"Is it only one child?" the king asked.

"Yes, according to my list," Falca replied.

"I will notify Solar of that myself," the king said. He rose to his feet and headed toward his suite. Wang felt disturbed and didn't know what to do except to race the king in order to warn Samar and Lillian. He looked from above to see Lillian holding the book in her hands and Samar standing next to her.

"Come on . . . very quick . . . the king is coming," Wang whispered to them. Samar locked the safe; and Lillian stood exactly underneath Wang, who stretched his hand after hanging his body down, and then Lillian jumped and grabbed his hand and pulled herself up. Samar was about to give the book to Lillian, but at that moment she heard the king trying to open the door to enter the room, so she threw the book under the king's bed, but part of it remained visible. The king entered his room, and Samar felt very confused, so she stood in front of the book to conceal it and started dancing with her eyes closed, pretending that she hadn't seen him coming.

The king looked at her for a while and said, "What are you doing, little devil?"

She played ignorant and surprised, inventing a wince, and said, "Oh! Nothing, Your Majesty. I have always wished to be a queen." She paused for a while and said pleadingly, "Would you marry me, Your Majesty, so that I become the queen?"

He looked at her contemptuously and told her to leave the room, so she took her broom sluggishly, trying to stay on that spot for as long as possible because the book was still in its place. Lillian tried to move the book using the power of her mind, but she failed. Wang grabbed her and said, "You can do it. Don't think of your fear. Only focus on the book."

With more concentration, she managed to move the book but very slowly. The snake became alerted, drew her tongue out, and leaped toward the bed. Samar went out of the room quickly while the king looked at her, suspiciously saying to himself, *These damned children are planning something.* He looked at his snake, which was moving her tongue and looking at the spot where the book was like she was telling him about the book. When the king tried to see what his snake was looking at and bent to see what was under the bed, Falca knocked at the door, saying to the king, "Your Majesty! We found them."

When the king heard that, he was delighted and rushed toward the door to open it. Falca entered the room and said, "Your Majesty, our scouts managed to locate the hideout of the runaways."

The king smiled and went out of the room with General Falca after taking the snake with him; and closing the door behind him, he had a final quick glance at the bed, but he saw nothing and carried on his way. Wang and Lillian heaved a gasp of relief for the departure of the king and his snake. Lillian went down again, took the book, and handed it over to Wang, who helped her go up again. They went through the secret passage together, but when they passed over the royal hall, Wang told Lillian to go on while he remained there to hear what they were talking about. He could see the commander of the reconnaissance team locating the runaways on a map stretched on a table for the king and Falca. Wang heard the king say, "I want you to send a huge force to obliterate them."

He looked at them and said, "I will not tolerate failure this time, understand? If you couldn't find the box, then you have to bring the commander of this group here alive so that we force him to tell us about the location of the box."

After Wang heard that, he crept slowly and went out of the secret tunnel. Once the other children saw him, they asked him about the reason why he was late, and he told them that he would tell them later and that they had to meet with Filda quickly. They all went to the jail after they had hidden the book in the clothes room. They told Filda what had happened regarding the book, and Wang told them what he had heard from the king and army commanders.

"It seems that these runaways own one of the two darzar bars, and the king wants to get rid of these convicts and capture the box," Filda explained.

"But maybe these runaways can help us somehow," Jamal said.

"Anyhow, we should do our best to warn them of the king's plan and tell them that their hideout has been discovered," Lillian proposed.

"We must find a way to get to them as soon as possible," Jamal said enthusiastically.

"I saw the details of the map they were viewing, and I can draw a copy of it," Wang said.

"This is of no use! We can't leave the palace," Shaun said desperately.

But the princess didn't pay much attention to what Shaun had said and said to Wang, "Draw the map and a portrait of Jamal's face and two more of Makashan's and Shakam's faces."

The kids looked at her with surprise, begging for an explanation, but she simply said, "I want to try something."

The princess's demands were surprising to the children, especially when she told Wang to do that as soon as possible.

⸷ STOM

S tom was one of the rare Shakams who worked with the Makash. He lived his life differently; he was the eldest son of one of the senior consultants of the older king, and when his father died, he left him with some diamonds that King Bermuda knew nothing about. Diamonds at the time of the older king were abundant and very cheap. When King Bermuda ascended the throne, he ordered his followers to confiscate all diamonds possessed by the Shakam, and he took their palaces and properties. He made diamonds the official currency of the kingdom of Scaba, so their value skyrocketed, and they became a very rare and expensive item. He gave the Shakam's palaces to his Makashan followers and turned some of them into headquarters for his government. Stom's father's palace was one of those humiliated palaces that were given to Commander Sikwel.

Stom used the diamonds he inherited from his father in making good relations with Makashan senior officials, and he thus became very influential in that he could enjoy the protection of the Makash themselves. Stom's dream was to collect as many diamonds as possible in order to buy his father's palace back from Sikwel, so he started working in many businesses.

He had no friends and trusted nobody, including human children. His father died in the small flat that he was forced to move to after his palace was captured, and before his death, his advice to his son was to trust neither King Bermuda nor the Makash in general.

He was very active in business, and added to this, he gained a fortune from organizing fighting games between the Makash. He used to share these profits with Sikwel, his covert partner.

He had no relationship with Sikwel other than business, but Sikwel wasn't a fair partner. He used to rob him the biggest share of profits, which was why Stom tried his best to hide as many diamonds as he could from Sikwel. He even arranged some fighting matches without Sikwel knowing about them to take profits for himself alone. He didn't lack intelligence and cunning, and he was very convincing, so he succeeded in pushing the Makash and Shakam to do what he wanted.

Once, while he was in the city and after the spread of the news of the homeless teenagers and their adventures, he saw the teenagers robbing a food court in broad daylight. He admired their courage and the gymnastic skills that they performed while attacking the Makashan guards who ended up in failure and frustration. The teenagers even dared to face the woufs, and when they were shot against them, they evaded them easily as if it was part of a movie that they were acting together with the Makash themselves. The teenagers' agility and courage was increasing the Makashan disturbance and floundering and always resulted in the guards' shooting and injuring themselves.

What was most surprising to Stom was that the onlookers weren't sympathetic with the Makash. On the contrary, they enjoyed watching them lose. Stom watched the kids while they were leaving the food court with stolen food and the Shakam who were clapping their hands for them in appraisal. Some other Makashan guards came forth to assist their peers, but the kids ran away as quickly as possible and hid among the crowds.

Stom decided to speak to these kids no matter what the consequences were. He understood that he wasn't allowed to speak or deal with the homeless kids, but that didn't discourage him from his decision. He saw in them a chance to make more diamonds and profit, and so he searched for them for three days but failed to locate them because the kids used to change their places and targeted food courts from time to time. They even wouldn't rob the same food court more than once every month, and some days the food that was brought to them by Sara was just enough.

On the third day of his search, Stom heard a strange voice while he was passing through one of the alleys. It was Steven warning his friends that someone was approaching. Sara was sitting with them when they heard the voice, so they hid and asked Kilsha to move around and see what was going on. Kilsha went out and saw Stom, who was looking around searching for the kids, so she went back to tell them that it was just a Shakam and there was no need to feel afraid of him. But they heard Stom shouting at them from his place as he saw some food leftovers in the alley, "Please go out! I came with a good bargain for you."

The kids exchanged looks, and then Steven went behind the buildings to see if there was anyone else with him; and when he saw that he was alone, he went back to his friends and said, "He is alone."

"What does he want?" Adam asked.

"What do you want from us? You shouldn't talk to us or you will receive a life sentence," Dana shouted at him.

Stom smiled when he heard them talking to him and was confident that he was in the right place.

"I don't care. I came here to help you," he replied.

"How?" Dana asked in a very high shrill voice.

"I want you to work for me—I mean, with me," he replied.

Dana looked at her friends indecisively, but Steven said, "If we wanted to work for you, we wouldn't become the homeless kids."

Stom agreed and said, "I know this for sure, but I have a different bargain for you, and I am sure you will like it."

At that moment, Dana and Adam came out of their hide while the others remained in their place as a precaution.

Stom said to them, "With me you will not have to change the routine of your life, and you will live the way you like. Also, I will provide you with the food you need."

Adam asked him what he meant by that, and Stom went on to explain to them that he managed fighting matches and would like them to join the game. He added that he admired their skills when they raided the food court and wished that they would take part in the fighting matches that he managed. They would play against Makash children of their age, and the Makashan children would be prevented from using their woufs. He also promised to work on lifting the stamp off their foreheads, which would be in their favor. All that they had to do was to practice the sport they liked, which was fighting the Makash; and they would not need to worry about food or housing because that would be made available by Stom, who also promised them Makash protection.

He asked them to think it over and gave them his address, and he told them that he would wait for a reply from their side within one or two days. Then he left them and went back where he came from.

The kids were divided while discussing the offer among themselves. Steven and Sara rejected the offer, saying that the Makash were stronger than them and they would kill them instantly and that they shouldn't trust a Shakam whom they knew nothing about. On the other hand, Dana and Nora believed that they should accept the offer as it would be a chance to study the Makash's points of weakness and get closer to them, which might help them access Sikwel's office and steal the carpet. They believed that it would be a rare chance that would never be offered to them again.

During that time Adam remained silent, so they looked at him expecting a decisive opinion from his side. He thought for a while and said, "I support Dana and Nora, and I think it is a chance that might not be repeated."

Dana rose to her feet and hugged him spontaneously, and when she noticed what she had done, she pulled herself back with embarrassment.

The next day, the children went to Stom's house. It was a grand one compared to other Shakam's houses. He welcomed them and asked them to enter, but they told him that they wouldn't do so until they made sure that there was no ambush set up for them. To this end, they asked Kilsha, who was escorting them along with Sara, to go inside and search the house. Meanwhile,

Steven monitored one side of the road that they had come from while Adam monitored the other side. It was an embarrassing and awkward moment for Stom while he was standing at the threshold of his house waiting for them to come inside. He exchanged smiles with Sara, and they didn't enter until Kilsha came out and told them that none of the Makash were inside the house.

The house was richly decorated inside, with thousands of ornaments and antiques. Stom took some time to show them the antiques and tell them where each had come from. After everyone felt at home, he said, "I will provide you with clean food and shelter, and you have to do the rest."

"What 'rest' are you talking of?" Dana asked.

"Training and fighting skillfully," he replied.

"But do you think we can defeat the Makash?" Sara asked.

"I am totally confident of that. I saw your skills, and I am sure you can defeat any Makashan," Stom replied.

"But what about the wouf?" Steven asked.

"They will not be allowed to use it during matches with you. Don't worry, there will be regulations." He added," You will be the first human beings to fight with the Makash."

"What about the guards who are desperately searching for us?" Nora asked hesitantly.

"I will take care of them," he replied with confidence.

"How can we trust you?" Adam asked.

Stom laughed at that moment and explained to them that, just by receiving them at his house, he was taking a risk and committing a crime of dealing with homeless teenagers, which would entail harsh punishment if he were caught.

Stom kept his promises to them and catered for them with delicious food and very neat beds that they had missed for a long time. It made them wonder where he could have gotten them. He always told them that he could get whatever he wanted in Scaba. After some days he took them to the underworld, the world of illegal fighting in the kingdom of Scaba.

THE NETHERWORLD

S tom took the kids to a palace on the outskirts of the city. It looked deserted from outside, but inside it was full of life as it was laden with male and female Makash and Shakam. In the middle of the palace there was a gigantic hole with a staircase on one of its sides.

Once the children entered the palace with Stom, everybody stopped what they were doing and looked at the children. They started whispering to each other, "These are the homeless street kids." Stom led the children with confidence toward the big hole; he went into it through the staircase, and the children followed. Sara and Kilsha were with them, and once they reached the bottom of the hole, he asked them to sit on the right-hand side. On the left-hand side were some Makash children who looked healthy and vigorous. They were aged between fourteen and sixteen, and their muscles were bigger than the average human being's. They looked at the human kids furiously and defiantly. The Makash and Shakam attendants were ringed around the hole, and Stom, who stood down in the middle looking up, said, "Ladies and gentlemen, today this palace will witness an historic event." He looked at the audience proudly and added, "For the first time in the history of Scaba, we will see human children challenge Makash in a fighting match."

The audience laughed contemptuously, as they believed that it was nonsense for week human beings to challenge the Makash.

"These street teenagers claim that they have special potentials that can help them defeat the Makash children."

The children looked at each other wondering who told Stom that they had special abilities, but they realized in a moment that Stom was lying just to make it more exciting for everybody to watch the match. The audience laughed again and again, and one of them shouted, "Come on! Let's see the fight."

The audience, all at once, began to shout, "Fight, fight, fight!"

Their voices terrified Sara who ran to hug Nora. Other children were afraid too, including Dana who dissimulated her panic and mustered up some courage to say to her friends, "Do what you used to do with the guards at the food courts, and don't forget their points of weakness that we have discovered through experience."

She then moved forward and said, "Anyone wants to fight?"

A Makashan child moved forward to fight Dana, and Stom said to him, "When fighting with human children, you are not allowed to use the wouf."

The Makashan boy opened his mouth in shock, and Stom proceeded in a high voice so that all could hear him, "Human beings don't have woufs, so woufs are not allowed in the matches with them. We want fair play."

Dana looked at the Makashan boy and said in a funny voice, "Are you afraid that you will be defeated by a human girl if you don't use your wouf?"

Filled with fury, the Makashan boy attacked her quickly, but she evaded him swiftly and started hopping here and there like a grasshopper. He went mad and started running after her while throwing his hand in all directions hoping to punch her.

Sara put both hands on her eyes to avoid seeing Dana punched by the Makashan boy, and the other children seemed unable to control their nerves, but they didn't stop directing and encouraging Dana.

Dana kept moving around her opponent until he lost his sense of direction, so Dana seized the moment and pulled him by his two tails. He fell down, and she jumped over his chest and tightened her hands on his neck until he surrendered. The kids realized that a quick loss of the sense of direction when confused and weak necks were two points of weakness of the Makash.

Stom announced Dana the winner. She jumped happily, and the other teenagers shared her happiness of triumph. The audience, meanwhile, felt disappointed, but Stom was happy too because he knew that all the attendants had bet on her loss while he was the only one who bet on her victory, which meant that he would gain the diamonds alone.

It was Steven's turn. He couldn't help shivering before the match. He tried to do the same as Dana, but he failed to make the Makashan lose his sense of direction and received a blow from his opponent that knocked him down and eventually lost the match. Stom announced the result grudgingly, and Steven's friends approached for support, but he said to them, "This is the last time I fight with a Makashan."

He was more discouraged and angry than hurt. Then it was Adam's turn to enter the ring courageously. He managed to evade his opponent's punches skillfully. He moved a lot to disturb his opponent while lowering his head and shoulders in a way that drove the Makashan mad because he couldn't punch him even though he was very close to him. Adam hit the Makashan strappingly at the right moment on the neck, which made him fall to the ground, but he shot a wouf at Adam, who evaded it miraculously.

Adam's friends ran to him, but he said to them, "Don't worry, guys, I am still in one piece."

Dana shouted at Stom, "This wasn't what we agreed on."

Stom felt embarrassed and started blaming the Makashan boy for that. He said in a high voice to be heard by the audience, "If you want to enjoy an exciting show, we shouldn't allow woufs to be shot at human children."

"No woufs, no woufs," the audience screamed in one voice.

Stom announced Adam's victory, and Adam looked very happy. Then it was Nora's turn, and she entered the ring dancing rather than walking. She poked her tongue out to tease her opponent, and she succeeded. He started chasing her; but she kept hopping, running, and slipping through his legs until he lost his sense of direction. Then she attacked him and punched him hard on his ear to drop him down in agony. That was the third Makashan point of weakness: when they are attacked from any side, their response is slow; and when they receive a hit on any of the ears, they fall down instantly with intolerable pain. This is why border guards cover their heads and necks with wooden shields that show only their eyes, but the city guards didn't do the same because they didn't expect to fight with anyone.

The teenagers had learned this from their repeated raids on the food courts, and they exchanged that knowledge among themselves.

The children's victory was a shock to the audience who attended that night, so they started shouting, "Kill these street teenagers! We won't allow these weak humans to defeat us." Then somebody added, "We won't allow these weak humans to defeat us. Kill them!"

Stom grew confused and stood in front of the children to protect them. They were horrified by the scene. Sara started crying as she could see no way out of this gridlock except through the staircase that led to the hundreds of enraged Makashan and Shakam in the audience.

"I told you not to trust him! You see, we will die now," Steven shouted.

"You promised to protect us," Dana said to Stom.

"But I can't protect you from all these," Stom replied in fear.

The Makashan fighter boys moved forward with eyes filled with wrath and fury, and Stom didn't know who to protect the children from: the Makashan boys or the audience upstairs. Suddenly, the audience's uproar was silenced, and Sara looked up to see what was happening. She saw Makashan soldiers surrounding the place. She told her friends to look up, and when they did, they saw Sikwel smiling triumphantly, and they realized that it was the end for them.

Sikwel ordered them to ascend, telling the Makash child fighters not to obstruct them. The children went up followed by Kilsha, and finally Stom and they were received by Sikwel at the mouth of the precipice, saying to them, "Welcome! Did you really believe that you would succeed in running away from me forever?"

He laughed deeply and ordered his soldiers to take them all to his office. They were put in a wooden wagon dragged by an elephant. As for Stom, he was handcuffed and put on another elephant. On the way to Sikwel's office, Dana said to her friends, "Sikwel's office! This is our golden chance."

"It is enough for me, Dana. I will not go on with you in this," Steven said angrily.

Dana felt disappointed about what she heard and started thinking about how she could make it up for him. She tried to say something encouraging, but he stopped her with his hand and said to her, "Please don't say anything. Adam was right when he said that all misfortunes that we had been through were because of your ghastly ideas."

Adam, however, interrupted, "But I was wrong. We are all in the same boat and must keep trying to the last moment of our life. We shouldn't give up, Steven."

"So go ahead by yourselves. I will not be with you," Steven said desperately.

Kilsha interfered at that moment and said, "I will show you which table leg contains the key of the file's safe."

They all agreed to that except Steven, who turned his face to the other side as if telling them that he was out of it.

ESCAPE PLAN

Wang started drawing a portrait of Jamal at the royal hall. He pretended that he was drawing the king but was, in fact, drawing Jamal for some time and then drawing the king for little time. He did the same with the other portrait of the Makash and Shakam. When he finished the paintings, he took them to the princess and showed them to her and to his friends. The princess gave the map to Jamal to keep it with him and told the kids in a faint voice that she believed the king wouldn't recognize the difference between Jamal and his portrait. To test this, she told them to try it that night at bedtime by standing at the end of the queue, and when it was Jamal's turn to stand before the king's portrait and say good night, Wang or Shaun would use Jamal's portrait instead. After that, they would put the picture on his pillow, and Jamal would sneak into the dormitory and sleep in another bed.

The kids were overjoyed when they heard the plan and started to regain hope, but the princess told them to be very cautious and precise so that they wouldn't fall into error. They were very fervent to try the plan, and when it was bedtime, they stood at the end of the line. When it was Lillian's turn, she wished the king a good night, followed by Wang who did the same; but instead of heading directly to his bed, he went back to the queue. Jamal waited until Samar stood before the king's portrait and passed smoothly from behind her into the dormitory. Wang put Jamal's portrait on his face and did the daily protocols, successfully followed by Shaun who did the same. Jamal rushed to his bed and put the other portrait that showed Jamal's eyes closed on the pillow, and then he went under the bed to sleep there that night. None of the kids slept easily that night, although a feeling of ecstasy overwhelmed them because the plan was carried out successfully, at least from a theoretical point of view.

The next morning, Jamal rushed to his bed and pretended that he was yawning to give the impression that he was on that bed all night. The group went to the food court happily and decided not to speak about anything in front of anyone until they meet with Filda and tell her about the success of their plan. Kameel sat lazily next to them as usual and after a while asked them, "Why is everyone happy this morning?"

"Because the plan succeeded," Shaun replied quickly and without thinking.

The other kids got confused, and Shaun noticed what mistake he had committed and started looking at them, begging for an outlet.

"What plan?" Kameel asked.

"The plan of Shaun joining the musical band," Samar replied promptly.

Kameel knew that Shaun couldn't play any musical instrument, and he looked in the faces searching for an explanation. Jamal rescued the secret by saying, "He will join the musical band as a secondary singer."

"How does that happen without the musical band's leader, which is me, not knowing about it?" Kameel asked.

"That was the plan," Samar replied with a big fake smile.

Kameel shook his head carelessly, and the rest of children scolded Shaun with their looks.

Princess Filda told Wang to draw other portraits of Jamal and some of Shakams and to make them into masks and distribute Jamal's to the group members so that they could use them alternately in misleading the king. Then, Filda told Jamal about another secret passage, which was located under her bed in her room. It was a passage that was designed for the king's family to escape in cases of war. They planned to send Jamal to reach out for the runaways and warn them of the king's intentions of attacking them and ask them for help to defeat the king and his followers. Meantime, the other children should try to send the *Doom Book* to the twins' parents so that they could help them defeat the Makash and liberate all children in Scaba.

She told Jamal that the secret tunnel would lead him to the outskirts of the city and then to a certain place he would recognize immediately because it was built upside down. There he would find Wajdbeer, an old man and loyal friend to her father, and tell him that the princess had sent him. The old man would ask why he should believe Jamal, and Jamal had to say, "Because Adlif said so." The kids asked her who Adlif was.

"It is me, but my name is inverted."

She explained to them that inverting her name was the emergency secret code between her father and Wajdbeer. Jamal was enthusiastic to go on with it, and everybody wished him luck. They agreed that Jamal run away on the night of the grand competition so that they could make the best use of time, and they all decided to do their best to win the competition in order to give the king a chance to celebrate the winning and, at the same time, give Jamal time and chance to escape.

"You have to win the competition; otherwise, all that we did will be useless," Princess Filda said.

KEY OF CARPET STORE

The city kids reached the big building that contained Sikwel's office and were taken to the office along with Stom. Kilsha ran quickly under Sikwel's desk and started rubbing her back on one of the legs of the desk to show the other kids the location of the key.

Sikwel was sitting behind his desk when they entered. He said to them, "Welcome, the team of the homeless teenagers."

None of them replied, and they remained silent, but he moved toward Stom and said, "What about you, Stom? How did it cross your mind that you would be able to get diamonds in my city without my knowledge?"

"I was trying to test these kids before I introduced them to you, sir," Stom replied, showing as much friendliness as possible to Sikwel.

Sikwel scolded him with harsh looks and accused him of greediness and readiness to betray anyone for diamonds. Then he asked the kids, "Do you remember the second punishment for homeless teenagers?"

They said nothing, and he looked at Sara as if he was seeing her for the first time and asked, "What about you? Why did you put yourself in that?"

"They are my friends," she replied in a very faint voice.

Dana interrupted her by saying, "She is not with us. I am responsible for all this; I am the one who forced them to rebel against you."

"No! It was me who forced them," Adam said.

"Why are you trying both to protect and cover me?" Nora said. "I am the one who you are looking for, sir."

Sikwel smiled sarcastically and asked, "Anybody else want to claim responsibility?"

"It is me! I am entirely responsible for this, sir," Steven replied.

They all felt happy when they heard Steven saying that despite what they had been through, but Sikwel said to them, "I like your courage. I can even lift the homeless teenagers' punishment and forgive you."

They exchanged looks and lent him their ears.

"But under one condition," he went on.

"What is that condition, sir?" Stom asked hurriedly.

Sikwel looked at the children and said, "You have to join the city team to compete against the palace team in the Grand Competition Day and win the competitions," he explained.

The kids didn't have much knowledge about the Grand Competition Day; so Sikwel explained to them that it was a day where all inhabitants of Scaba and some inhabitants from other worlds gather to watch the grand competitions between the city kids and the kids who lived in the palace in many events, including music, sports, and dancing. There were no rules in the completion, and victory would go to the better team. He also told them that King Bermuda was the one who initiated the competitions and had never missed watching them.

If the city team won, the members of the team would be rewarded with a year off in which they would be allowed to do nothing except enjoy their time and get whatever they wanted. Other children would have two days off, one on the competition day and the other on the following day. There was also a draw in which one kid would be selected and that lucky kid would be sent back into the human world without being made to lose his mind but only made to forget the period he spent in Scaba.

Steven looked at his friends and said in a very faint voice, "I wish I were that lucky person."

Sikwel also told them that if they were defeated, they had to work relentlessly for two years until the date of the next grand competition came once again, and they would then have another chance.

"But if the spoiled children of the palace win," Sikwel said, pressing hard on the word *spoiled*, "the celebrations will be in the palace only."

He looked at them to study their impressions and added, "The king loves the children of the palace, and the celebrations if they win will be of very special type. They are indeed very lucky to be endowed with the king's love. The only thing that I know of their reward is that they will become like supervisors and will have a rest for a whole year."

Before any of the kids could reply, Steven hurriedly said, "We agree, but what should we do from our side?"

Sikwel told them that the only thing they had to do was to train and prepare themselves for the big day in the big building that was built specially for the matter, and Mr. Solar would come then to evaluate their performance. Dana was very happy to know that the building that Sikwel was talking of was exactly across from his office building.

Sikwel called one of the guards and whispered something in his ear, and the guard rushed out. Then Sikwel looked at Stom and said, "And you, my friend, will be in charge of their training."

Stom got closer to Sikwel and said to him, "But in this way we will not get diamonds from that."

When Sikwel heard that, he remembered the diamonds and asked Stom, "Oh, by the way, where is my share of diamonds for today's event?"

"Do you want us to make our accounts here before these children?" Stom asked hesitantly, as if trying to evade payment.

"Yes! I have nothing to hide. Come on, give me my share now," Sikwel said.

So Stom put his hands in his pockets and took out some diamonds and gave them to Sikwel, but he looked furiously at him and said, "I want the revenue of the whole day, not part of it!"

Stom took out more diamonds hidden in the folds of his clothes and gave them to Sikwel, but Sikwel looked at him again unsatisfied, which made Stom take out more and more diamonds until Sikwel was pleased. Meanwhile, the kids where watching details of the office very closely. The guard came after a while with a bottle that contained very little liquid in his hand. Sikwel took it and gave it to Dana and said, "When you reach your beds at the new building, wipe your foreheads with this liquid, and the stamp will be removed instantly."

Seven guards came in and took the kids to the new building, but before they left, Sikwel said to them, "I hope that you win because if you don't all kids in the city will blame you for the hard work they are going to do."

The kids went out, and Stom remained with Sikwel, who said to him, "If these kids win the matches on the big day, the king will give us more diamonds than ever, more than enough for both of us for the rest of our lives."

Stom was glad to hear that and felt very enthusiastic about starting to train the kids. When the kids reached the new building, they met in one of the rooms, and Dana said to them, "Now we know the details of Sikwel's office, and all we have to do is plan how to get inside it and take the key."

"All we have to do is sneak into that building and reach Sikwel's office," Nora said.

"But there are guards outside and inside the office building, so we must plan this time very cautiously and wisely," Adam said.

But Steven interrupted him, saying, "No matter what your plans are, I am not with you in them."

They looked at him with reproach, and Dana said to him, "But we heard you say something more positive and manly to Sikwel. What does that mean?"

"It means nothing. I will join the training and take part in the grand competition, but I will never join you in your failed attempts of escape," he replied. "I strongly believe that it is impossible to escape from Scaba and go back to the human world, and you should live with this fact. The only chance for any of us is to get our names picked in the raffle. Give up your dream. It's over. We are staked here forever."

None of them agreed with him, so he went out while the other children remained in the room, planning how to reach Sikwel's office after they had all wiped their heads with the liquid that Sikwel had given them.

That night Adam and Steven slept in one room; Adam gave the small bottle to Steven without exchanging a word with him, and the three girls slept together in another room. The next day, they woke up early, and to their surprise, the stamps on their foreheads had gone. They went to the training hall to see scores of children filling the building. There were different groups of children: some were talented at music, some athletes, others dancers. Every group has their specific type of training as a preliminary stage prior to the selection process for the big day.

The street teenagers started their training, but Steven didn't join them and preferred to stand away from them, which saddened them all, but Dana said to them, "We have to concentrate on our mission."

She looked around and said to them that their chances of succeeding in getting into the other building would be better if things remained as they were, but Sara interrupted, "But how can we know for sure that Sikwel is not there in the office at the moment?"

"When he comes here, along with the so-called Solar, to select the team for the Grand Competition Day, it will be the right moment for us to sneak into his office and steal the key," Adam explained.

"I wish Steven were with us." Sara sighed.

The kids were told that Solar was coming in just two days to select the team. Dana's plan was that one of them would take a bucket and a mop outside the hall when Sikwel and Solar came. He would go to the office building pretending that he was going to clean, and when he entered the building, he would go to Sikwel's office and take the key. Then, he had to go the store and take a carpet, put it in the bucket and go back to the new building.

"But who will fly the carpet?" Adam wondered.

"Let's first get our hands on the carpet and then search for a pilot for it," Dana replied.

"Maybe we can convince Stom to fly the carpet for us," Nora suggested.

"I don't think so. That Shakam is not trustworthy," Dana replied.

"I know the right person to do that," Sara said, not very confidently.

"Who is that?" they all asked in one voice.

"It is Shishar, the one that I work for. He was a senior officer in the old king's army, and he hates the Makash, which means he'll do anything to help us take revenge on them," Sara explained.

"But can we trust a Shakam?" Adam inquired.

"Yes! From the first moment I went to serve them in the house, he kept telling me that he wished he could send me back home to my family," Sara said.

"So let's capture the carpet and take it to him," Dana said wholeheartedly.

They were very happy to hear this and started jumping and hugging each other while Steven sat at one of the corners watching them and feeling sorry for them.

By the time that the day that Solar was due to come had arrived, the children had prepared themselves for the plan and selected Adam to carry it out because they were confident that Sikwel would notice if Dana was absent. Dana had no difficulty providing the cleaning tools; she went out to the street and took a bucket and a mop from the first child cleaning the street she ran into, leaving him in astonishment of why anyone would take such valueless items from him.

The training hall was full of children who looked very eager to show their best in order to be selected. Sikwel and Solar came into the hall accompanied by Wajdbeer, the physician, who sat in the front seats to help in cases of emergencies.

Once Sara saw Solar, she remembered him and told everyone about it while Solar looked at her, smiling maliciously as if he knew what they were talking about. The kids discovered that they had all

126

been kidnapped by the same person, the only person in that world who kidnapped his own species to be enslaved by these creatures.

The show started, and Solar and Sikwel sat in opposite seats along with scores of Makash, whereas the attendant children who came to watch the rehearsals sat on the sides of the stage. The seats were arranged in a semicircular shape around the stage, but they were thirty meters away from the stage, and the empty lot was meant to be an assembly point for the teams. Once Solar arrived, the organizers told Adam to prepare himself because boxing would be the first event followed by running on tight hanging ropes.

Adam looked befuddled, but Dana told him to start his second show once he finished his first one. Adam nodded approvingly and entered the ring to play against one of the children while his mind was absent. He kept looking at Dana during the match, so his opponent used that and knocked him down with a powerful punch. Sara worried about him because, if he was hurt badly, he might fail to go on with the mission. Therefore, she hurried toward the exit door cautiously and, along with Kilsha, went outside backward with slow steps. Wajdbeer noticed this, but he remained in his place. Steven saw her go out and got confused as to what he had to do, but he soon settled his mind to stay where he was and do nothing.

Sara went out with her heart beating fast, picked up the bucket and mop, put on a hat, and went out of the building. She headed toward the office building quickly and, once she approached the entrance, started walking slowly and lowered her head. The guard at the main gate asked her, "Where to?"

"To clean the lobby," she replied.

He allowed her to enter the building, so she went inside with Kilsha walking beside her. She went up the staircase, which was short but looked endless to her. She arrived at the lobby where she saw some Makash who worked in the building. Nobody was alarmed to see her in that spot because it was normal for human children to come regularly to clean the place. When she reached Sikwel's office, she put her bucket down and started looking left and right with her heart beating faster and faster. She opened the office door, which was unlocked, and took a deep breath for a moment to regain her bravery. She went inside and closed the door behind her. She looked around, as if she were seeing the office for the first time; and when she again tried to control her heart beat by taking deep breath, Kilsha said to her, "Come on, Sara, you have no time to waste."

She bowed to open the leg of the table and remove the key of the safe but failed, and so she asked Kilsha if there were certain numbers or pass codes to be used to open the leg, but Kilsha said, "No! All you have to do is to turn the leg twice to the right and once to the left." Kilsha told her that, if she moved it the wrong way, the Makash would be alerted and come to the office in seconds.

"But is it my right side or yours?" Sara asked. The question made Kilsha think for a while, and then she said, "It is on your right."

Sara was about to turn the leg of the table when Kilsha said, "Wait, wait, maybe it is on my right and not yours."

Sara got confused and told her to think again, "Is it my right or yours?"

Kilsha approached Sara and said, "It is your right."

"But now we are standing next to each other, which means that my right and yours are the same."

Kilsha thought it over and said, "Yes, it is our right. You should turn the leg toward the right."

Sara turned the leg of the table slowly, as described, and when she opened it, there was nothing inside the hollow leg except a candle. She wondered about that and asked Kilsha about it; Kilsha inferred that the candle must have been the key to the safe, telling her that she had definite information about that. Sara looked at her and asked, "Information? You mean you are not sure?"

Kilsha said shyly that she had once heard two Makash guards talk about the key and the children's files. Sara took the candle and said, "They must have been talking of a candle, not a key."

Kilsha felt confused, but she insisted on what she had heard, "I am sure of what I heard."

"Don't worry, dear. We all make mistakes," Sara said.

Kilsha became angry and said to her, "Why don't you believe me?"

"I believe you. Maybe Sikwel took the key with him today," Sara replied nonchalantly.

Sara noticed a chandlery with places for three candles, but there were only two candles in the chandlery; and as she approached it, she said to Kilsha in sarcasm, "Maybe Sikwel heard about the plan and took the key with him."

Kilsha got annoyed and said, "I am leaving."

Kilsha was about to go out of the room, but at that moment Sara put the candle in the chandlery, and instantly one of the walls opened. Sara gasped with panic, but Kilsha smiled and turned back. "I told you that I am sure of my information," she said triumphantly.

The file store was another large room that was full of huge shelves. Inside, there were files for all children that contained photos with names written neatly. Sara and Kilsha went inside the store, dazzled by what they were seeing. Sara took one of the files, which happened to be for one of the girls; the file contained information about her age, date of arrival in Scaba, her hobbies, and what she was good at. Sara put the file back and started pulling files randomly, looking for the store's key. While searching, she noticed another section inside the store for the missing children. She opened a file and read some information about a boy that was concluded with a note revealing he was still missing. She read seven other files that ended with the same note: missing. Kilsha told her to focus on what she had come for instead of reading files. "Sara . . . we should find the key of the store."

Sara stopped reading at that moment, looking around as if she were talking to Sikwel. "Where did you put the key, Sikwel? Where?" She went out of the file room and back to the office again and started searching for the key in the file shelves. She noticed a file with Sikwel's image on it, so she smiled and said to Kilsha, "I think I found the key."

She opened the file to find that it was hollow, and there was nothing inside but the key; she took it, and while putting the file back into its place, she heard the footsteps of some Makash approaching the office, so she started searching very quickly for a place to hide.

Outside the office, the Makash officer saw the bucket and the mop, and he asked his group who had put the bucket in there. They told him that a girl had come inside the building to clean, but he looked at them angrily and said, "You idiots! There is no work for the kids today at this time. It is the selection day."

He ordered them to search for that girl, so they went inside Sikwel's office but couldn't find her because she had hidden herself inside the file room after she had told Kilsha to remove the candle in order for the wall to close. Kilsha herself, after doing that, hid herself in one of the drawers; and once the guards went out of the office, she went out of her hiding place and put the candle back in its place. The wall opened, and Sara went out of the file room with the key in her hand. They removed the candle, and the wall closed, and then they returned the candle to its place. Sara then went out of the office and went toward the lobby in order to go out of the building. She walked slowly at the beginning, but the nearer she got to the exit, the quicker she walked. She noticed the alert guard standing at the entrance with his face turned inside the building, so she hid behind one of the pillars and started thinking with the key in her hand. She concealed the key in her clothes and screamed loudly, "Help! Help!"

Kilsha was bewildered by what she heard and asked Sara if she was fine, but Sara put her index finger on her mouth, telling Kilsha to keep quiet. The guard came to see who was shouting. Sara waited until he passed them and then moved quietly toward the exit. She ran as fast as she could, but the guards who were coming from Sikwel's office saw her and started shouting and warning the unaware guard, telling him that the girl was running away. He looked back and saw her heading toward the second building; he shot her with a wouf and managed to hit her shoulder. She screamed with pain, but despite that, she was able to continue running until she reached the backstage door. She then walked with a slower pace in order not to raise attention of anyone, but

Wajdbeer again saw her and saw how she was groaning with pain. Even Steven noticed it, so he came nearer to her and supported her, as she was about to fall. He made up a smile as if he were celebrating the victory of their friends with her. She put the key inside his clothes and said to him, "Here is the key, Steven. Don't let us down."

Steven looked at his friends and saw Adam and Dana watching them with anxiety, as if asking for permission to come and help as well, but Steven looked at them with disapproving looks. Nora at that moment was on the stage dancing; Solar and Sikwel were taken by the interesting show, and in order to grab more of their attention, she started doing risky and unusual leaps and hops in the air. This astonished all attendants and left them speechless; some of the kids from the audience were driven by the show to start dancing enthusiastically in their places. The same was the case with the other attendants, including Sikwel himself, who was moving his head in ecstasy with the music; but he stopped when Solar looked at him. Moments later, the guards came into the hall, and one of them came closer to Sikwel and whispered something in his ear. Sikwel looked at the kids who smiled back, but the guard pointed toward Steven and Sara, who smiled as well despite the agonizing pain she had. Sikwel whispered something in reply to the guard, who immediately ordered the others to follow him.

Solar asked Sikwel if everything was okay, and the confused Sikwel replied that there was nothing unusual and nothing to worry about. The guards approached Steven and Sara, whose fear increased, and the senior guard asked Sara to show him her shoulder. She looked at Steven slowly, searching for a savior, and Steven said to her, with a big pretentious smile while giving her the violin, "Sara, it is your turn."

She took the violin from him and prepared to go to the stage, but the senior guard stopped her and said, "Not that fast. Show me your shoulder first."

Solar sensed that there was something going on and asked Sikwel, who replied with a smile and said, "They are only security procedures."

Sara turned back to show the guard her shoulder; and they were all surprised, even Sara herself, that her shoulder was normal, so they allowed her to go up the stage. She played so sweetly that all the attendants forget what they had been through, and they closed their eyes to go into a dream journey. Even Solar enjoyed her playing and closed his eyes to fly with her music to a different world, but Sikwel looked numb, as if he were hearing nothing. He was busy thinking of what exactly was going on, who the girl who broke into his office was, and what she was looking for. He looked at the children and saw them smiling with joy and cheering for their friend.

After the test performance, Solar selected the city team members and told Sikwel to take good care of them so that they would trust him and do their best to win the competition. Then he said to him, "They've got to realize that winning the competition is their only chance to have an easy life in Scaba." He left Sikwel without knowing what had really happened. Sikwel was more afraid of the crystal ball than of Solar, the king's representative.

Sikwel rushed back to his office and immediately checked the leg of his desk where he hid the candle to find it still there in its place. He demanded a report of the incident as well as a list of the items that had disappeared from the place, if any. After some time the guards reported to Sikwel that everything was fine and nothing had disappeared.

Sikwel looked angrily at them and shouted, "So what was that girl doing in the building?"

He then told them to try to figure out what the thing in the building might be that human kids might risk their lives to get. The senior guard said, "Food?"

"Do human children eat our food? Twit," Sikwel commented resentfully.

They couldn't figure out what had happened and grew even more bamboozled as to where the girl had disappeared, especially seeing as they had checked all the girls after the departure of Solar and none had a mark on the shoulder. Sikwel sank to his desk after he had failed to infer anything with only one idea lingering in his mind, *I must know what these bastards want from this building.*

WAJDBEER,
THE PHYSICIAN

When Wajdbeer saw Sara enter the place in that state, he concluded that she was having a certain problem, so he went toward the gathering of the kids between the stage and the audience and headed toward Sara and Steven who felt very afraid. He took an herb out of his bag and passed it to Sara cautiously, telling her to put it on her shoulder and she would be fine. Then he said to Steven, "Tomorrow, bring your friends and meet me at the fifth house before the inverted house."

He went back to his place without being noticed by anyone except Sara and Steven, and once Sara put the herb on her shoulder, her wound healed instantly, and her pain vanished gradually; and so when the guards inspected her, they found no wounds.

When she started playing the violin, she looked at Steven and smiled encouragingly as he was grabbing the key tightly in his hand and smiling back. After the tests had finished, Stom came to the group happily and told them that Solar had selected them to be members of the city children's team, and they had to train more diligently so that they could win over the skillful palace children's team and that they had no excuse whatsoever because Solar the magician had decided to exempt them of any tasks and chores to focus on training for the big day.

The kids met together after that to celebrate the seizure of the key and to plan for the next step. Dana hugged Sara fondly, eulogizing her courage; and so did Nora, Adam, and Steven, the last of whom apologized to all of them for thinking of letting them down.

"Thank you, Sara, for such an unforgettable lesson of courage," Steven said.

Kilsha tried to attract their attention, but it seemed that they had forgotten about her in the midst of their celebration; and when Sara noticed this, she paused and said, "The real heroine in all of this was Kilsha."

Once Kilsha heard this, she felt shy but very happy, so Sara hugged her and said, "Without Kilsha's help, we wouldn't have gotten the key."

The other children thanked Kilsha for her role in the mission and her courage. Adam asked Steven to show them the key, so Steven took it out of his pocket and showed it to all of them. It was a very old and normal key, but they celebrated it as they had never celebrated anything before in their lives because it was their only means of getting out of that world.

Sara and Steven then told them about what had happened to them with Wajdbeer the physician and their interview with him the other day. They all decided to go there to meet him and thank him for what he had done for them.

The next day, the kids went to the fifth house before the inverted house. They waited for Wajdbeer, and after some time, he appeared. He was masked and said nothing to them except for telling them to follow him. They couldn't recognize him in the beginning, so he said to them, "I am Wajdbeer, the physician."

They were assured and followed him inside the house that they were waiting in front of. The house looked very neat and clean but empty of tenants. Wajdbeer opened one of the doors. A staircase led to the bottom of the basement. He went down, and they followed him; and when they reached the basement, Wajdbeer went to one of the corners and pulled the lantern that was dangling from the ceiling, instantly opening one of the walls. They were all taken by surprise, but Sara saw the funny side of it and commented, "Everyone in this world has a secret wall that opens in a magical way."

When everyone had recovered from the hilarity occasioned by Sara's wit, he told them to follow him; and when they crossed to the other side of the wall, Wajdbeer pulled another dangling lantern, and the wall closed again. He did the same with many walls until he reached the inverted house. They were surprised to know that they were in the upper floor of the inverted house and not in the basement. This was a normal sensation because everything in that house was built upside down, including the pictures and paintings that were hanging on the walls. The kids asked him about why the house had been built in that way. He smiled to them and said that everyone who visited the house asked him the same question, and he elaborated by saying, "This house had been built by the most competent Shakam architect."

He explained to them that the house was a maze. Anyone who got inside would never manage to leave again, and it was built that way to help the Shakam hide in cases of war. If anyone thought he was going up in that house, he was, in fact, going down; if they thought they were on the right side, the truth is that they were on the left side and vice versa. He added, "This gives the Shakam the needed time to get as far as possible from the scene before they get caught by the Makash."

The children shook their heads, trying to digest what had been said, but they couldn't, and they were content to gift him with a smile and to thank him for treating Sara, but he said to them, "I have been searching for you for a long time, but I have not been able to find you."

"We had no certain location. We were the homeless street teenagers," Dana explained sarcastically.

He looked at her and said to them all that he admired their survival skills and techniques despite the jurisdiction against them in that regard and that he very much liked their organization, determination, and courage, which all made him search for them.

"But what do you want from us?" Nora interrupted.

He paused for a while and said, "I want you to join me."

They exchanged looks and started inquiring about what he meant, and he explained to them that he was not content with the rule of King Bermuda. He told them that he had been a loyal assistant of the late former fair king, and he was trying to find any way to defeat Bermuda, but he needed their help.

"But how can we help?" Adam asked.

He rose to his feet and told them to follow him upstairs toward one of the halls.

"We are now in the bottom of the house, although we are up," Steven said to Nora.

Nora looked at him unaware what he meant, and when they reached the end of the corridor, which was full of closed doors on each side, Wajdbeer sat on his knees and opened a small niche at the corner of the wall and said to them, "Don't be afraid and just follow me."

Wajdbeer squeezed himself into that opening, and the other kids did the same. They were immensely surprised to see a large hall at the other side of the wall. Half of the hall was made into a lab, and the other side was designed for the training of martial arts. They were even more surprised to see six other children of the same age as themselves—three girls and three boys.

"I know you. Your name is Brian," Sara shouted while waving at someone.

The boy looked at her in wonder, and so did the others.

"Do you know me?" the boy asked.

"Yes, I saw your file in the 'missing' section in Sikwel's office," she replied promptly but felt sorry for revealing a matter that shouldn't have been revealed.

"Is there a section for missing people in Sikwel's office?" Wajdbeer asked.

"Yes. The day you treated her she had been there searching the file. What a naughty, nosy girl," Dana said jokingly.

Sara quickly supported the point, saying, "Yes, yes, that's true. I entered the office out of curiosity."

"I didn't know that there are missing kids in Scaba," Nora said, trying to change the course of the conversation.

Wajdbeer explained to her that the Makash didn't announce the disappearance of these six kids because they didn't want the news to spread among other children who might try the same. Then, he introduced them to each other; and when Brian shook hands with Dana and deliberately left his hand a second or two longer than normal in her hand, Adam's jealousy moved up, so he quickly gave his hand to Brian, introducing himself with "My name is Adam." Brian smiled and pulled his hand sluggishly to shake hands with Adam. Dana smiled shyly at that.

The six children were Brain, Nancy, Alex, Nadia, Joseph, and Monika.

Steven approached the lab and started asking Wajdbeer about what type of lab it was. Wajdbeer explained to him that it was not only a lab to make new medicines but also a lab in which to conduct experiments.

"Experiments on animals? Are you dissecting them?" Steven asked curiously while looking at Kilsha, but Wajdbeer told him that he was trying to do what Nafarit had done to some human beings. Then he opened a book on one of the tables in the lab and said to them, "This book contains the entire history of Scaba. Nafarit wrote it herself."

They didn't understand what he meant, so he looked at them and said, "Nafarit enabled some human beings to release woufs."

He went on fervently revealing these secrets to them, but when he noticed that they were lost, he said to them, "It seems that you need a lesson in history."

The kids were seated for the lesson about the beginnings of the kingdom of Scaba that they needed very much. He spent some time educating them about it, and when he finished, Nora said, "What an exciting history!"

Wajdbeer told them that even many Makash and Shakam did not know that Nafarit had taken a certain hormone out of the Makash and instilled it into humans, who became able to shoot woufs afterward. She wanted these humans to be like a sleeping cell at her disposal and to use them when needed, but Hercules killed her before that.

"Do you think that we are these humans?" Steven asked naively.

Wajdbeer laughed and told him it was unlikely but explained to them that he was able to identify that Makash hormone and he wanted to form an army and use it to defeat King Bermuda. He told them that he needed their help in the matter.

The kids were silent for a while, as they didn't know what to say to him. Then Dana said, "We want to, but we can't be of any help to you because we decided to run away from your world."

Wajdbeer and the six children smiled vaguely at them, but the smile was made clearer by Wajdbeer when he said, "You can never escape from Scaba."

"But we arranged for everything," Adam said defiantly.

Wajdbeer looked at him compassionately and said, "The only possible way to reach the Hill Gate is with a flying carpet, which is restricted only to Makash. Human children can never fly it by themselves."

"I stole the key of the carpet store from Sikwel's office," Sara said in a loud voice.

"What!" the physician exclaimed as he opened his mouth wide with surprise and shock.

The other kids, and Sara herself, felt worried for a moment that Wajdbeer might not be the right person to reveal such secrets to, so they looked at Sara in blame. She felt confused and said, "It was you who told him that we plan to escape in the first place."

Wajdbeer looked at them and said, "Don't worry. I am with you, not against you."

"We were wondering if you can fly the carpet for us, doctor," Dana said.

"But how?" he asked in amazement.

"Since we have the key now, we can arrange to steal the carpet," she explained.

"But that will be almost impossible, even if you stole the carpet," he said, and after a little while, he added, "I don't want to discourage you, though."

The kids were very tentative and waiting anxiously for any word from him, so he explained to them that not all Shakam and Makash can fly the carpet because flying needed skills that he didn't have, and even if he had these skills, he explained he wouldn't go into that very risky matter and that he had another noble cause to follow, which was the liberation of Scaba from the tyrannous King Bermuda. He told them he couldn't give up that cause, and then he offered to help in any way other than flying.

"Why don't we work as one team, try all possible ways and, whichever is most feasible we go on with it?" Steven suggested.

"Now look who is saying that with enthusiasm," Dana said.

"This time it is different because we have the key and this kindhearted doctor on our side," Steven explained.

Dana got permission from Wajdbeer to consult privately with her group members. She took them aside to one of the corners. She told them that they should make use of Wajdbeer until they realize their goals but explained to them that she herself didn't trust Wajdbeer and felt that he wanted to use them as Stom had done before.

Sara interrupted her by saying, "No, he is different from Stom. He has saved my life and saved all of you; without him, our secret would have been revealed."

"Anyway, I don't think of coming back here ever. When I go to my world, I wish to forget all about this place, and I will never think of coming back to help anyone," Dana said promptly.

"Me too. Let these children liberate themselves. They haven't helped us when we needed them. I will never come back to this place to save anyone when I am back in my world," Nora said.

Steven and Adam agreed on that and added that the tyranny of King Bermuda was not their issue and that they would prefer not to come back to this world after running away from it.

Therefore, they all agreed grudgingly to use Wajdbeer to get the power of wouf because, if they managed to do so, they would be more powerful and their chance of getting their freedom would be better off; and if they didn't, they still had the key, and they would go on with their plans anyway.

"We shouldn't lose this old creature. It is of our benefit to make him think that we are his friends," Adam explained.

"We have few Shakam friends, and in case Shishar refuses to fly the carpet for us, we will try to convince this old doctor to do so and take us to the Hill Gate."

"This is what we should do to get out of this place. It is not our problem who will be left behind."

They all agreed to make use of Wajdbeer, so they showed him their desire to help. He told them that, before he even started anything, he needed some materials that would help him build his army and weaponry.

"Can I ask you something risky?" he said.

"Our life from the first day here has been full of risks. Ask whatever you want; it will change nothing," Dana said.

He thought this over for a while and then said to them that he wanted them to use their skillful techniques to bring a piece of Makashan tail for him.

They were puzzled to hear that, so Adam asked him, "But what for?"

"Makashans are like human beings. Any cell of their bodies carries the genetic code of the whole," he explained. He added that he needed only a small part of a Makashan tail with which to produce the hormone that was used by Nafarit.

"Are you going to dissect the small piece?" Steven asked curiously.

When Wajdbeer said yes, Steven added without thinking, "I will help you in that."

They all wondered how he had rushed into such a decision, but he explained to them that he loved lab work.

"But how can we get a Makashan tail?" Sara asked.

"Stom is the answer. Stom told us that he can find anything in this world," Dana explained.

They all agreed to this except Wajdbeer who couldn't imagine that. He thought they would get the tail in another way, perhaps by cutting it somehow.

Nora asked him whether he had some diamonds, and he told to her that he had lots of diamonds. Nora said, "So don't worry. You will get the tail that you want."

The kids divided themselves into two teams: one team—composed of Steven, Sara, and Nora—visited the Shakam family that Sara was working for, and the other team, Adam and Dana, went to meet with Stom. The division was made for security purposes—in case something bad happened to one team, the other would still be safe.

In the training hall at the big building, Adam and Dana met Stom and revealed to him their desire to get a piece, regardless of its size, of a Makashan tail. Stom listened to them carefully and thought for a while. He looked at them suspiciously, which made them confused.

"We will pay you diamonds," Dana said.

"Diamonds! Where did you get them?" he asked anxiously.

"If you want diamonds," Adam said promptly, "bring a piece of a Makashan tail for us, and let us arrange the diamonds for you in our way."

Stom laughed with his eyes swollen with greed. "In that case, I will bring you not only a piece of the tail but the whole of it if you want," he said.

He looked at them suspiciously and asked again, "But what do you want it for?"

He received no reply, and after a moment of silence, he said, "It doesn't matter. I will not ask you again about the tail. This is none of my business."

Adam and Dana heaved a gasp of relief to hear that, and then he said to them, "Meet me at the abandoned palace where I organize my fights and bring the diamonds with you."

When the other team reached the house of the Shakam family, they were all gathered, as was usual at that time, at the dinner table. They welcomed Sara, Steven, and Nora compassionately. The family members hugged Sara fondly asking her anxiously where she had been all that time. She told them all of what had happened to her with Stom and Sikwel, and then she introduced them to Steven and Nora. After that, she asked them a favor with hesitance. The wife answered her with an encouraging smile to ask whatever she wanted without feeling shy. Suddenly, Sara started weeping, and when they asked her what made her weep that way, she explained to them that she missed her family and the world back home. Then she pointed to Steven and Nora and said, "We all want that; we can't stay here any longer, and we were brought in the first place against our will."

The husband agreed with her and said, "I totally understand what you feel. Oppression is hard for anyone to accept."

"We came here hoping for your help," Nora said hesitantly.

The wife looked at her husband wondering what type of help she could mean, but Nora explained to them at once that that she knew from Sara that Shishar used to work in the former king's army and that he had a good military background.

Shishar was touched by what he heard, and it seemed to remind him of his past glorious days, so he blew out his chest like a turkey and said to them, "Yes, and I was the best at work. I was about to be promoted and become a lieutenant, but the coup that happened in Scaba changed everything."

"This is why we need you, sir. You are our only hope in this kingdom, and we promise you that we will pay as much as you need of diamonds," Steven said.

"I don't want diamonds, and I never think of them, but tell me how I can help you."

Nora looked at Sara and Steven as if begging them to speak, so Sara said, "We want you to help us reach the Hill Gate."

Shishar and his wife were shocked to hear that, as they knew it was impossible, so Shishar said immediately, "But that needs a carpet, and we, as you know, are not allowed to fly carpets."

"Please help us. You are the only one who can do it," Steven said.

"But how can I do it? I don't have a carpet they took mine when they disbanded the army," he wondered.

"I stole the key of the carpet store. It is with me," Sara explained with her eyes were still full of tears.

The couple gasped and asked in one voice, "Really?"

She agreed with a nod of her head.

"But you have endangered yourself by doing that," Shishar said.

"We are willing to do anything to go back to our world," Nora explained.

Shishar and his wife exchanged looks and then the wife, understanding what her husband was thinking, nodded her head in approval. Shishar stood up and moved toward the door, where he opened a niche and took out a mask and a shield from it.

"You even have a secret place?" Sara said.

Shishar looked at his mask and shield proudly. They appeared to have taken him back to old service days and memories. He said, after taking a deep breath, "You have selected the right Shakam."

The wife started telling the story of her husband and his days in the army of the former king and how he had received many medals of honor and courage. But when King Bermuda ascended the throne and disbanded the army, he disallowed her husband his most beloved thing that was his work. They even confiscated all his army belongings, such as the carpet and the medals, but he managed somehow to keep his mask and shield and hide them. She told them that the day he had to submit his carpet to the store was the most difficult day ever that it took him years to learn to live with its bitterness.

Shishar put on his mask and shield, which made him look like any Makashan soldier; the only distinguishing mark was his long single tail. When the kids looked at once at his tail to grab his attention, he said to them, "Don't worry."

He brought a tall cloak, similar to that worn by Sikwel, and put it on in order to cover the tail. He then said, "Now we have to choose the right time to break into the carpet store and fly."

Flying on a regular day would raise the suspicion of the guards who would probably stop them, so they had to plan to fly on an irregular day, a day in which air traffic would be very active, and to steal the carpet on a day when Sikwel wouldn't be in his office. Shishar suggested that the best day to do that would be the day of the Grand Competition because everyone was busy on that day including the king watching the events, and air traffic would be at its peak.

He added that city kids must win the competition because if they did there would be celebrations everywhere in the city and more flying carpets than on any other day of the year, whereas their loss would mean that celebrations would be held only at the palace and there would be very little traffic, which would make it almost impossible for them to fly without being noticed or stopped.

When the city kids gathered that night in the big building and exchanged this information, they were filled with joy and ecstasy and felt that their departure to their homeland was close, so they decided to do their best to win on that day. The rest of the day went on sluggishly, with only one idea crossing their minds, how to get a piece of the Makashan tail, to prepare themselves for unexpected happenings.

It was time for them to meet with Stom according to the scheduled plan, so they took their needed precautions as usual; Dana and Adam went to meet him, whereas Steven, Sara, and Nora went to meet Wajdbeer. Adam and Dana went to the rear of the abandoned palace and waited for Stom there. Dana had the diamonds with her, and she kept checking every now and then that the diamonds were still in her pockets, but she felt safer with the presence of Adam with her. It became obvious that Adam had certain feelings toward her despite his many attempts to hide it.

The fights started inside the palace, and Stom waited impatiently for the injury of any Makashan, which was likely to happen as usual. The first match passed without any accidents to the Makashan tails, so Stom put the most resilient and harsh Makashan fighters in to fight against each other in the second match. The audiences heightened the violence of the two fighters with their applause and cheers. Stom watched the four tails very closely, and it wasn't long before one fighter jumped in the air and hit his opponent's tail hard. A piece of it was cut and fell under the feet of the other fighters who were waiting for their turn. Stom watched the spot where the piece fell and thought about how to get it without attracting the attention the other fighters. He announced the Makashan who had cut his opponent's tail winner even before the end of the match, which raised some objection from the other fighters as well as the audience. In order to silence the uproar and hostile cries, Stom announced that there would be a new way of fighting, whereby all fighters would get involved in one grand match and the winner would be the one who survived until the end. The audience liked the new idea and shouted enthusiastically, so Stom told the fighters to gather in the middle of the fighting ring, whereas he himself headed toward the piece of the tail, took it, and put it in his pockets. Then he went up the stairs, and in the middle of the staircase, he gave the signal to start the fight. The fighters attacked each other fiercely, and he went up and went out of the back door to meet Dana and Adam.

When they met, he told them he wanted to see the diamonds first, but Dana insisted on seeing the piece of tail first. Stom took the piece out of his pocket and showed it to them, and Dana gave him diamonds in return. He couldn't believe his eyes, and Adam took the piece and put it in his pocket.

"I will not ask you where you got the diamonds, but in the future, even if you need a hand or a leg, I am your Shakam," Stom said and rushed back into the palace while Adam and Dana went to see Wajdbeer who was waiting, along with the other kids, impatiently for them.

They entered the lab, and the others circled them anxiously. When Adam took out the small piece, Steven took it and showed it to Wajdbeer, who told him to put it on the experiment table. It was the size of an index finger, but it was more than enough for experiments as Wajdbeer asserted in reply to their questions.

"You are heroes! Real heroes," he said to them encouragingly. "Now I will start dissecting it at once; I don't want to waste time because it is a long-awaited moment."

Steven approached him slowly and said in a low voice, "Can I take part in this, sir?"

Wajdbeer welcomed him, which made him happier than ever, and said to his friends, "Finally I will perform real dissection. Hurray!"

The kids' morale was raised after Shishar agreed to flying the carpet and getting the piece of tail, which would enable Wajdbeer to produce the hormone that would make them more powerful. Things appeared to be moving in the right direction for the first time in that strange world. They agreed to act cautiously until the coming of the Grand Competition Day and to try to escape immediately after the end of the events. They decided not to let the palace kids win over them no matter what happened or they would lose a chance that might never be repeated. Dana said to them, "Always remember our objective when we meet them in the competition. We have one goal: to go back home."

They wondered about the absence of any rules for the games of the competitions, but Wajdbeer cleared the mystery to them by asking, "What happens when competitions take place without rules?"

They all replied that it would urge for cheating, and Wajdbeer said, "And this is what the king wants." He explained to them that lawless games and cheating would raise the spirit of hostility and dishonest competition among them, which would lead to mutual hatred between palace kids and street kids and minimize any chance of cooperation between them, a hatred that would go on until the next competition, and so on.

Kilsha felt sad for the fact that Sara was going to leave Scaba and go back to the human world, but Sara told her that she could visit her anytime she came to the human world.

The kids started training hard every day because they didn't want to raise suspicions while Wajdbeer worked seriously on his experiments to extract the hormone using Nafarit's books as a reference.

GRAND COMPETITIONS

The Grand Competition Day was the only day in which all palace children went out of the palace. Jamal said to them before they left, "Remember that we have a noble cause: the liberation of Scaba and all the children who live in it in tyranny. So we have to use the chance of winning and do what we planned for." He didn't forget to remind them that losing the matches meant the loss of their efforts.

The kids were told to assemble in the front yard of the palace where the Makashan soldiers were waiting for them with their carpets. They ordered groups of four onto each carpet. The kids were very excited to do this because they knew that their days in Scaba were about to end and the fugitives would rescue them and also because they had trained very well for that day. They saw King Bermuda flying on a carpet along with General Falca and a group of Makash guards flying around them. The Makash pilots flew the carpets with the children on them above the city. Jamal told the children to try to locate the inverted house of Wajdbeer from above. The kids tried to but couldn't. They arrived at the Rainbow Desert and saw the majestic building in which the competitions were to take place. It was kind of a stadium that contained huge theaters and a small lake with green grassy spaces and hills around the middle. It didn't look like any Olympic stadium they had seen or expected to see in the human world. The king occupied a magnificent platform that overlooked the competition playground. Next to him sat Falca and Sikwel. "I don't want the city kids to win. Make sure they lose the competitions today," the king whispered to Falca.

He didn't want them to win and gain more popularity because if they won they would become an example for all other children to follow or join them. Many creatures from other planets attended that day in response to an invitation from the king, who wanted to demonstrate his control over the city in front of them. All the children of Scaba attended the event, and the king ordered that they be divided into two sections: one that supported the city team and the other that supported the palace team. The two audiences exhibited hostility to each other even before the matches began. In the beginning, some young clowns performed a funny show, and after that the king announced the beginning of the competitions.

The competition contained four contests, and the winning team had to win more than two of these contests to be considered the overall winner. In case of a draw, a decisive final contest would be held between the two to decide the winner of the grand competitions.

The relay contest on hanging ropes was the first event of the day; there were two very thin ropes that stretched for four hundred meters. The contestant had to run as fast as he could on the thin rope to give a small stick to another member of his team who would do the same and run and give the stick to the third, and the third had to give it to the final contestant who was supposed to conclude the contest. The first of the contestants from the palace team was Jamal, and his counterpart from the city team was Nora.

They balanced themselves on the ropes waiting for the signal to start. Silence drowned the place, and the audience held their breath. Nora looked at Jamal furiously and contemptuously, but Jamal smiled at her. The king himself started the contest, and shouts and cheers filled the stadium. Jamal was lighter than Nora, so he managed to outrun her despite the fact that Nora was zippier. At the end of the first one hundred meters, Wang was there, waiting anxiously to take the stick from Jamal. Jamal lost his balance and almost fell off the ropes, but he managed to regain control and balance amid the encouraging shouts of his fans and hostile ones from the other audience. He reached out for Wang followed six seconds later by Nora, who gave the stick to Steven. The time difference helped Wang outrun Steven, who tried his best to catch up with Wang and managed to reduce the difference to four seconds. Wang gave his stick to Samar and Steven gave his to Sara. The king was watching all this very tentatively and excitedly. He tried not to show much enthusiasm toward the palace children out of pride but couldn't control himself and started shouting. Sara surprised all the children with her agility and speed, managing to reduce the difference between her and Samar to only two seconds, which made the competition much hotter between Lillian and Dana, who were both fast. Lillian ran as fast as she could, and all members of her team encouraged her fervently. She was running gracefully, as if she were running on solid ground, and Dana tried to catch up with her but couldn't. Lillian lost her balance some meters before the end and fell off the ropes, down into a pool of mud. Dana won the match, and the palace team ran to see if Lillian was all right while the city team celebrated their first victory.

Lillian wept for her loss and apologized to everyone with a bitter feeling of disappointment and guilt. Her friends stood by her, and Samar said, "It doesn't matter. It is not the end of the world; we still have three competitions ahead of us. Come on, stand up and get ready. We are not finished yet."

The king was disappointed by the city team's victory. He looked angrily at Falca, who dared not look the king in the eyes. As for Sikwel, he didn't know about the king's desire at that moment, so he looked at the king wearing the broadest smile ever; but when he saw the king frowning at him, he looked away. The king patted his snake on the head and kissed it as he released it to go somewhere.

The second contest was dancing. The two teams had to stand at the side of a very steep hill opposite each other, one ascending and the other descending. The two teams started dancing, each selecting a dance of their own. Once dancing starts, the hill will start turning, slowly at the beginning and then increasing speed with time. The contestants will feel dizzy and start losing their sense of direction, but despite that, they have to keep their rhythmic dancing with the music and keep moving in body as one team. The first team to lose balance and harmony loses the match. Nora led the city team whereas Samar led the palace team. It was uncomfortable for both members of the two teams to perform their dances over that slope, but they started their dancing with the playing of the music, and the crowds started shouting and cheering them on. The movements of the city team were more graceful than those of the palace team thanks to Nora, who blended in her dancing different traditional dances of the world and hip-hop. As for Samar, she only performed ballet and a little of hip-hop, but according to the rules of the games, what mattered most was the harmony and rhythmical dancing between members of the team.

After half a minute of speedy spinning, the palace team started losing their control and harmony, and they looked fatigued. They were about to collapse and give up, but in the dying moments, Nora saw the king's snake coming closer to sting her; so she jumped back with panic and fell down, spoiling the movements of the city team, which made them lose the match to the palace team. Once the hill stopped spinning, the palace team went down supported by each other because of dizziness while the other team was very upset and disappointed because of what Nora had done. Nora told them that she had seen a snake, but nobody believed her; one of the dancers told her to be honest and admit the fact that she made them lose the match. Her friends comforted her with some encouraging words and listened to her telling them about the snake. They believed her although they haven't seen any snake nearby.

Falca jumped for joy for the winning of the palace team because he knew that this would make the king happy. The king smiled maliciously while looking at a certain spot. Seconds later, the snake appeared from that spot, so he took it and patted on its head and said to her, "Well done."

Sikwel was confused and couldn't understand why the king rejoiced over the city team's defeat. The two teams were level at one to one, and both decided to work harder to win the competitions.

Dana said to her friends, "We will not let this group of children defeat us and deprive us of going back home."

"It seems that this group of children receives certain type of illegal help," Nora commented.

"Don't forget that these villains are the king's infiltrators and his adherent followers."

"It doesn't matter. We will win over them," Adam said and smiled at Dana who smiled back.

The third competition, which was underwater musical playing, started. The rules of the competition were simple: the title would go to the team that could endure playing music underwater for the longest time. Sara headed the city team whereas Kameel headed the palace team with his saxophone. The two teams went underwater and started playing a piece of music chosen by the king. It was a lovely piece of music that could be played with all instruments. The audience was able to hear the music although it was performed underwater. The kids started to come out of the water one by one after a while, all, that is, except Sara, who closed her eyes and went away with her imagination as she always did when she played music. Nobody could compete with her except Kameel, who fought hard to stay underwater as long as he could up to the last moment; but he finally had to leave the water, leaving Sara, the winner, behind. She even continued playing after that and went on playing unaware of when to stop. All started to feel worried, and Steven jumped into the water for rescue amid the two audiences' clapping and shouting.

The king felt bad about it and said to Falca, "You should do something. Otherwise, these devils will turn into heroes."

Falca rose to his feet when he heard the king say this.

The result meant the city team was leading two to one, and they started to celebrate their victory in front of the disappointed palace team.

The fourth and final competition was over the flag of Scaba. There were four circular wagons, each of which barely could accommodate one person, pulled by zebras. The two teams had to occupy four wagons and fight against each other to seize the flag of Scaba, which had the picture of King Bermuda. The flag was put midway between the wagons of the two teams, and whoever succeeded in grabbing the flag first had to cross a very narrow bridge that ran over a very dangerous space full of thorns and slivers of very sharp glass. The team had to cross the bridge over to the opposite side and plant the flag on a hill. The weather was very bad at that particular part of the arena; it was windy and snowing, which made it hard to see around. The kids had heavy jackets on to withstand the harsh weather. Sara didn't take part in that competition, nor did Shaun and Kameel from the other team. Before the king gave the signal to start, Falca came back and winked to him, and he smiled in turn and started the competition.

The city team went immediately toward the flag, whereas Jamal went toward the bridge and parked his wagon there. Wang and Samar stopped at the middle near the flag.

"What intelligent kids," Dana said to herself.

Adam, Steven, and Nora obstructed the way of the other team and started colliding with them to prevent them from moving farther, but they were very surprised when the wheels of their wagons started to fall apart. Adam said, "This is cheating. This is unfair."

Steven shouted, "These kids have sabotaged our wagons."

"We will not let you win," Nora said while she was trying to prevent Lillian from passing despite the fact that the wheels of her wagon were broken.

Jamal looked back to what was happening and didn't like what he had seen.

Dana made her way to the flag and was able to seize it after she performed an acrobatic movement; she hung herself from the wagon with her legs, pulled her body down and picked up the flag, and then she pulled herself back into the wagon again amidst the audience's clapping and shouting. She went to the bridge where Jamal was waiting, but she pushed him back with her wagon and went on.

Jamal's wagon started to spin around, and when it stopped, he chased her. The king looked at Falca angrily when he saw Dana passing Jamal and mounting the bridge. The wheels of Dana's wagon started to disengage slowly. Suddenly one of the wheels fell off, and the whole wagon slowed down and almost fell off the bridge. Jamal reached her, and although her wagon had only one wheel, Dana didn't give up; but after that the second wheel fell down, and when Dana saw her wagon about the fall off the bridge, Dana threw the flag up into the air and jumped to clutch Jamal's wagon. Jamal grabbed the flag before it fell down and went on to the other side unaware that Dana was holding onto his wagon.

"I will not let you defeat us," Dana shouted at him.

Jamal was confused and didn't know what to do, but when Dana tried to take the flag back using her free hand, he pushed her hard, which made her fall down, whereas he went on his way while shouting, "I am sorry, sorry."

He got off the wagon and hurried up the hill. The snow made it very hard for him to climb up, and Dana was there, trying to catch up with him. He reached the top. He started to put the flag in place, but when he saw Dana still chasing him with determination, he dropped the flag twice before succeeding in putting it in place and raising the flag over the base, winning the match for the palace team.

The fans of the city team were very frustrated and shouted with fury every time a wheel fell down, and after the end of the contest, they started throwing their shoes into the ring. The other audience retaliated with the same. The king felt happy to see them in that state of hostility and mutual hatred as a result of his unfair competition from all sides: from one side, the members of the city team were older than the members of the palace team, and from the other side he interfered to tip the palace team over their opponents, but after all, this is what he had wanted all along.

The four contests ended in draw, a result that neither was satisfied with but had to accept. The members of the city team called their opponents cheats, but Samar shouted back, saying to them, "And you are older than us. Go and compete with kids your age."

The two teams had to do conduct one final decisive contest to determine the winner. The last contest was about taming a wild tortoise, and the team who managed to stay the longest period would win. The kids of both teams laughed when they heard about this because the tortoise is one of the slowest animals and the task would be very easy.

Sara joined her team for this final competition, and so did Shaun. There were ten tortoises in wooden boxes. Each box could be accessed only from above, where the roof of the box was open. The children entered through that opening and rode the tortoises. There were no ropes for balance, but it didn't matter for the kids as they knew that the tortoises would by very slow; but when the boxes were opened, the tortoises went out very fast with the sun glowing in their eyes.

The kids didn't expect this and started to fall of the tortoises' backs. Shaun was the first to fall, followed by Steven, Samar, Sara, Adam, and then Jamal. Only Lillian and Nora remained. Moved by the audience's fervent applause and clapping, Lillian remembered how she had controlled her unruly horse one day, so she patted the neck of the tortoise while holding her very tightly. Nora couldn't stay on any longer and fell off while Lillian remained on the back of her tortoise until it calmed down and stopped by itself as Lillian kept patting its neck and smiling for her victory.

The city kids were very frustrated by the final result and blamed the *deceptive* palace kids, as they called them, for their defeat. Dana said to her friends, "Don't worry, we will convince Shishar to go on with our plan despite everything, but we have to do it very quickly."

They agreed to go on with their plan and forget their defeat in the competition and the fact that things had become more difficult. The king announced the palace team the winner, and the celebration was to be held in the palace immediately. He said, while looking at the fans of the city team, "The celebrations will be in the palace only, and the rest will go back to their work as usual. The kid who will be selected through a draw to go back to the human world will be selected from among the kids of the palace only."

The palace kids were happy to hear that, but Lillian said to them, "Did you hear that? There will be a random draw to select one of us."

"Don't buy that; the king is lying. Each year someone we've never heard of wins that fake draw," Samar explained.

"Don't let him spoil our day; what is important is to go on with what we planned for," Jamal said happily. "I hope I will make it and escape today."

SHISHAR

O n the day of the Grand Competition Day, Shishar put on his shield and mask and kissed his wife and children before he left his house. He knew what he was going to face, and despite his worry, he felt proud, as if he were back in his real life again. As he headed toward the big building that contained the magical carpet store, he knew exactly where to go. His heart was beating fast, but he controlled himself. He passed by the guard at the outer gate who didn't suspect him at all. He entered the building and had to pass in front of Sikwel's office to reach the store, but he noticed that the place was heavily guarded, especially in front of Sikwel's office. He passed them by without being notice, but suddenly one of the guards said to him in an investigative way, "Stop."

He stopped without turning his body, and his heart started beating very hard. He felt that his heart would jump out of its place but was saved by the guard saying to him, "Go to the uniform section to change yours because it is very old."

He heaved a sigh of relief and continued walking after he had said yes to the guard. He reached the carpet store and looked around cautiously. Once he felt assured that there was nobody around, he opened the door with the key given to him by the kids. He closed the door behind him, and inside the store there were great heaps of carpets that made him stunned. He walked between the shelves touching some carpets and smelling others. The carpets reminded him of his past service with the former king. He took one carpet, spread it on the ground, and sat on it; he was happier than ever to see the carpet fly inside the giant store. He went down and wrapped the carpet, tied it with a rope, and took off his tall suit to put the carpet on his back. Then he tied the carpet with the rope to his body and put on his suit again and left the store quickly.

When he passed the guard who had asked him to change his old uniform, the guard noticed the swollen suit and told him to stop, "Stop! What are you hiding under your clothes?"

Shishar smiled while turning his body to face the guard and pulled another uniform from behind his suit, saying, "It is the new uniform. I followed your advice."

Then he walked away, leaving the guard behind smiling and went out of the building.

After that, he looked around, and when he saw nobody around, he pulled out the carpet and flew it up. There were many Makash soldiers flying their carpets on that day to secure the place for the competitions and the king. Shishar flew his carpet beside them without being suspected by anyone. He couldn't believe he was flying, and when he came closer to the Rainbow Desert, he watched the assembly point for the pilots. Once he had got it right, he landed his carpet, as it happened at exactly the moment the competitions had finished.

The Makash divided the children into two groups: the city kids and the palace kids. Jamal tried to apologize to the city kids for the unfairness that they faced in the competitions, but nobody listened to him because the city kids had agreed to ignore the palace kids. Jamal swore to them that they had no hand in all of what happened, but Dana screamed in his face and said, "Shut up! We don't want to hear your excuses."

Jamal had to be quiet grudgingly, but Lillian said to him, "Don't worry, they will thank you one day when they discover that it was for their benefit."

When the kids passed in front of the audience, the fans of the city team started shouting at them indiscriminately and one of the audience said, "You deprived us of a one-day rest and diminished for all of us the chance to dream of returning home."

They threw their shoes and rotten fruit at them, and when the audience of the palace team saw that their heroes were also being beaten, they attacked the other audience and started a fierce fight that made the king nothing but much happier. Sikwel stood up and was about to go and break up the engagement, but Falca prevented him.

The city children were taken to the carpet assembly point, which was far away from the audience's assembly area, in order to be taken back to the city, whereas the palace children were taken to another assembly point on the opposite side of the competition stadium. Shishar waved his hand when he saw the city children who ran toward him and seated themselves on the carpet. The carpet was big enough for all of them except Steven, who couldn't find a place on the carpet. The Makash pilot who was parked near Shishar told him to come on board of his carpet, but Steven said to him, "But we came on the same carpet."

"But now you will ride with me. Come on, don't argue," the Makash said in a harsh voice.

It was clear from the military suit that the Makashan was wearing that he had a higher rank than Shishar. On the other carpet there were some city children whom Steven didn't know, but they looked at him contemptuously while he was trying to ride with them. Sara cried quietly, but Steven smiled to her and moved his lips without uttering a sound to say to them, "Don't worry, I will follow you."

Shishar flew the carpet immediately because the more time they wasted the easier it would be for them to be discovered. After they were high in the sky, Shishar asked them, "Did you win?"

They all shook their heads shyly, which was enough for him to understand that they lost. "So we will not be able to do it. We will get caught."

"Please, Mr. Shishar, we beg you to do that; we have passed through lots of difficulties to reach this stage," Dana begged him.

Shishar looked at them pathetically and said, "But this is suicide."

Sara, with her eyes filled with tears, said, "Please, sir, please. I can't stay one more day in this world."

Shishar thought for a while and said to them, "We will fly over the Rainbow Desert, and when we make sure that everyone has left, we will go to the Hill Gate quickly."

The kids became happy to hear that. Steven was watching them from afar knowing that they were getting closer to their freedom. His eyes glazed with tears but showed nothing to the Makashan pilot who landed the carpet close to the training building and didn't fly again until he saw Steven go inside the building. Moments later, Steven came out of the building and went to see Wajdbeer.

Shishar flew the carpet over the Rainbow Desert, and while on their trip, they saw the carpet that carried the twins, Samar and Shaun, who exchanged looks with them. Shishar headed toward the Hill Gate and started to go down gradually as he was at a great height. They all noticed the heavy guarding of the hill, so Shishar decided to try to bring his carpet to the front side of the gate so that he faced only the guards at the gate after passing the other guards who were situated before the gate. Dana said to him, "It seems that we will need more than a delivery from your side."

Shishar understood what she meant, so he lowered the carpet down. The guards weren't alarmed to see the carpet with the kids on board because they knew that this wouldn't have happened without orders from the king and General Falca. Shishar lowered the carpet to the level of a man's height that made the guards suspicious, and they prepared themselves for any unexpected happening. The kids started kicking the guards on their ears, which made them drop one by one. At that point, the guards situated before the gate turned back and started shooting woufs at the kids and Shishar, who was doing quick maneuvers with the carpet to evade them.

The kids got off the carpet, and Shishar attacked the other guards with the wouf to protect the kids and give them a chance to reach the gate. The kids ran toward the gate, fighting many guards on the way as they felt that they were getting closer than ever to freedom. When the last guard fell, Adam smiled to Dana and said, "Here we are."

Adam was the first to enter the gate. Dana had to wait for a while for Sara and Nora who were still behind. She urged them to hurry up, and once they arrived at her place, they heard Adam's voice shouting from behind the gate, "Run away. There are many of them here."

Then they heard him screaming in pain; Shishar looked back to see the kids retreating and coming back from the gate, so he turned back and on the way he saw Adam going out of the gate injured, barely able to walk. Shishar lowered his carpet and helped them on board quickly, but they had to wait for Adam, so they flew over the place very slowly, but Adam was too slow because of his injury, and the guards started to attack the carpet again from both sides.

Adam shouted at them, "Leave me! Save yourselves!"

But Dana stretched a hand for him and said, "Hold my hand. Come on, you can do it."

Adam tried to walk faster with his hands stretched to grab Dana's, but the guards were getting closer, so Shishar had to go up, leaving Adam down amid a huge pack of fierce guards while Dana was still stretching her hand toward Adam who was now too far away.

They all started crying seeing the guards arrest Adam, who was now looking up at his friends as they got higher and higher. Dana asked Shishar, crying, "Can we come back to liberate him?"

Shishar didn't reply but simply looked at her with compassion. She put her head between her hands and started crying, blaming herself for all that had happened to them. Sara got closer to her and said, "Don't worry, you will find a way to get him back."

"I am the one who let you down. My plans all end in disaster. I am a loser who is good at nothing but putting friends in trouble."

Sara hugged her fondly and speechlessly; then suddenly Shishar noticed that there was a group of Makash chasing them on carpets, so he shouted, "It seems that we have company. Hold on."

He sped up while the Makash were chasing him and shooting woufs. He evaded them skillfully and gracefully and took them over the competition area, which had become vacant now. He lowered the carpet to a level at which the kids had to raise their legs up to prevent them from crashing to the ground. Shishar told them to pick anything on the way that might be useful as a weapon. The kids got off the carpet where Dana picked up a wheel from one of the malfunctioned wagons, and Sara took a wooden rod from Dana's wagon that broke down, and so did Nora. They rushed back to the carpet, and Shishar rose up again while a group of Makash was approaching them on another carpet. Shishar headed toward the city and flew low, and a Makashan got closer to them. Dana threw the heavy wheel at him, and a direct hit dropped him off the carpet, which continued to fly without a pilot for a while and then fell to the ground. Shishar flew even lower to a height of about two meters, causing a state of chaos and disturbance in the streets that were crowded with children and Makash. The shoppers were disturbed and alarmed to see that number of carpets in the air chasing each other. Sara threw the wooden rod at the Makashan, and he managed to evade it, but it hit one on another carpet and knocked him off it. A Makashan got very close to them and jumped at their carpet so gracefully that he filled the kids and Shishar with wonder and amazement. The girls attacked him fiercely, and Shishar had to focus on flying the carpet while at the same time trying to shoot the Makashan with a wouf. Nora hit him with the wooden bar on his feet, which made him fall on his back. Nora and Dana attacked him and hit him on the ears, but he pushed them back hard, which made them almost fall off the carpet. They grabbed the carpet by each end with their bodies hanging in the air. In the meantime, the Makashan rose to his feet and headed toward Sara, but Shishar flew the carpet up a little and shot the Makash with a wouf, which made him fall to the ground. Sara ran and helped the two girls back on board the carpet.

They arrived at the fifth house before Wajdbeer's house and landed there. Shishar wrapped his carpet up and gave it to Dana, telling her to keep it because she would need it someday, and then he went back home as the girls went inside the fifth house to look for Wajdbeer.

Sikwel was in his office when he heard about the attempt to break into the gate. He couldn't believe what he heard and said to the guard who told him the news, "What? How did that most secure and sensitive place get attacked and breached that way?"

The guard explained to him that a group of children attacked the Hill Gate on a carpet, but Sikwel couldn't digest it, "Flying carpet? But how? And who helped them?"

Then, as if he had suddenly remembered something, he opened the leg of the table that contained the candle, took it out, and put it in the empty slot of the chandlery. When the file store opened, he rushed inside and opened the file that was supposed to contain the key to discover, with dismay, that there was no key.

He threw it to the ground and said, "Those damned kids. So that was their plan that day. They deceived us. I will kill them before the king kills me."

"It seems that a Shakam helped them in that, sir, because the wouf that was released from the pilot of the carpet had Shakam characteristics."

Sikwel got angrier and said, "Kids and a Shakam who dares attacks Makashan guards? That's intolerable!"

He thought over this for a few seconds and then asked whether the kids had managed to escape, and the guard assured him that they managed to arrest one of them.

Sikwel said in a low voice, as if speaking to himself, "Why do I have a hunch of who did it?"

"But who is that Shakam who endangered his life to help these kids?" he went on.

He pondered the matter, trying to work out who had done it while looking at the guard. All of a sudden he rushed to the files as if remembering something, opened Sara's file, and smiled on the sly.

The kids arrived at Wajdbeer's place where Steven and the six children were working. Steven and Wajdbeer were busy dissecting the tail, and each of the other six children was doing something. When they saw the girls back with their eyes full of tears, they were afraid, and Steven asked promptly, "Where is Adam? What happened to Adam?"

Sara ran and hugged Steven and said, "They arrested him."

Wajdbeer asked them what exactly had happened to them, and she told them the whole story in detail while sobbing.

When Shishar arrived home, he said, while opening the door, "Honey, I am back," but he heard no reply. When he entered the house and saw her sitting in the middle of the room, he instantly suspected something abnormal. He was right because Sikwel came out of one of the rooms and said sarcastically, "Welcome back, hero."

Shishar panicked and realized that it was the end for him, so he said to Sikwel, "My family didn't know about that. I alone am to blame only for it."

"Come with us, traitor," said Sikwel.

The guards arrested him amid his wife's and children's crying and begging. They tried to do something to help their father, but the guards pushed them away.

Furious King

The king heard about the breach and got very furious. It was Falca who told him the news, so the king said to him, "I have never trusted that Sikwel."

Falca bowed his head in humiliation and shame. "You exaggerated his skills and praised him day by day," the king added. "Remember when you told me that he is the bravest of the Makash? It seems that none of you is competent, and that's why the Shakam used to rule you despite your power."

"It is treason, Your Majesty, treason by this Shakam who helped the kids to breach our security," Sikwel replied.

"But the Shakam wouldn't do it unless they feel that you are weak," said the king.

Falca continued, as if he hadn't heard the king, "Sikwel identified the traitor and arrested him."

The king ordered him to summon the Shakam and the boy in order that he could decide what to do to them himself.

"The crystal ball showed me where the other girls, who were with the boy, went to, so send a troop of Makash and tell them not to come back without these kids."

Falca bowed in humiliation, and before leaving, the king said to him, "I will order them to search all houses nearby. Never trust anyone!"

"We hear and obey, Your Majesty," Sikwel replied.

Sikwel went to the meeting hall to meet the king, bringing Shishar and Adam along with, both handcuffed. He was drowned in fear of the king's fury, but the king said nothing to him. Instead, he gazed at Adam and Shishar for a while and said, "The only way you can save your lives is to tell me where the rest of this gang is."

Adam and Shishar remained silent.

"It is better that you tell me because the crystal ball will tell me anyhow."

They nevertheless remained silent, and the king said while trying to suppress his anger, "Falca, I want you to announce that these two will be hanged if their friends don't surrender."

"We hear and obey, Your Majesty," Falca replied.

But the king turned to Sikwel at that point and said, "They humiliated you, Sikwel, and made you a subject of ridicule and laughter. Now these two are yours. I want you to continue torturing them in front of all the inhabitants of Scaba until their friends show up."

Sikwel swallowed his saliva and couldn't but agree with the king for giving him the chance to avenge them.

The guards arrived at the fifth house and broke its door down to search it. They went down the basement, but it was empty; the same was the case with the attic and the upper stores, so they went out and searched the nearby houses, where they broke and smashed the doors and shouted at its Shakam inhabitants, calling them traitors and ordering them to bring the kids out of their hideouts. They reached Wajdbeer's house, and when he asked them who they were looking for, they pushed him aside and went into the inverted house to search for the kids. Some of them went up to discover that they were still down, and some went down to discover that they were in the upper floor, so they couldn't find anyone; but the kids were in the basement and could hear the guards running around, so they held their breath.

It was announced in the city that the runaway kids had only two days to give up before Shishar and Adam were to be hanged. They tortured them in front of other inhabitants in a public square where they put up two gallows to hang the two prisoners.

Dana cried when they prevented her from surrendering to the guards to stop Adam's and Shishar's suffering and to protect them from death. Wajdbeer begged her to be patient because he thought he was very close to extracting the hormone from the tail and said to her, "They will kill you without any mercy if you give yourselves to them. Never trust them."

Dana replied desperately, "Who shall we trust, then? You and your imaginations and dreams that will never come true? You can't make Makashans out of us."

Suddenly Steven shouted with joy, "I think I did it! I extracted the hormone, doctor."

Wajdbeer rushed to him anxiously and looked through the microscope. He couldn't believe his eyes; the hormone was separated from the rest of the cell, so the old physician jumped with joy and hugged Steven, saying to him, "You are a genius, Steven. You are a genius."

Steven had never felt happier and looked at Sara who was looking at him fondly, but he soon asked Wajdbeer, "Do you think that this amount will be enough?"

"Of course, it is even more than enough," he replied happily.

Wajdbeer asked them to give him some time to prepare the hormone, which made the six children who had been living with Wajdbeer in the house even happier than the other kids because they had waited for that moment for a long time.

"I will take some of the doctor's diamonds and give them to Stom to help me save Adam," Dana whispered to Nora. Nora didn't agree with her, but Dana had made up her mind to do that.

Wajdbeer finished preparing the hormone and put it in a small bottle and said, "It is time, heroes."

Then he told the six children to come nearer one by one and dripped one drop of the hormone from the bottle in their ears. Sara said in astonishment while she was watching the six children, "They haven't altered a bit. Why is that?"

Wajdbeer explained to them that there would be no superficial noticeable change but that they would change from within and that the change would enable them to shoot woufs like the Makash and the Shakam, but the human wouf would resemble the Shakam woufs, and the hormone would start working after twenty-four hours. When the six children had finished, he told the city children to do the same. Even Kilsha wanted to have a drip, but Wajdbeer told her that it wasn't suitable for her.

"But I want to get the wouf to become stronger!" she screamed with indignation.

But Wajdbeer explained to her that Moback bodies weren't able to incorporate the hormone and that it would be of more harm than benefit, and it could even kill her. When Sara heard that, she took Kilsha in her arms and said to her, "You don't need that."

Dana couldn't believe that the hormone could change anything, and her mind was occupied with only one idea—how to release Adam and Shishar—so she waited till everybody was not paying attention and stole some diamonds and went out to meet Stom without being noticed by anyone. Stom was the last hope for her.

JAMAL'S ESCAPE FROM THE PALACE

Jamal couldn't escape that night after their victory because too many Makashan guards had come to the palace, and the kids were told to go to sleep early. The palace children heard nothing of the city children's attempt to escape. They only noticed that traffic that night in the palace was not normal and that the king was irritable and shouting at everyone. Jamal decided to postpone his escape for another night. The kids met the next day with Princess Filda and told her all that had happened the previous night, and she told them that it was fine to postpone to another night, but she asserted that this had to be done as fast as possible.

The night the king decided to go to the city to see what was going on, Jamal put his picture on the bed and asked Shaun to take the picture from the bed every morning and put it back on the bed every night. Jamal sneaked out of the dormitory and went to Filda's room where he searched for the clothes of Shakam that belonged to Dushan, which Filda had told them about. He found the clothes and then he looked for the secret tunnel under the bed, and when he found it, he went down through it. The light was dim, so he walked slowly down that very long tunnel that went under the city. Jamal could hear creatures talking and walking above. He felt exhausted, so he took a rest and then walked again until he reached the exit. There he put on the new clothes and the Shakam mask and went out of the exit, located on the outskirts of the city, and walked slowly and cautiously. He saw some fatigued children heading to sleep after a long day's work. They looked at him nonchalantly and went on their way. He started searching for Wajdbeer's house but didn't know where to start. He saw some Makash soldiers who were passing by, so he lowered his head and walked at a faster pace, and while he was passing them by, one of them looked at him suspiciously, but he didn't stop him. Jamal was relieved for that; but the same guard stopped, thought for a few seconds, looked again at Jamal, and said to his friend, "Look at that Shakam. He doesn't have a tail."

They shouted at him and told him to stop, but he ran away as fast as possible, so they ran after him, shouting, "Stop, weird creature."

Jamal ran faster than he ever had in his life, looking for a place to hide. He saw a child unloading a pack off a zebra's back, so he jumped over the animal and ran with it with the Makash still running after him amid the astonishment and resentment of the zebra's young owner.

He noticed a narrow alley, so he jumped off the zebra and ran through, hiding himself behind some empty cartoons. The three guards came forth and entered the alley, searching for Jamal. Jamal felt as if they were about to discover his place, so he climbed the wall and jumped to the other side to see himself somehow out of the city. He walked aimlessly and hid himself in the darkness that was as thick as a blanket. After walking for some time, he noticed a light in the vicinity coming out from one of the buildings and decided to go there. When he arrived there, he discovered that it was an abandoned palace and stood up there for a while unsure to get into it. He heard the voices of the three guards who were chasing him approaching the place, so he made up his mind to hide inside. When he entered it, he found himself behind a huge audience of Makash and Shakam who were all cheering fervently and realized that there was some kind of competition going on. It was an ideal place for him to hide himself, so he squeezed himself into the crowds and mingled with them while watching the three guards who were still searching for him. Nobody noticed his presence, but after a while, one of the Makash became alarmed and shouted, "A strange tailless creature."

Jamal, before the others could notice, jumped gracefully here and there, sometimes over others' shoulders and some other times between their legs until he reached the edge of the ring underneath where the wrestlers were fighting. He lost his balance and fell into the ring between two wrestlers, which made the audience more thrilled, and the wrestlers more embittered. Stom tried to discover what the creature that fell from above was, but he didn't have time because one of the wrestlers grabbed him by the hands. The other wrestler came forth to hit him while he was still between the hands of the other wrestler, but Jamal was faster and kicked the feet of his jailer, which made him leave him. Jamal lowered his head very quickly, making the wrestler hit his opponent rather than Jamal. The audience had never been more excited, which filled the injured fighter with frenzy and ire, so he stood up and kicked his opponent very hard. Jamal at that moment ran up, and the three guards tried to reach the staircase to arrest him, but the place was overcrowded, and it thus took them longer than should have. Jamal went up and pushed himself inside the crowd searching for an exit. The audience were applauding and shouting for the two fighters, which gave Jamal a chance to look around and see the back exit, so he crept until he reached it and went outside. He ran into Dana who was about to go inside and surprised her.

"You," said Jamal.

She looked at him wondering who he was, so he took off the mask; and when she saw him, she screamed with surprise.

"You? What are you doing here? And how did you get out of the palace?"

"It is a long story," he replied.

Then he begged her to help him hide from the guards, but she hesitated and grabbed the diamonds very tightly; and before she said anything, the three guards were on them and shouted, "You are under arrest. Stop, both of you."

Dana said in a low voice, as if she were talking to herself, "We aren't yet."

She threw diamonds at the guards, who immediately bent to collect them, and took Jamal by the hand and ran away from the guards. Dana took Jamal to Wajdbeer's house, and Jamal kept asking her on the way where she was taking him. When she entered the basement of the fifth house, Jamal asked her if she knew about someone called Wajdbeer and where he lived, but she didn't reply to his question. She reached the lab where everyone was sleeping. She woke them up, and when Steven saw Jamal, he shouted, "Are you crazy to reveal our secret place to this child?"

"I am not a child. I recently turned ten," replied Jamal angrily.

"Can't you remember him? He is—" said Dana.

"We know who he is. He is the fraudulent child from the palace team," Sara said promptly.

"We didn't cheat, and I apologize for—"

Wajdbeer interrupted him, asking, "Who are you, boy, and what do you want?"

"His name is Jamal, and he is one of the palace kids," Dana replied on his behalf.

Wajdbeer was astonished to hear that and asked, "But how did you escape from the palace? No child has managed to escape from the palace before."

"He must be one of the king's loyal servants who came here to spy on us," Steven muttered. "Princess Filda helped me to escape," Jamal replied, ignoring Steven.

"Princess Filda? Do you know her?" Wajdbeer asked in a disturbed tone.

"Yes, she was the one who helped me and told me to search for an old man whose name is Wajdbeer," said Jamal.

"And what do you want from Wajdbeer?" asked Wajdbeer.

"It is secret that I will reveal only to Wajdbeer himself," Jamal explained.

"I am Wajdbeer. What do you want from me?" Wajdbeer said.

"But how can I verify that you are Wajdbeer?" Jamal asked.

"He is Wajdbeer. Didn't your princess tell you how to identify him?" Dana asked.

"Yes, I should identify him by his place; it is a weird house," explained Jamal.

So Dana took him around to take a close look at the inverted house. Jamal was astonished to see that everything was upside down, but he was happy to see himself in the right place. To go back to the gathering, Jamal and Dana went up to practically go down to the basement.

"I need your help to reach outside the borders of the crystal ball," Jamal said to Wajdbeer.

"But why should I help you in that?" Wajdbeer asked.

"Because Adlif asks you to," Jamal replied promptly as if he were expecting the question.

When the old physician heard that, he smiled but said, "Not until you tell us how you managed to escape from the palace, hero," Wajdbeer said.

"Not until I apologize to everyone for what had happened in the competitions," Jamal said.

Then he told the city kids that they hadn't cheated, but they had done their best to win in order to allow Jamal a chance to run away and save Scaba from Bermuda. He then looked at Dana and said, "I want to personally apologize to you."

"Don't worry, I forgot about it."

Before Jamal started revealing to them how he had run away, Brian shouted while he was looking at his hands, "I feel something strange in my hands. It's like there are insects creeping on them."

Nancy, Monika, Alex, Nadia, Joseph, and Monika all felt the same.

Wajdbeer grabbed Brian's hands to check them and said, "It seems as if the hormone has started working, even faster than our expectations."

Steven felt the same, followed by Sara, Nora, and finally Dana; only Jamal was standing there in the middle, unaware of what was going on.

DANNY'S DEPARTURE

Children at the palace stopped their work after they saw the Makash guards headed by General Falca dragging Danny to send him back to human world. Danny was crying and resisting them furiously, begging them to leave him there in Scaba and promising them to be as obedient as ever.

"It is not a matter of obedience and hard work," Falca said while stressing the words and raising his voice to make everyone hear the message. He looked at the children and smiled contemptuously. "You will all have the same fate when you turn eighteen. You will be sent back to your world," he added, "after we make you lose your small brains, dear."

Children felt disappointed and sympathized with Danny. Shaun looked at Lillian, Samar, and Wang, asking them for permission to release his energy against the guards; but they all showed disapproval of that intention. Wang, who was sitting next to him, grabbed his hand to prevent him from doing anything, but Shaun ignored all that and focused on one of the guards. The guard sat down promptly with a heavy thud. Falca and the other guard looked at him, trying to figure out what was going on, but to their surprise, the same happened to them as well. Every time one of them stood up, one of the others would sit down. It looked like they were playing a game. They stood up after Shaun got tired of releasing his power quickly and stood back to back, preparing themselves for an attack from an enemy they didn't know and couldn't locate.

In the meantime, Danny ran away, and Wang pressed hard on Shaun's hand to stop the flow of energy he was releasing. Falca, still baffled by what had happened, ordered the guards to chase Danny. The other kids also were surprised to see that happening to the sturdy guards.

The two guards caught Danny and dragged him outside the palace in order to return him to the human world.

The kids met with Princess Filda. They were in a state of resentment and agony about what Shaun had done.

"You almost exposed us and revealed our secret by what you have done, which would have destroyed all we planned for," Lillian said to him.

"I couldn't stand seeing Danny in that situation. I wanted to do something to save him," he replied.

"You need to save yourself from yourself. You are good for nothing, Shaun," Samar said sarcastically.

Shaun was embarrassed by Samar's outburst, but Filda told them not to judge him because he had good intentions and he had only failed to control his feelings. She added that this would certainly not happen again and that she had found the best way to take the *Doom Book* to the human world in order to be given to Jamal and Lillian's parents. Hearing this, the kids gathered around her in order to hear what she had to say.

She told them that every time Solar went to the human world with some Makash to kidnap children, they took some Moback with them to deceive children who would run after them until they fell in the hands of Solar. She suggested sending the book with Sisami because nobody would suspect him, and when he arrived there, he would go to Jamal and Lillian's parents and give them the book. Lillian asked her whether Sisami would be able to explain what he wanted to them, but Filda told her that she opposed the idea because human beings weren't used to seeing animals talk and would thus be very frightened. She said that Sisami was intelligent and would figure out another way to convey the message to the parents.

Jamal's picture was fixed on a mop and put in front of the king's picture in the prison. Filda told them to be cautious when putting Jamal's picture up. The kids met with Sisami to see how he would carry the book. They came up with the idea of wrapping the book around his abdomen and tying it with a piece of clothing. He was then asked to practice walking with the book wrapped around his body.

Sisami put himself onto the carpet and went to the gate along with many Makash who were heading there. He squeezed himself in among the crowds of Moback that entered the gate and walked inside but in a weird way, which raised suspicions. When asked about it, he said that he had fallen and broken his back and that some children had treated him. The other Moback started laughing at him, but he didn't care; he had a specific mission, which was to reach out for the parents and give them the book.

The next day at breakfast time, when all the kids were gathered in the food court, Jamal's place was vacant. Wang made a picture of Jamal as a mask to wear on the back of his head so that anyone seeing Wang from the back would think it was Jamal. Wang sat with his back to the wall to hide the mask from the children, and whenever he had the chance with nobody around, he put his back to face the king's picture. Kameel asked the kids about Jamal, and Lillian told him that he had been sick for two days.

PUNISHMENT DAY

S hishar and Adam were tied to a wooden structure that the children had built according to the orders from Falca and the king. The two appeared totally shattered and drained. They were unable to raise their heads. They exchanged looks, and Shishar smiled to Adam and said to him, "Don't worry, your friends will come and save us. I am sure of it."

"I hope they don't. Can't you see how many guards are around? It will be suicide if they try to release us," said Adam sadly.

The square was in the middle of the city surrounded by high-rise buildings from all sides. It was overcrowded with children and Shakam who had come to see the execution of Shishar and Adam or the surrender of their friends. The king was sitting on a makeshift stage that was built specifically for the occasion. Near him sat General Falca while Sikwel was with Adam and Shishar on the stage waiting for the deadline to carry out the execution that was scheduled for that evening.

The Makashan guards were everywhere in the area waiting for the kids to come as expected and rescue their friends, so they were prepared to arrest them.

Adam's friends had conjured a plan to save their friends, and they had benefited from information given to them by Jamal, so they made up six masks of human faces and gave them to the six runaway children who were supposed to put them on and mingle in the crowds in different places in the square. Meanwhile, the city children wore Makashan masks with tall cloaks to hide their lack of tails. Each of them positioned himself in one of the buildings surrounding the square, and Jamal and Wajdbeer positioned themselves right behind the building where the execution stage was built. Sikwel looked around and said to himself, "Show yourselves, you damned ugly kids!"

Meanwhile, Bermuda said to Falca, "Do you think they will give up?"

"It is better for them to do so," replied Falca.

"I want you to kill them all in front of all these crowds," the king said. "I want them to be a lesson for the other kids in the city."

"The grace period is finished now, Your Majesty," Falca said.

The king looked around and then looked at Sikwel who was gazing at the king. waiting his signal to hang Shishar and Adam.

The king moved his head as a sign to start the execution, so Sikwel stood up to deliver the speech for the occasion and said, "Good citizens of Scaba, the king has given orders to hang these two traitors because they betrayed the kingdom of Scaba and because of their attempt to breach the security and terrorize citizens."

Many in the crowd grew excited about what they heard, and someone shouted, "Hang these traitors," which the audience repeated in one voice. Sikwel ordered the nooses to be put around their necks, and once the guards did that, the whole crowds heard a shrill order uttered by Brian, "Attack now."

The guards prepared themselves to fight back, but they started receiving fatal woufs from among the audience. Two of these hit the guards who were standing next to Sikwel on the stage. The six children threw their masks away and attacked, and at the same time the city kids came out of the buildings and ran down while shooting woufs at the guards who were taken by surprise and could thus only retaliate after some time. Chaos ensued, and the crowds started to run in all directions. When the king saw this, he said to himself, "These damned kids discovered the secret of Nafarit."

Then he looked at Falca as if inquiring about what had happened even though he realized exactly what was going on but preferred to keep that secret because only a few knew the secret of Nafarit. None of the guards succeeded in shooting any of the kids because of the chaos, and when Sikwel tried to shoot back at the kid, he was shot with a wouf by Steven who was positioned in one of the buildings. When Sikwel tried to retaliate, he received another wouf from Dana and then another one from Sara and another one from Nora, which made him fall to the ground. Despite his injury, however, he could identify Alex and shouted, "The disappeared kids."

Suddenly, the carpet flown by Wajdbeer appeared in the scene, almost hitting everything around it. Wajdbeer wasn't a skillful pilot, so the carpet kept going up and down while Jamal was guiding him to reach the stage, sometimes telling him to go down and at others up. When they got near the stage, Jamal jumped onto it while Wajdbeer remained on the carpet to maintain it at a certain height in order to be ready to take off after Jamal succeeded in untying Shishar and Adam.

"Faster, faster, I can't control that carpet anymore while these Makash are throwing woufs."

Alex and Dana reached the stage. Dana shot Sikwel with another wouf, but he trundled to avoid it and fell off the stage to the ground. Dana didn't run after him but instead ran with Alex to untie Adam and Shishar who were totally stunned to see their friends shooting woufs miraculously.

"I am happy that you came to save me," Adam said to Dana.

"Did you think that I would leave you?" asked Dana.

The guards shot the woufs at Dana, Jamal, and Alex; so Jamal stopped in front of them and released the protection aura around the group, which protected them from the woufs. When Dana and Alex finished untying their friends, they all jumped over the carpet, and Shishar flew it. Once the carpet started to fly up, the king took out the iron bar from his pocket and threw a red ray from it at them. It hit the carpet and burned it, but Shishar, who took over, didn't stop and rise up with the burning carpet. Meanwhile the other kids ran away from the square. They were chased by the guards who shot at them, but the kids shot back and managed to run away from the guards.

The passengers tried to extinguish fire on the carpet, but it ate up most of it, so Shishar landed it somewhere and ran away together with the group between the houses and alleys with the rest of the kids helping him and Adam.

The king had never been as angry as he was that day, so he reproached Falca, "Human kids shooting woufs and defeating guards? Nothing like that has happened in Scaba before."

Falca remained silent and lowered his head, and the king went on with the same tone, "Tell me what is going on, Falca. Tell me! And what is that aura that young Makashan used, which protected them from the woufs? What type of magic were they using?"

Then he said to the injured Sikwel, "Where were these children hiding all that time? How did street kids gain these capacities to shoot woufs?"

Then he looked at Falca and said, "You must kill them all, General Falca. I don't want to see any of them alive, including that small Makashan and the Shakam who were standing behind them and supporting them. I want you to chop their heads off and hang them in the middle of the city as a lesson for all others."

He then raised his hand calling for the Makashan pilot to bring the carpet; the guards brought it quickly, and when the king got on board, he said to Falca, "I want answers to all these questions today. I don't care who you put in jail or kill to get the answers."

Then he asked his pilot to take him back to his palace.

Falca looked at the injured Sikwel who was moaning in pain and said to him, "To the office now."

Falca met with Sikwel in Sikwel's office and gave him no chance to say anything but told him that he must find these kids along with anybody supporting them from Makash and Shakam and kill them mercilessly, or he should step down to give them a chance to someone who can do that mission. Sikwel hesitated a little and then said to Falca that the kids were very intelligent and they had developed themselves in a miraculous way. When Falca heard that, he got even angrier and said, "So you must be more intelligent than they were and develop your potentials in a faster way."

Sikwel swallowed his saliva in fear and promised Falca that he would find them, but Falca insisted to know how, and Sikwel said, "These kids are located in the city, and I am sure that there is someone helping them who is close to us."

Falca wondered who that person would be, and Sikwel replied that the only person who was knowledgeable and could enable the kids to shoot woufs was Wajdbeer, the physician. Falca pondered this for a while. It looked convincing to him, but he said to Sikwel, "But Wajdbeer wasn't with them today."

Sikwel replied while trying to depress the horrible pain that he had learned from those kids that not all that appeared at the surface was the truth.

"I don't know what they are doing, but they are always deceiving us."

Falca ordered Sikwel to take his guards and go at once to Wajdbeer's house and search it, and if he didn't find anyone, he should demolish the house and flatten it to the ground.

Sikwel and the guards rushed to the house, broke down its door, went inside, and searched it, breaking the furniture on the way; and when they found nothing, they flattened the house.

DIVULGING OF THE
CHILDREN'S TRICK

The king returned to his palace in a miserable state of disappointment and ire. His fury almost killed him, and he desperately wanted to know how these children had acquired the power of the wouf. He realized that the secret of Nafarit to give humans such a weapon was known by only very few, most of whom were dead. He decided not to rest until he discovered the secret behind it and said to his snake, "At first, I gave priority to runaways, and now it is the runaways and the children. Damn these children, I will obliterate them all."

He made up his mind to first attack the runaway fugitives and capture the iron bar that they had in order to dominate both Scaba and the human world; if that happened, children would be powerless by default because, with the two iron bars, he would crush them easily.

He looked at his crystal ball to see what the kids were doing and to try to search for the street kids. He noticed something weird when he looked at Jamal's location: he was in two different places at the same time, in his bed and near the jail. The king reviewed this many times and concluded that what was on the bed was a portrait of Jamal with his eyes shut, and the one near the jail was another portrait of him hanged upside down on a broom. He got furious and shouted, "These insignificant kids have deceived me!"

Then he shouted, calling from his suite and running out like a crazy person, "Falca, you idiot, where are you?"

But Falca didn't reply because he was still there in the city. It was a good time for the king to think over it for a while. He didn't want anyone to know about the disappearance of Jamal from the palace as it would be an indication of the king's weakness. Falca came from the city and headed to the royal hall where the king was sitting alone with his snake. Falca was reluctant to proceed or talk, but the king looked at him and said, "These children have fooled you, idiot!"

Falca didn't understand what the king meant, so he remained silent.

"Send one of the guards to the children's dormitory and let him bring the picture on the bed of a boy named Jamal," added the king.

Falca immediately ordered one of the guards to bring the picture. "And send another guard to bring me Wang, the artist child, immediately. Also, bring me the picture of Jamal that is on a mop near the iron jail," the king said.

The king then sat on his chair whereas Falca moved restlessly around, unaware what to do.

"How did these insignificant children deceive you, Falca?" asked the king angrily.

Falca hesitated a little while, thinking that the king was still talking about the city children, and proceeded, "We concluded that Wajdbeer is the one who is helping them." The king thought for a while and nodded his head agreeing with Falca.

"For the first time in your life, you figure something out correctly," the king said. "That Wajdbeer! Go chop his head off and bring it to me. I will not accept excuses this time."

"We have already sent the guards to bring him forth, Your Majesty," Falca said.

The king looked at him and then told him that there were more children who had deceived him. Falca replied that he did not understand what the king was talking about.

"You know nothing about anything, Falca," the king said angrily.

"Here in my palace they have deceived me. Where were you when all that was happening?"

Falca remained silent and confused, and minutes later, two guards came forth carrying a portrait, one for Jamal, and the other guard came in and brought Wang with him. A third guard came with a mask for Jamal fixed on a mop. The king took the mask that was identical to Jamal and said, "This is what I am talking about."

Then he looked at Wang and said, "Is that everything, or do you still have more for us?"

Wang didn't reply and lowered his head. The king searched him and found a mask under his clothes and said, "You thought you could get away with it, idiots?"

He turned around and said to the confused Falca, "Go immediately and bring me all the friends of this detestable boy."

Falca went outside toward the food court, and the king looked at Wang with all the wrath and evil in the world and said, "Where did your friend run away to?"

Wang didn't reply, so the king slapped him on the face, but he remained silent and showed no signs of pain. Falca came back with Lillian, Samar, Shaun, and Kameel and said to the king, "There is one missing, Your Majesty."

"It is because he ran away, stupid!" the king said.

Falca didn't understand how this had happened, and the king looked at the children and said, "Where did your friend run away to?"

"I don't know who you are talking of, Your Majesty," Kameel said.

"None of them know anything. It was me and my brother who planned his escape," Lillian said.

The king laughed and looked at Wang. "There must be someone who drew these pictures."

"It is I, Your Majesty. I was the one who helped them," Wang said.

"My brother has joined the fugitives, and they will all come to rescue us from your tyranny," Lillian said.

The king laughed again, but it was obvious this time that he was very wrathful and resentful.

"The runaways, huh? You think they can save you, stupid?" asked the king.

"Yes, they can! And they will defeat you," she replied defiantly.

"They would have saved their own souls if they had been able to," the king explained.

He then asked them who helped Jamal out of the palace, telling them that if they didn't confess he would kill all the palace children.

Samar approached and said, "I am the one who helped them."

Lillian looked at her disapprovingly, but she didn't stop, so the king asked, "Who else?"

Nobody said anything, and the king ordered Falca to put them in jail until he could think of a punishment worthy of their deeds.

The king looked at Kameel in a threatening way, and Kameel lowered his head in fear and dismay and then ordered them all to leave to have a private talk with Falca. After they all went out, he said to Falca, "Be very careful! I don't want the news of this execrable boy to be leaked to anyone, not even to our followers."

Falca saluted the king in obedience.

RESOLVING THE PUZZLEMENT

The children were taken to the old palace's jail, the one that had hosted Falca once upon a time. It was a narrow cell with a wooden door, and the guards pushed them inside roughly.

Shaun went to the princess feeling ashamed because he had not confessed cooperation with Jamal to the king, but the princess commended his actions, saying that he had done the right thing because there must be someone outside the jail to help the others.

Shaun revealed to the princess that he felt that he was a loser and couldn't do anything right. He confessed to her that the king wouldn't have discovered Jamal's escape if he had put the picture away from the bed and that he had failed to perform the easiest task, which was simply putting the picture on the bed at night and taking it away in the morning. He almost wept with feelings of disgrace.

The princess patted him on his shoulder and told him that everyone made mistakes and that he should learn from those. She told him to focus on the future plans, mostly on the *Doom Book*.

He repeated what she had said, as if he were thinking aloud, "The *Doom Book*."

Then he added, "Can you please repeat what is written on the cover of the book?" he asked.

"But I told it to all of you," the princess replied.

"I just want to check something," he said.

So she repeated what was written on the cover of the book, "A couple of opposite genders unite into unconditional love. Through their veins runs amalgamated blood and possessing an invaluable duo of pearls."

He thought for a while and said to her, "But how did you arrive at that conclusion and decide that it must be a human husband and wife?"

She explained to him that this was what could be inferred from the sentence and that even their ancestors had arrived at the same conclusion centuries ago.

Shaun said in a low voice, "The twins."

The princess picked up on what he said and thought on it for a few minutes while repeating, "A couple of opposite genders unite into unconditional love. Through their veins runs amalgamated blood and possessing invaluable duo of pearls."

Then she said promptly, as if she had discovered something, "What a genius you are, Shaun. Yes, it is the twins!" She added that the invaluable duo of pearls would be their parents, not the other way around.

Shaun felt happy and proud of that, and the princess, based on the new discovery, explained to Shaun that Hercules wanted to make it too hard for Shakam and Makash to open the book, and he exploited the fact that they didn't give birth to twins. He made it even harder by selecting human twins, a boy and a girl, to make options as limited as possible. By doing so, he managed to mislead the Shakam and the Makash for centuries.

"Does this mean that Sisami will kill all of us?" asked Shaun.

Filda shivered before she replied, "Yes! If he succeeds in giving the book to the twins' parents, we will all be dead."

When they then realized how critical their discovery was, the idea terrified them, and they immediately started thinking of ways to evade it, but there was nothing in hand to be done because their discovery came too late, and nobody could reach Sisami to prevent him. It was shocking to Filda, and she started blaming herself for everything. She was now helpless and unable to do a single thing either for herself or for the others. It was now the end of life in

Scaba, she thought, and she had decimated her people because of her reckless behavior. She shouldn't have jumped to conclusions and carried out whatever crossed her mind. Shaun went out brokenhearted and desperate, wishing Lillian, Samar, and Wang had been there with him in that moment. He met with Kameel in the corridor. Kameel blamed him for keeping the news of Jamal secret from him, but when he saw him in that gloomy state, he asked him what was wrong with him. Shaun didn't want to reveal it, even that to Kameel; but Kameel insisted on knowing, saying, "I am your friend, Shaun, and I really want to help in any possible way, so please tell me what is going on."

Shaun was encouraged to reveal the big secret to Kameel, especially that the end of life was approaching and that there was nobody else around to help in listening to him. He told him to promise not to reveal what he had said to anyone, and Kameel promised not to do so. Shaun told him what had happened, which was very shocking and terrifying to him. He said to Shaun, "I will go now and take the book back from Sisami."

"But Sisami by now is on Earth. That's why princess Filda couldn't telepathy with him," Shaun replied promptly.

"Don't worry, I can reach there. I have my ways. You just give me the address," Kameel said.

Shaun looked at Kameel in amazement, trying to digest what had been proposed, but desperate as he was, he gave him the address without even waiting to hear an explanation; and once he did so, Kameel ran fast, and that was the first time Shaun saw him running.

CONFESSION TO WAJDBEER

Sikwel and the guards rushed to Wajdbeer's house, broke down its door, went inside, and searched it, breaking the furniture on the way. When they found nothing, they flattened the house.

Wajdbeer and his young friends were in the basement listening to the footsteps of the guards above. Wajdbeer wept silently, so the kids gathered around to comfort him.

"I must reach the runaways in any way near the Mirror Mountain to ask for their help, sir," Jamal said.

Sara asked who the runaways were, and Wajdbeer told her that they are all from the Shakam, and they were all devoted supporters or the former king. So she said to him, "So it is of no use because they will not be able to defeat the Makash."

Jamal rejected the idea and explained to all that the *Doom Book*, which was being sent at any moment to his parents—it had maybe already reached them—and the secrets that would be revealed by his parents would help them defeat the Makash with the help of Shakam. Jamal then asked Wajdbeer to show him to the shortest way to the mutineers' place.

Wajdbeer said that the shortest possible way to the Mirror Mountain was through the twisted jungle, but once he mentioned it, horror showed on the faces of the six disappeared children. Brian said to Wajdbeer, "Oh no, not the twisted jungle again!"

The other kids started asking curiously about the secret behind the jungle, and Wajdbeer explained to them that they had dug a tunnel that led to the twisted jungle and that he had advised the six kids not to use that tunnel unless they felt that they were ready to pass through that dangerous place to reach the runaways or if their hiding place was discovered by the Makash guards. One day, though, Barry, who was one of the missing children, due to his adventurous spirit, had entered the tunnel to discover the jungle and the trees devoured him.

"Carnivorous trees?" Nora asked shocked.

Wajdbeer said to her that it was true. Kilsha held Sara tightly because of what she heard about the trees.

"We don't have any time to waste. I have to go through that jungle," Jamal said resiliently.

Then he told them that the king had ordered an army to eradicate these runaways and that he should reach there before it is too late in order to warn them.

"I can create a shield of light around me to protect me from these trees," he added.

"I will go with you to protect you with my woufs," Dana said.

"Me too," said Adam.

But Wajdbeer told him not to go because he was still in need of further treatment.

Then he told Dana and Jamal to go in order to warn the runaways. Wajdbeer's plan was to warn these mutineers, and when they received the revelations of the *Doom Book*, they were to attack Bermuda's army. Meanwhile, Wajdbeer and the rest would launch their attack from inside Scaba.

He gave them a bag full of human food that he had prepared before and a red zebra, telling them that it was one of the fastest animals in Scaba.

Dana and Jamal hugged him and bid their friends farewell. Adam took Dana aside and said to her, "Be careful and don't run wildly."

She looked at Jamal and said to Adam, "Don't worry! This courageous child will protect me."

Adam and Jamal exchanged smiles, and then before departure, she said to Wajdbeer, "Please forgive us, good doctor. We had agreed to stay with you in the first place just to use you and take advantage of you, and we didn't want to join your army."

Wajdbeer smiled to her and said, "I knew that, but it wasn't of any concern to me. I knew you're going to come around."

Then he helped her ride the zebra behind Jamal who rode the animal toward the twisted jungle.

THE SERPENTINE JUNGLE

J amal and Dana arrived at the serpentine jungle following the directions given to them by Wajdbeer. They entered the jungle cautiously, and the trees were so twisted and marvelously entangled that the zebra they were riding stumbled and dropped them to the ground, so they decided to walk. They were astonished by the fruit they saw, one of which looked like red peppers the size and length of Jamal. The fruit was everywhere, as if it were an unwanted wild tree. Many enar animals were flying over the jungle. Jamal and Dana strived to evade the trees, but it was very difficult because the trunks and twigs were interwoven with each other. All of a sudden one tree attacked them with one of its boughs, but they managed to dodge it and run away. They continued to walk, looking around cautiously. After they went deeper and deeper into the forest, another tree attacked. It clutched the zebra and raised it above the ground with one of its boughs and attacked Jamal with another, but he jumped away as he had done before. The tree also attacked Dana; she threw some woufs at it, which made it let her go. The tree then opened what looked like a mouth in the middle of its trunk and swallowed the zebra before they could help it. Jamal and Dana were so terrified that their hearts started to beat faster and faster. They could not differentiate between ferocious and nonferocious trees, so they took more care and started to walk more cautiously. They arrived at one of those furious trees that were gripping three flying tigers, enars. The enars were resisting strongly but in vain. When Jamal and Dana saw the suffering of the enars, they looked at each other, and Jamal said, "Let's help them."

Dana replied, "It's none of our business. We've got a special mission. Don't get us involved, Jamal."

But Jamal didn't pay attention and ignored her call to stop, so she was obliged to join him. Dana started to throw woufs at the tree, but it was useless. Jamal retreated several steps away from the tree looking for anything around him. He could only find some red peppers. He dragged two of them closer to the tree; they were very light. When he was close enough, he threw one pepper into the mouth of the tree, and then he threw the other. The tree devoured it and soon started to move its boughs frantically, which gave the enars the chance to run away. Jamal and Dana hurried away, advancing toward the Mirror Mountain. They noticed that the daylight had started to fade, so they were afraid that it might get dark while they were still in the jungle. They decided to walk faster but with caution. After a while, they noticed that the fruit of the red peppers had disappeared from the ground, and some thorny fruit had begun to appear instead. They proceeded alertly trying not to step on those thorns, but much to their surprise, the thorny fruits were only wild hedgehogs, which unfolded themselves and started pursuing them.

Dana started throwing woufs at them and managed to kill some. Instead, though, they multiplied and began chasing Dana and Jamal, who tried to run away but found it really hard to move in that entangled jungle. Dana repetitively pelted woufs at the hedgehogs, which were determined to attack although the woufs killed many of them. Jamal and Dana stopped running as Jamal asked; then he released the aura out of his mind. The hedgehogs tried to penetrate the aura but couldn't. They kept striking against it until they got fed up and pulled back. When the last hedgehog disappeared, Jamal regained his normal state, exhausted because of keeping the aura up for a long time.

Dana asked Jamal to rest for a while, but he refused and insisted on going on. They felt that something was following them and were terrified, looking over their shoulders fearfully to find out that the three enars that they had rescued were following them. They stopped and looked at the enars, but they were still terrified. They noticed that the enars grew frightened and disappeared behind a tree. When they felt reassured that the enars were harmless, they decided to keep walking. The enars followed them again, and when Jamal and Dana stopped, they ran away as before. The same thing occurred several times. The last time, Jamal crouched on his knees, as if he had been calling a strange dog. Dana looked at him with amazement and disapproval of what he was doing while she reminded him that they did not have much time to waste. The enars advanced a little, stopped, and stared at his eyes. Jamal tried to encourage them to advance more, but they refused. Jamal started focusing, trying to communicate with them by telepathy after he remembered the princess's talk about telepathy with the Scaba animals.

Jamal tried for quite some time, but none of the enars responded. Dana vowed to leave him and continue by herself. It got dark, and they found themselves close to the entrance of the cave that they have to pass through to reach the Mirror Mountain according to Wajdbeer's instructions, so they decided to rest and spend the night in the cave. They entered deep inside the cave looking for a safe place when, surprisingly, they saw a light that looked like sunlight, although it was night already. They walked toward the light and discovered that the cave was only a passageway leading to an empty space of an open plain with trees of very thin trunks. The trees were so high in the sky that they reached beyond the clouds. To their utmost surprise, they discovered that the sun was still shining. The thin trees surrounded the plain from both sides, and there was only a passage in the middle that led to a lake. They also saw some giant rocks behind the trees, so they knew they were in the bottom of a cavity of a mountain. The lake was not large, and the land on the other bank led out of the cavity. They approached the lake to inspect how they could cross the lake to the other side, but no sooner had Dana put her hand in the water than an ugly giant frog with big sharp fangs appeared out of the water and tried to bite her hand. She just avoided it. Then another two ugly giant frogs appeared from the water and stared as they lay in wait for them. Dana and Jamal returned back to hide behind the trees and started to think of a way to cross the lake without being attacked by these ugly frogs.

Dana looked around her, and then she had an idea. "Let's try to cut one of these trees," she said to Jamal.

Jamal looked at her and said sarcastically, "Are you trying to make a ship?"

She looked at him but said nothing. She started throwing woufs at one of the trees, and Jamal, seeing this, pushed the trunk until it fell down. Dana lifted the trunk and said, "I am going to cross first; then you follow me!"

Jamal asked, bewildered, "But how?"

She shouted while carrying the trunk and running toward the lake, "Do what I'm doing."

Dana ran quickly until she came closer to the lake, dropped the trunk tip into the bank of the lake, and then the trunk bent and she continued up and forward, making use of the reaction force of the trunk when it straightened up as if she were a pole-vaulter in the Olympics, until she reached the other bank. Jamal opened his mouth with admiration while looking at her and shouted, "Wow, do you think I can do it?"

Dana threw the trunk in the lake and pushed it toward Jamal, who dragged it, and then she told him, "I saw you in competitions, and I know you can do it."

Jamal took a deep breath while looking at those terrifying frogs that were lying in wait for him. He walked back some steps and rushed forward. He flew high in the air, smiling when he found himself high above the frogs. But all of a sudden, the trunk stopped in an upright position. Dana got scared on seeing this and stood still. Jamal closed his eyes when he started falling down, but before he reached the awaiting mouths of the frogs, he felt something hold him and carried him high in the air. It was two of the enars, and they took him to the other bank.

Dana felt happy, and Jamal was smiling with joy and pleasure, as he was safe. The enars put him near Dana and flew away. Dana then said, "I missed you there for a moment."

He replied, "I had surrendered to death."

Dana explained that whoever did well to others would surely be repaid, and those enars were repaying him. They decided to complete their journey despite all difficulties and were determined not to stop until they crossed that jungle. Once they went out from that cave, it was morning, and the sun was just starting to rise.

FACE-TO-FACE WITH THE SHAKAMS

The enars followed them again. Jamal tried to communicate with them by telepathy, but Dana asked him to stop doing so. He was about to surrender, but after several attempts, the enars slowly approached him as if they could understand him. The enars started communicating with him, which made him pleased, and so he asked them to take him and Dana to the Mirror Mountain. Jamal then said to Dana, "Let's follow them. They'll take us the Mirror Mountain."

Dana asked him how he knew this.

"By telepathy . . . by telepathy," he replied with a smile.

They followed the enars, but as they were about to come out of the jungle, the enars fell in a big hole with webs and got stuck. Jamal would also have fallen in the hole had it not been for Dana who gripped his hand at the last moment. The enars asked Jamal to help them, so Jamal and Dana started looking for something to throw to the enars so that they could come out of the hole. While they were doing so, some Shakams appeared and captured them. The Shakams pulled the webs to help the enars get out and led all of them somewhere.

It was the first time that they had been arrested by Shakams. Dana and Jamal tried to communicate with them but couldn't because the Shakams ignored them, so they kept silent. On their way, they passed by the Mountain of Mirrors. Seeing this, Dana and Jamal knew that those who led them were the fugitives for whom they were looking.

They took Dana and Jamal into a cave and the enars into another. Jamal wanted to know where they were taking the enars and what they were going to do to them. The Shakams ignored Jamal again and kept silent. The cave in which they kept Dana and Jamal was huge, and there was a great number of Moback animals everywhere in the cave. They were singing a sad song. Dana and Jamal were amazed to see a lot of Shakam males and females—some of whom were lying on the ground, others standing near the walls, and others sitting on the rocks, which were projecting from the top of the cave close to the ceiling—and all of them were looking at Dana and Jamal. Dana noticed that all the Shakams were slim; none of them were fat. They came to the leader who was taller and had bigger muscles than the others. When he approached them, they noticed that he was lame.

The commander asked them while gazing at them who they were. Jamal replied, addressing everybody, that Dana and he were friends and that they had come to warn them of an imminent attack from the king, who had discovered their place of hiding. The Shakams marveled at this, and the commander asked how he could make sure of it. Dana responded that they didn't have proof, and the Shakams were risking their lives if they stayed there. She told them that they could move to another place temporarily until they could be sure of what they told them. The commander looked at them suspiciously and asked what made them risk their lives. Jamal told him the story of the kids and how Princess Filda cooperated with them. As soon as Jamal mentioned Filda's name, the commander said, "Filda? Is she still alive?"

Jamal looked at him with amazement and asked him how he knew her. The commander absentmindedly replied that she was his wife. Jamal kept silent for a moment and then hesitantly asked, "Are you Commander Medan?"

The commander responded that he was. Jamal then said more hesitantly, "Impossible. The princess told us that her husband had been killed . . . or that's what she was told."

The commander sat on one of the rocks after hearing this and said to Jamal, "Here I am before you . . . alive and well."

Then he added that he also thought that his wife had been killed because when he ran away she was almost dead. Jamal explained what had happened to her and that she was pregnant. The commander felt so happy and started asking about his son. The commander trusted them and asked them to sit beside him when Dana asked about what had happened to him.

MEDAN, THE LEADER

Medan had been known for bravery and military experience before he married Princess Filda. He led most of the wars against the Makash and won all of them. He was an amiable person and was loved by his followers. He was even loved by the Shakam themselves, so the king didn't mind his daughter's marriage to Medan with whom she was in love. He was promoted until he became the king's deputy and assistant. Since he didn't like Falca and suspected his behavior, he told the king to throw him out of the palace, but the king had another point of view. Falca had the same feelings toward Medan, and on the day Falca decided to kill the king by surprise, Medan noticed that the Makash were behaving suspiciously. He didn't know what they were up to but decided to keep an eye on them, especially on their leader. Medan didn't expect an assassination attempt but instead expected something stupid. He saw Falca that day where he looked confused while heading toward the king. He watched him more closely, and Falca couldn't notice him because he was much confused and disordered. When Falca entered the hall, Medan followed him; and when Falca tried to shoot the king with a wouf, Medan stopped him immediately with a faster wouf that made him fall unconscious. He was almost sure that Falca was not alone in that, and he suspected Bermuda to be the other person in on the plot. Even though Bermuda had tried his best to become friends with Medan, this didn't diminish his suspicions toward him. Medan always felt that Bermuda and Falca were planning something evil, but he had no evidence of it; he had only his hunch.

When Commander Medan was young, he used to play with Solar, so he gained some kind of human experience. He didn't hate human beings; but he was very cautious about dealing with them, unlike the king and his wife, who loved humans and was ready to make anything that would make them happy.

One day the king came to him and told him that he wanted to go to the human world for a little adventure. Medan insisted on accompanying him, but the king refused and warned him of even following him, telling him to take care of the kingdom until he came back.

Medan was sitting with his wife when the king came back from his journey fatigued and sick. He had the *Doom Book* and the dazar box with him. When the king entered the royal hall in that state, Medan and his wife hurried to support him because he was about to die. Medan was facing the door when he kneeled down to help the ailing father-in-law, whereas Filda was in the opposite direction. The king was so sick that he was unable to speak easily. Medan told his wife not to cry so that they could hear what the king was trying to say. The king was only able to tell Medan to take care of his wife and protect her from someone. Medan couldn't figure out who that person was and asked insistently about the name of the person, but the king said, "He didn't know everything . . . I didn't tell him everything, but he—"

No sooner had the king uttered this than he received a wouf that killed him at once. Medan looked up to see Solar up there and couldn't believe his eyes, but when Solar shot the princess with another wouf and she fell down, Medan thought she was dead and decided to take the book and the box with him and run away, especially considering that he had seen Solar with a dazar in his hand. He knew he wouldn't succeed in defeating him, so he ran as fast as possible; and because he didn't have enough time, he managed to take the box with him but not the book. Solar shot him with a wouf that hit his leg and left him with only one limb. Medan ran away beyond the crystal ball, and after a short period, his loyal followers managed to escape as well and follow him there. They were also followed by their wives and some who rejected the ruling of Bermuda. They started destroying all construction works of the Makash that aimed at expanding the kingdom beyond the scope of the crystal ball.

By listening to what Jamal and Dana have to say about what had happened to them since the first day they arrived in Scaba, things became clear to the commander Medan and his troops, and they realized that Solar and Bermuda had planned to kill the king and capture the throne. Medan ordered his troops to prepare themselves to move to another place, and when Jamal asked him about the three enars, Medan told him that they hunted them to benefit from the fire that they breathed, and when they died, they threw them away. Jamal objected to that and said to him that they could benefit from the enars' fire in a more effective way without letting them die. Medan couldn't understand what Jamal meant by that and told him that they had to treat the enar in that way. He also blamed "Brometheos," who deprived them of fire, saying that the only option they had to get fire was to make use of the enar in this way, and since they were very wild untamable animals, they tied them down and forced them to breathe in these holes.

Jamal told Medan that they could use enar's fire to light wood, which would then burn, but the rest of Medan's followers laughed at that because they couldn't imagine that such a thing could happen. Jamal insisted it was true and promised to show them once they reached their new hideout.

HUMAN LAND

S isami reached the twins' house and started pushing the door noisily. The twins' parents were sitting together inside overwhelmed by sadness for the loss of two children when they heard the door being rung more than once. The mother went out to see what was there, and to her surprise, she saw a beautiful small very strange creature that she couldn't identify. She patted Sisami's head fondly and hesitantly. When the mother noticed that the creature was tame and placid, she called her husband who also looked at the new creature with surprise and admiration, so they took her inside. Sisami started jumping and playing with the parents, which changed their mood. They wished that their two children had been there to play with that beautiful animal. Sisami slept on his back to help the parents see the book that was tied to his abdomen. The mother noticed the book and told her husband to come closer and see that. They took the book and read the puzzle written on its cover but couldn't figure out what it meant, so they decided to open the book.

In the meantime, Kameel had come to the address that was given to him; his heart was beating faster as he was getting closer to the book because he was expecting perdition and destruction at any moment. Breathless, he reached the door of the twin's house and knocked it hard and fast. The twins' father opened the door, and the first thing Kameel did was to try to see through the opening. The father asked him who he was and what he wanted, but he didn't reply and only kept trying to look inside, and when he saw the mother about to open the book, he screamed at the top of his voice, "No, no, no!"

But the mother opened the book, which made Kameel jump down on the ground, flat on his stomach, very quickly covering his face and head like someone expecting an explosion to happen at any moment. It took the father by surprise and astonishment to see the fat boy doing what he did. Kameel remained in that position for a while, but when he noticed that nothing happened and that he was still alive, he stood up again embarrassed and unaware what to say to the twins' father. Sisami came in time to save his face and jumped on him fondly. Kameel said to the parents, "I was just looking for my little pony."

He was about to leave with Sisami when the mother called him to take his book and said, "I am sorry. I had to open it to look for any evidence that might lead to the animal's owner."

Kameel thanked her.

"You should write some information about yourself in that book and not leave it all blank like that," the mother said.

Kameel smiled stupidly, took the book, and went together with Sisami confused and full of surprise.

GETTING TOGETHER WITH THE RUNAWAYS

When the fugitives reached a new hideout along with Jamal and Dana, the two kids went out to bring some wood from a tamed jungle assisted by some Shakams and a large number of Mobacks. They were ignorant of what Dana and Jamal saying about the nature and uses of wood. Unconvinced, they cut some trees, but they were following Medan's orders to help Jamal and Dana and give them what they wanted.

They came back with some wood and put it in a big hole. Jamal asked them to call the three enars forth, but they all laughed at that, especially when he said, "My three friends." Even Medan couldn't help laughing at that, but Jamal didn't care about it. When they brought the three enars, Jamal telepathized with them to blow fire into the wood in the hole, and they did so; but the wood didn't burn at once as Jamal expected, so he looked in dismay at Dana who wasn't any less dismayed. The enar tried many times, and Dana said to Jamal, "It seems that their fire isn't able to light wood."

The two kids were about to give up, but at that moment, thick white smoke started coming out of the wooden logs and branches. All Shakams and Mobacks gasped with wonder at what they saw while Jamal and Dana started jumping happily. Wood burned, and flames came up amid the attendants' bewilderment. Jamal told the enars to stop blowing and looked at the audience with pride. They couldn't believe what they were seeing.

"Now you can make use of fire without killing and exhausting the enars," Jamal said to them.

He then hugged the enars lovingly and joyfully.

Dana suggested that Commander Medan prepare a strong army to face the king and the Makash, but Medan looked almost desperate about it as he believed that the Makash were much stronger than they were especially that the Shakam voices no longer had an effect on the Makash because they had somehow learned to overcome it. He believed that if he sent an army there, it would be annihilated by the Makash, but Jamal reminded him of the *Doom Book*, which had already been taken by the kids and would be sent to the human land, and all its secrets relating to the killing of the Makash that were revealed by Hercules would be revealed. Jamal advised them to be prepared for everything and to try to make use of their surroundings to strengthen their army and enhance their defenses.

"Your environment is full of materials that you can use to become stronger," Jamal added.

"All right, I will go along with that and imagine it is true. I will make an army, but believe me that we will not be able to defeat the Makash if we don't discover a way to kill them."

He explained to them that the Makash would come back again and again to fight them and there was no way to destroy them at all. Jamal thought for a while and asked Medan about the box that he had. Medan appeared hesitant to answer, but Jamal told him that he wanted to try to release the power from the dazar, and if he managed to do so, they would have a significant power.

Medan was all in all eager to believe that and hurried at once to bring the box. It was a wooden box wrapped in red zebra leather. He gave it to Jamal who opened it cautiously to see the remaining dazar inside. It hadn't rusted even though it was centuries old. It was as shiny and dazzling as ever and looked like a new one. Jamal took it with his hand and focused on it to release the power from it, but he was unable to do that. He gave it to Dana to try, but she also failed.

Medan felt disappointed, but Jamal assured him that the *Doom Book* would teach them all the secrets of the dazar and defeat the Makash.

DISAPPOINTMENT

In the backyard of the twins' neighbor's house, Kameel and Sisami sat down to talk with the book in their hands. Kameel opened the book in fear and turned its white pages. "Not even a word? The *Doom Book* is only a lie made up by Hercules," Kameel said then added, "All these years the inhabitants of Scaba have dreamed of opening a hoax book."

"This is impossible. We all know the reality of the *Doom Book*," Sisami said.

Kameel asked why the book was blank then, and Sisami said that maybe what they had wasn't the real one.

"What do you mean? Didn't you steal that book from the king's safe?" Kameel asked curiously.

"It is true, but this doesn't mean that this is the real book; the king must have probably expected that to happen one day and replaced the book."

Sisami said to Kameel that they had to go back to Scaba as soon as possible to inform everyone of that in order to help them act as quick as possible, but Kameel was hesitant to do so. Sisami moved forth, and Kameel remained in his place, so Sisami looked back and called him.

"There is nothing that is worth coming back for. I am sorry. I have reached my world, and I hope everyone will understand me," Kameel explained.

"Never be a coward and rogue and never let down your friends in that difficult time," Sisami said angrily.

Kameel explained to Sisami that the king had jailed all the children and it was impossible to rescue them all, but Sisami reminded him that they were his friends and he should try to help them out of it.

"They are not my friends. They didn't involve me in their plans," Kameel said excitedly and then added spontaneously, "King Bermuda also promised me to send me back home."

"King Bermuda? Are you working for the king?" Sisami asked in dismay. "What a traitor you are!" Kameel kept quiet and looked down in shame.

Sisami left him and hurried to the gate that opened to let him in. Kameel remained alone and went back to the neighbor's house where he found King Bermuda in wait for him.

"There are news of great matter to you, Your Majesty," he said.

The king looked at him and said nothing when he heard that the children had stolen the book after they had discovered the couple who can open it.

"And who is that couple?" the king asked curiously.

Kameel explained to him that the kids made a mistake when they thought that the twins' parents were the ones who could open the book, and when they discovered their mistake, it was too late because Sisami had it with him in the human land, so he rushed to help in saving the two worlds.

"So this husband and wife couldn't open the book, could they?" the king asked suspiciously.

"No, Your Majesty, they discovered after they had sent the book to the parents that the real couple that was meant by the puzzle was the twins themselves and they are the ones who can open the book."

The king looked at him with astonishment, not believing what he heard, and said, "Which twins do you mean?"

"Jamal and Lillian."

"What?"

Kameel explained to him that it was true and the kids were confident of that, but the irony was that the parents opened the book and there was nothing in it. The king laughed and moved closer to Kameel who felt restless and afraid.

"Do you know where I hid the real book?"

Kameel said he didn't.

"It is here in the human land, in this specific house. In this way neither the Shakam nor the Makash can find it."

Then he laughed contemptuously and told Kameel to keep the other book with him as a souvenir, saying to him, "All right, now prepare yourself. We are going back to Scaba."

Kameel was hesitant to say what he wanted to say, but at the end he said, "You promised me, Your Majesty, to send me back home when I had revealed to you the kids' plans."

The king laughed and said to Kameel, "None of the children will ever leave Scaba, idiot!"

"But—" Kameel said with disappointment, and the king looked at him ferociously, so he lowered his head and said nothing.

THE NEIGHBOR

S olar, the magician, was a lonely man who didn't like to socialize and mix with others. He lost his father when he was a small child, and ever after he was faced with many nightmares. He usually woke up in the middle of the night sweating, and because he was a bag of bones, he used to face ridicule and laughter from other students at school. He hated everyone and hated his childhood and all children in the world. He usually sat by himself and spent hours alone gazing at emptiness, and then when the sun set, he would go back to his mother. On one occasion after sunset, while he was sitting in his favorite spot near the woods, he saw some mirrors coming out of ground. He panicked and ran to hide behind the thick bushes and trees of the woods. He almost fell down because of shivering and panicking. He was only eleven years old at that time. When he felt the chill in the air, he rubbed his hands to get some warmth. He kept watching the horrible scene, and after a while a number of strange creatures came out of these mirrors. Their heads resembled those of lions, and their bodies were like normal human bodies. One of the creatures was wearing a crown decorated with dazzling gems; he appeared to be their leader or king. Solar, despite being very frightened, wished to own that crown.

Suddenly, the mirrors vanished, and the creatures went away after a while. Solar ran away and went back home where he told his mother everything, but she didn't believe him and accused him of lying. Solar felt upset because of his mother's response and decided to prove to her that he wasn't lying, so he went to that spot many times waiting for the mirrors every day but in vain; nothing showed up. He kept doing the same for four years until one dark moonless night he saw these creatures standing in queues, and then the mirrors appeared, and they walked right through them one by one. He hesitated for a while but couldn't stop himself from following them and going through the mirrors as they did. He closed his eyes and lowered his head while going through the mirrors because he thought he would break the glass. It was very surprising to him to see that he could go through them as the other creatures did. He saw them going down a glass staircase, so he went down and followed them to a strange world.

Despite the beauty and magnificence of that world, Solar was full of shock and horror, and he felt very sorry for what he had done and decided to go back home, but it was too late. The other creatures noticed him when they looked back and wondered how he had reached there. They looked at their king who told them to bring him to the palace.

He was taken by surprise when the carpet began to fly, carrying him along with some other creatures. The place was wonderful on the way to the palace. He wanted to ask about everything but remained silent in fear. When they reached the palace, he found it was too magnificent and beautiful to describe in words. They took him to the royal hall where the king asked him in a friendly way who he was.

"I am Ben," Solar replied.

The king smiled to him to make him feel at home and asked him how he had managed to enter that world, and Solar told him honestly what had happened to him and that he had waited for them for four years to see them again and had never missed a single day. "But why?" the king asked.

He explained to the king that he wanted to prove to his mother that he wasn't lying and because he hated his life where he was always lonely and without friends and wanted to try another one in which he might gain some significance and respect. The king sympathized with him and decided to keep Ben at the palace.

He named him Solar, and it didn't take long before he knew everything about the place. He knew that the Shakam and Makash are two different tribes who lived with each other in harmony and peace, but their history was marred with lots of wars that normally ended with the defeat of the Makash, and that's why the ruling elite was always from the Shakam. He learned that the Shakam usually defeated the Makash with their voices; they shouted at a certain pitch that was intolerable by the Makash who were paralyzed by the voice. It was surprising to him also to know that the Shakam couldn't kill the Makash with their woufs, and the best thing that they could do was paralyze them and arrest them. Meanwhile, the Makash can kill the Shakam with their woufs.

The king taught him how to release his power and use his utmost mental potential and taught him many other tricks that made him stronger than other human beings. He felt very significant in Scaba and wished to spend the rest of his life there, but the king was preparing him for a far greater mission—he wanted him to serve as a link between the two worlds—so he gave him the keys to move easily between Earth and Scaba and trained him for the greatest mission, which was to find the couple mentioned in the riddle of the *Doom Book*.

That mission made him even more important than Shakam themselves.

Solar was very happy when he returned back to Earth for the first time; a whole earthly year, which was equivalent to ten Scaba years, had passed since he had first came to Scaba. He felt that he had become significant and confident, but when he turned back, he discovered that his mother had died earlier the same year, and he felt very sad for her death.

When he went back to the human world, he was much stronger than ever, and he decided to take revenge on his friends at school who used to make fun of him. The king didn't know what in Solar's mind; he loved him and treated him like a son, trusted him to be his deputy on earth without knowing how much evil he had in his mind and soul.

Solar felt that nobody could defeat him and started thinking with conceit of ruling both Scaba and Earth, so he made up his plans to sour relations between the Shakam and the Makash. He knew that the leader of the Makash didn't like the Shakam and waited for the right moment to kill them all, so he started getting closer to General Falca, convincing him to rebel against the king by telling him that the king and his tribe were weak and that the Makash were more powerful. He taught him how to betray them and kill them by surprise. General Falca was convinced after long hesitation and started to prepare for the plan, but Solar wished that the two tribes would kill each other.

The Makashans killed some unprepared Shakam, but the Shakam, headed by Commander Medan, managed to control the situation and arrest the rebels, including Falca who was fainted by a wouf. Solar felt disappointed but didn't lose hope and helped Falca's loyal followers to help him out of jail.

Years later, Solar convinced the king, Princess Filda's father, to visit him on Earth in order to open the *Doom Book* after he had claimed that he had found the right couple for him, so the king took the dazar box and the *Doom Book* to Solar unaccompanied by anyone. He told his daughter and her husband that he was to go on an adventure that would last some days. When the king didn't find the couple mentioned in the *Doom Book*, he asked Solar about it.

"I am sorry, Your Majesty, but it was the only way to convince you of coming here with the book and the box," Solar explained.

Then he explained to the king that it was true that their ancestors had warned them that opening the book by any person other than the intended ones would lead to their end and the end of the kingdom of Scaba, but opening it in the human world would not lead to the same result because the human world was a different place that was governed by different rules. He told him that he should open the book no matter how high the price was because its secrets would enable him to manipulate the only two dazars that were left by Hercules.

The king hesitated for a while and said that none of his ancestors had dared do that before, but Solar kept encouraging him to do so and said to him, "History will remember that you were the most courageous king for the Shakam."

The king liked that and enjoyed imagining himself with that status, but then Solar asked him to show him the dazar, so the king opened the box, which contained the two iron bars. They were unique. Solar had never seen anything like them before. He picked one, and the king told him to be very careful. Solar looked at the dazar in complete admiration and astonishment. Meantime, the king opened the book slowly and cautiously, but when he opened it a little, thick black smoke came out, so he closed it immediately. But a small amount of smoke had entered the king's mouth. Nothing happened at first, and Solar saw what had happened but didn't care about it as he was occupied with the dazar. He asked the king to allow him to see the other dazar, but the king refused. In a moment he started to feel very dizzy, so he told Solar to put the dazar back into the box, but Solar didn't agree to do that, especially when he saw the king in pain and agony.

"You deceived me, damn you!" the king said to Solar.

Solar started laughing and told the king that he had become much stronger with that dazar and that he would take the other one from him to rule the two worlds. Then he pointed the dazar toward the king, and when he did that, the mirrors appeared instantly and helped the king enter them instantly but only after he had received some of the lethal radiance of that dazar.

THE PALACE

The cell that Lillian, Wang, and Samar were put in was narrow and small with a very thick wooden door guarded by two sturdy Makashans. They were fatigued but hopeful that Sisami might succeed in reaching the twins' parents and give them the book to read it and save everybody. When they were put in jail, they started looking for an exit, but they failed. They decided to spend their time telling stories; each one had to tell their own story from the beginning. Samar told them about herself and that she was from Pennsylvania, USA, and hailed from a medium-sized family. She had two other elder brothers with whom she spent her time quarrelling. She hated to be treated as the only girl in the family. She wanted always to be a rival for them, and now she wished she had the chance to go back to her normal life to fix all the matters with her brothers and never fight with them no matter what the reasons were because she missed them a lot. Her mother was a teacher in one of schools in Pennsylvania and always encouraged her to read, but Samar was lazy and hated reading books. This upset her mother; but after some time in Scaba, she promised herself that if she ever returned home, she would have read all the books in the world to please her mother. She missed her mother and father, who was working in the military, and wished her father had known the way to Scaba so that he could come along with the army to rescue her and the other children. She told them that on her ninth birthday she had seen two Moback animals in the garden of her house, and she liked them very much. She followed them to a deserted place and heard on the way someone saying to her, "Come to the party," and then suddenly, a tall man with a scary smile appeared. She tried to run away, but he called her, "Come and join the party."

She didn't understand what he meant because there was no party around, but suddenly a gathering of elegant people in formal evening wear, long gowns and tuxes, appeared and who looked and behaved as if they had been in that spot for a long time. When they appeared and disappeared again, she panicked and fainted; and when she regained consciousness, she was in a totally different place: Scaba.

Wang told them that he was from China and the only child in his family because the law in China prohibits families from having more than one child. He always wished that he had a brother or sister. His parents noticed his talent in drawing when he was three years old, so they registered him in a talent program. All he remembered was that he used to draw a lot. He used to draw portraits of his father and mother, and he loved in particular to draw his mother whom he loved greatly. He showed his friends a portrait of his parents, and they liked it very much. He told them that he missed his parents a lot and missed his homeland in Beijing where he used to be treated with love and favoritism.

"Nothing has changed; you are still special here," Samar said to comfort him.

He laughed but with a sigh in the heart. He told them that one day, all of a sudden, he had started to hear a strange voice that sounded real. It invited him to go to a certain place to attend a party. The sound kept calling him for three consecutive days, and gradually it became stronger and clearer. He went to the school's backyard, and there he saw a strange scary tall man who didn't look Chinese with some strange people attending a party in that open place. The tall man smiled to him and called him to join the party, but when Wang stood there to try to figure out what was going on, all the people disappeared except the tall man. Wang fainted, and when he woke up, he was there on the hill along with Samar and Kameel.

Lillian told them what happened to her and to her twin brother, Jamal, in detail and how their new neighbor was the one who kidnapped them after they had the same dream for three days.

They all realized that the one who kidnapped them was the same person, and it must be Solar, the magician. While they were chatting, they heard a noise outside the cell. They hurried to the door and looked through its holes to see Dushan and Sisami confronting the two guards. They shouted at Dushan, telling him to go away because the guards would kill them, but he didn't listen to that and started screaming, which made the two guards fall to the ground. Dushan shot them with a wouf that made them faint, and then he searched their pockets for the keys. When he found them and was about to open the jail, Falca appeared behind him.

"What do you think you are doing, prince?" Falca said.

Dushan and Sisami looked back in fear, and Dushan threw the keys to Sisami and started screaming, but that didn't affect Falca, who smiled and said, "Don't bother yourself doing that because I have a secret weapon against your screams."

Dushan shot him with a wouf, but Falca retaliated with a more powerful wouf. Dushan resisted Falca but was defeated by him because he was much stronger, but suddenly Falca sat down on the ground as if someone had forced him to do so in a way that made Falca puzzled.

"Not again," he said.

He tried to stand up, but something forced him to sit down again and again. Dushan rushed to the cell and opened its door, helping the kids who went out. Shaun was there, very tired and trying to control Falca who stood up after Shaun couldn't concentrate for a long time. Falca tried to shoot them with a wouf, but Wang was faster and released energy that blinded Falca temporarily. Samar took part in that and paralyzed him, and Lillian, in her part, pushed him to jail. Prince Dushan closed the door and ran away with the group.

They decided to go and release Filda, and on the way, Samar asked Dushan, "When did you learn to release that scream and use the wouf?"

"The princess taught me some rules, and Dashan was a good student," Sisami replied on his behalf.

They saw the king with Kameel in the royal hall and felt disappointed because they discovered that Kameel had betrayed them and that he was working for the king.

"I was about to tell you that," Sisami said.

He explained to them about the *Doom Book* and Kameel's betrayal to all the palace's children. They were disappointed and felt that their efforts had been in vain. Wang interrupted their silence by saying, "Let's run away. We have no time to waste; at least go and try to join the runaways."

"But what about Princess Filda?" asked Samar.

"We will come back for her," replied Lillian.

Dushan and Sisami refused to join them and run away through the secret tunnel that leads to outside the palace although the others begged them and promised them that they would come back to save the princess. They insisted on staying and rescuing the princess.

At the royal hall, the king searched for Falca and ordered the guards to bring him forth. He had decided to teach the kids a lesson that they would never forget after he felt that the rug was pulled from under his feet. This was especially the case with the revolting of the palace's kids and their new skills and power that they gained in Scaba, and with the running away of one of the palace's kids and the stealing of the *Doom Book* from the private suite of the king. All these things could make the king appear as a weak person, and the news, if leaked, would mean that he would lose his prestige and status. He made up his mind to kill the kids who stole the *Doom Book* and tried to open it to learn how to defeat the Makash. He said to Kameel.

"I will kill them all."

Kameel was frightened to hear that and felt sorry for collaborating with the king against his friends. The king laughed and said that he would make them an example for all human kids in Scaba who dreamed of running away.

Falca came after a while disappointed and heartbroken. He couldn't look the king in the eyes. The king looked at him in an investigative way and said, "I decided to kill all the children in jail in front of the children of Scaba and not only in front of the palace's children.

"This time there will be no grace period," he added. "Take them now to the city and hang them in front of all."

Falca lowered his head and said in a very low voice that could barely be heard, "They ran away, Your Majesty."

"What are you saying? I can't hear you," the king said.

He raised his head and looked at the king with fear and said, "The kids ran away, Your Majesty."

The king rose to his feet and pushed Falca hard with anger.

"How did they run away, loser?"

He waited for an explanation of how they managed to run away, but before Falca said anything, the king came very close to him and asked, "Are you with them, Falca? Are you a traitor?"

Falca denied the accusations and tried to defend himself by telling the king details of what had happened with them, which made the king nothing but more furious.

"It is Filda who taught them all those skills. I will kill her and her human friends," he added. "Damn all these Shakam; they turned the kids into weapons against me, but there will be no tolerance from now on."

He ordered Falca to put Dushan in jail with his mother and told him to summon all army leaders because he decided to go himself and eradicate the runaways and to make sure that nobody was left alive. He was sure that all children would join the runaways to have protection, so he decided to destroy them all.

"I want you to send the azoufa with the army."

Falca and the other guards felt afraid of that, and the king smiled triumphantly.

Dushan and Sisami were hiding behind one of the doors and listening to what was going on. One of the guards captured Dushan who tried to resist but in vain. They brought him inside the hall.

The king looked at Dushan and said, "I should have killed you while you were still in your mother's womb."

Dushan replied with a shrill scream, which made the king laugh.

"Your scream doesn't affect me, stupid."

Then he ordered the guards to take him and throw him in jail with his mother. Dushan winked at Sisami who ran to the secret passage.

Dushan was sent to his mother who hugged him and felt very happy to see him there with her. The king went to her and passed through the iron bar without being harmed. Although the princess knew that the king could touch iron without being affected by it, she was bewildered to see that for real in front of her eyes. He said to her after he saw her hugging her son, "Enjoy the company of your son because soon you will die with him."

She looked at him defiantly and said, "I am no longer afraid of your threats."

He looked at her furiously and said, "I will punish you hard after I kill all the runaways."

He went away to meet the army leaders. Kameel was still in the royal hall with the book in his hands. He was afraid and unaware of what to do next because what the king had said about killing all children made him restless and uneasy. He stood up lazily and went to work at the clothes store.

KIDS JOINING
THE GROUP

L illian led her small team—Samar, Wang, and Shaun—
through city streets until she reached the serpentine jungle
in a way that showed previous experience of the place.
Streets appeared familiar to her, as did the jungle because she
started warning them of the wild ferocious trees in the jungle.

"Have you been there before?" asked Samar.

Lillian didn't reply, and that was typical of her since she ran
away. She ordered them to stop and hide behind a tree. They
obeyed and started peeping from behind the tree to see a number of
wild hedgehogs. Lillian thought for a while, but the hedgehogs gave
her no choice as they attacked them and forced them to run away.
Lillian said to her friends that they should use their mental power
to protect themselves from the different hazards. They concentrated
on the hedgehogs for a while, and that made them collide with each
other randomly and stopped in their places. Some others lost their
sense of direction and ran into trees where they were devoured by
them at once.

After that the four kids went on toward the mountain. They
reached the cave and went into it, where Lillian warned them of
the fierce frogs and instructed them to cross to the other side and
to rest for a while to prepare themselves to face the frogs. They sat
under the thin trees for a while, and after a while Shaun fell asleep
whereas the others watched the lake carefully. It looked peaceful

and safe, which made Wang ask Lillian suspiciously, "Are you sure that there are wild frogs in that lake? It looks normal and quiet."

"Sure," Lillian replied. Wang stood up and said, "I will try my luck and swim to the other side."

"Please don't try it," Lillian begged him.

But he insisted and went forth, and the two girls followed him. Wang went into the lake very slowly and cautiously and waded through water. As he proceeded, the water became deeper and deeper until it covered his chest, so he said to Lillian and Samar, "Come with me. There are no wild frogs here. It is too shallow to host such hostile populations. Come down."

Samar looked at Lillian, approving what Wang had said, but no sooner had she put a foot in the water than a wild frog appeared and attacked Wang. It captured him with its long tongue, which made Samar retreat in panic. Wang screamed, "Help! Help!"

Lillian told Samar to paralyze the creature with her brainpower. Samar concentrated, and she managed to neutralize the frog's muscles, which made it release Wang, who fell into the water making a huge splash of water. Another two frogs emerged from the water and captured Lillian and Samar with their powerful tongues. Wang went back and used his power to blind the frog that was capturing Samar, and that made it move randomly and throw Samar away to the other side of the lake. The other frog that had been paralyzed by Samar was in wait there as it regained its power, so it captured Wang again. Lillian used her power and forced the frog to land her peacefully to the other side of the lake. Wang was still wrapped and twisted in the tongue of the unruly creature when the two other frogs came forth to have a share of the human flesh, but the frog defended its belonging and fought with them to eat him alone, but Samar and Lillian helped him again; Samar neutralized the frog, and Lillian forced it to throw it to the other bank of the lake. They ran away as fast as they could, trying to get out from that fearful jungle. No sooner had they gone out of the crater of the cave than they heard Shaun calling them.

"Hey, you, wait for me."

"Oh, Shaun, we totally forgot everything about him," said Samar.

"You should cross to the other side, my friend," Wang said to him from the other side of the lake.

"But how can I do it with these ugly frogs lurking in the lake?" Shaun wondered. Lillian promised to help him and said that he should trust them, but Shaun said, "You mean to trust my friends who were about to leave me alone?"

"We didn't mean to leave you here. Come on, be brave!" Samar said.

Shaun moved toward the lake where one of the frogs tried to attack with its tongue, but he evaded it and shouted to them, "How can you help me?"

"We will release our mental power, and you should pass quickly," Wang replied.

The kids agreed that each one should concentrate on a certain frog, and when Shaun noticed that his friends were controlling the place as one of the frogs got blinded, another was paralyzed, and the third was sent away to the extreme end of the lake, he crossed the lake very quickly in a way that astonished them all, including himself. When he reached his friends, they all went out of the cave quickly.

In the fugitives' new place, Jamal left what was in his hand and looked around as if he heard something. The Shakam and Moback wondered what he was looking at, and Medan asked him what happened, but he didn't respond and moved slowly as he was chasing or tracing something. The three enars, Medan, and Dana followed him.

"Lillian, my sister Lillian," he said.

He started running, followed by the enars and Dana; and when he reached a big tree, he found Lillian along with Samar, Wang, and Shaun.

"It was Jamal who was leading me all the way through the jungle," Lillian said to them.

Jamal was overexcited and happy to meet them; he hugged them and Shaun said, "I am the one who deciphered the puzzle and figured out that the couple meant in it was you and Lillian, and you are the ones who should open the book. I am a genius."

Jamal asked him about it, but Samar said to him, "We will tell you everything later. Now we are very tired, so please take us somewhere to rest."

Jamal told them to follow him, and while they were walking, they wondered when they saw the enar and asked him about them. He told them about the names that he gave to them and that he could telepathize with them.

✝ REUNION

T he children reached the assembly point of the army, which welcomed them. Jamal introduced them to Commander Medan, and they wondered how it was that he was still alive. Jamal told them it was a long story and he would tell it to them. When Samar saw Dana, she asked, "What is this girl doing here?"

Jamal told them that she was his companion during that entire dangerous trip. Dana promised to tell them her story later.

They all gathered around the kids to hear the latest news about the palace. They listened to them, and Medan felt proud and happy for Dushan and what he did, but he was afraid about the rest when he knew that the *Doom Book* that the kids captured was not the real one and that Kameel had turned out to be a traitor and that defeating the Makash would be impossible and they turned back to zero point.

They all felt disappointed except Jamal and Dana who started to encourage the rest and cheer them up. They said to everyone that they shouldn't rely on the book and should rather come up with a strategic plan to defeat the Makashan troops that would be sent by the king. Dana added to them that the children are a power that can be added to the Shakam.

They felt somehow enthusiastic and decided to go on with what they had started despite their despair and weakness. Medan cheered them up when he said to all, "If we have to die, let's die with honor defending the glory of our kingdom."

The Shakam loved the children who joined them and exchanged their knowledge and experience with them. The kids told them about humans, and the Shakam told them everything about the Shakam. There were many things about the Shakam that the kids didn't know; they only knew that the Shakam were lazy creatures that rely on human children in everything. They learned from them that the Shakam were the ones who founded and built Scaba, and they were the ones who developed life there in Scaba. They learned that the Shakam were active creatures and would die if they put their bodies and minds in a long period of rest from work for long times.

They hadn't enjoyed their enthusiasm for long before Sisami reached there with the news that the king was coming to them with a huge army and the azoufa. Medan felt very sad and desperate to hear that. They all knew how brave he was, and now his fear was making him angry. He sat by himself after he heard the news of the army and refused to speak to anyone; the rest of the Shakam felt desperate, and the Mobacks sang for defeat and death.

The kids also felt defeated and desperate.

"I will never see my parents again," Shaun said.

They all drowned into a state of matchless sorrow and gave themselves to defeat even before the battle started. They all lost any desire to fight. Even the enars shared in their big grief and gloominess.

Dana gave up for the first time since she came to Scaba, and she lost every hope that was lightening her soul and heart.

EXODUS OF BERMUDA
AND HIS FOLLOWERS

The king led a huge army to fight the fugitives. The army looked endless and contained three azoufa animals, the only three left alive as the others were all extinct. They were very huge animals that looked like ducks but with relatively smaller wings compared to its colossal size. They had small legs compared to their big bodies and they couldn't fly, but they were extremely powerful as they could spit stones and pebbles from their abdomens. They were viewed as perfect and had no points of weakness, and their favorite foods were the enars that they turned into stones inside their bellies. Each azoufa had twenty soldiers on its back to control and steer it all the way through. Another twenty Makash had to walk alongside these three animals to guide them from down. The king himself was riding a zebra striped in yellow and red, which stood out from all the other zebras that were ridden by other Makashan knights. Some troops in the army were riding elephants, and some others were on foot. A troop was up there on flying carpets. The army was well organized and headed by the king and Falca, who was riding a yellow zebra next to the king. All their shields and masks were made of wood. The army bypassed the jungle by turning around it to reach for the runaways, but scouts came forth to tell the king that they had changed their place, and they managed to locate their new place. The king didn't like that because changing the course of the army meant it would take longer to reach there and defeat them, but he had no other option.

DOOM'S BOOK

The next morning Sisimi returned from a reconnaissance mission and informed everyone about the coming army, and they all woke up in a desperate and gloomy state. Children were unaware of what to do and they looked at each other with silence drowning the whole place. Suddenly fourteen silhouettes appeared on the horizon, moving toward them. The kids and some Shakam moved ahead to identify them. Medan ordered the Shakam to be prepared, and the enars surrounded Jamal to protect him. When Sisami identified the shadows, he smiled, and before he uttered anything, the identity of the newcomers became clear to all of them. It was Filda, Dushan, Wajdbeer, and Shishar along with Kameel, city children, the disappeared children, and Kilsha. Kameel came forth with the book still in his hand. The children smiled and ran to receive the new guests. Medan was so excited and happy that he didn't know what to do or say. He waited for them, whereas the other children ran toward them. Princess Filda was very happy to see all the kids in one piece and hugged them all. Kameel stood aside filled with shame and disgrace for what he had done to them, and the palace children looked at him with admonition, but Filda told them that it was Kameel who helped her and Dushan out of jail, and so the kids welcomed him and forgave him. The kids took Filda to Commander Medan, and there she couldn't control her tears when she saw her husband still alive. She looked at him for a moment, and they smiled; then she ran toward him as he did to her. She noticed lameness, but that wasn't important at that moment. They hugged each other for a long time, and she said to him, "I missed you. They told me that you were a traitor and they killed you for that."

"I missed you more, but I thought you were dead."

Dushan got nearer to them, and when Medan saw him, he looked at Princess Filda, seeking a confirmation from her; and when she nodded her head, he took him in his arms while crying with joy, "I am your father. I am your father."

Dushan hugged him happily and said, "Dad, Dad."

Then he looked at his mother and said, "This is my father, Mom. This is my father."

Mother said yes with tears filling her eyes.

Wang asked Kameel, "How did you find us?"

"Princess Filda took us to this kind old doctor, and he brought us here," Kameel replied.

"Commander Medan sent someone to guide me through the way in case he needed my help," Wadajbeer said.

Sisami approached Kameel and asked him why he had changed his mind. He was silent for a moment, and then he apologized to everyone for what he had done and for his treason and selfishness. He told them that when the king refused to send him back home, he realized his mistake and decided to avenge the rights of all children in Scaba and that he replaced the fake book with the real one without the king knowing and kept it with him all the way back to Scaba. He was very afraid that he might be discovered by the king and all the efforts would be lost. It wasn't what the king said about his intention of killing children that made him sweat during the journey. He planned to help Filda to escape when a chance appeared, and when the king went out of the city with his army, he went with a group of children, whom he told about what had happened, and attacked the two guards at the gate of the prison and liberated Dushan and Filda. Most of the palace children took part in the attack including the young concert, dancers, clowns, and others. They attacked with chairs, mops, buckets, and whatever they found on their way and took the guards by surprise. Filda took the lead when she was out and guided the kids in the fighting against the Makash who came to the spot in great numbers. Dushan and Filda started shooting them with their woufs and evading their woufs, and when the children realized that it was impossible to defeat the Makash who outnumbered them, they suggested that Filda and her son run away because they were the only hope left for them to get away from Scaba.

Kameel gave the book to Jamal and Lillian who took it amid the attendants' great anticipation, and before they opened it, Kameel said to them hesitantly, "Jamal, Lillian . . . I want to apologize to both of you for another matter."

The twins looked at him and waited to hear an explanation amid attendants' deep silence.

"I was the one who told the king about your attempt to escape in your first night in Scaba," he said in a low voice.

"So it was you who caused them all that pain!" Samar shouted at him.

Kameel lowered his head, but the twins got nearer to him.

"We forgave you, Kameel," Lillian said.

"You don't have to feel ashamed of yourself. Consider it forgotten," Jamal added.

The twins then went into one of the caves to be alone with the book. Shaun said to everybody, "I was the one who solved the puzzle on the cover of the book."

But none of the kids and Shakams heard him because they were occupied with a much more important matter; the twins went into the cave in fear and reluctance. They didn't know what to do. Lillian wondered if there some certain rituals to be performed before opening the book, but Jamal told her he didn't think so. They read the sentence on the cover:

"A couple of opposite genders unite into unconditional love. Through their veins runs amalgamated blood and possessing invaluable duo of pearls."

Jamal said, "We are the couple of different genders, and our parents are the invaluable duo of pearls."

"And we love each other unconditionally with one blood running through our veins," Lillian said.

They sat next to each other and held the book together with all the fear in the world. They agreed to open the book after counting to three. "One, two, three," Jamal counted.

They opened the cover of the book, and a mild wind blew, so they went back a step and read what was inside:

You will read a fair book that will do no injustice to anyone. I wrote it to help the weak over the tyrant. You have the same blood and are not the same gender. Each one of you loves the other and feels their presence even if you are apart. Scaba doesn't give birth to twins, so you are the best judges. Take from the book what can help further your cause and leave what you feel is redundant. There are great secrets and hard consequences, and you, humans, don't like to live in Scaba but prefer to live in your world, so you are the best to act as assessors and referees. This is the responsibility that lies on your shoulders, so carry it out honestly and vigilantly.

Hercules

When they finished reading that introduction, they realized that they were about to read the most dangerous secrets on Scaba in the next pages, so they took a deep breath and moved to the next page to discover it was blank. The next one wasn't different; they turned pages until they reached page 7, where they read:

The azoufa's favorite food is the leaves of the untamed trees. Shakam have to cut these leaves with their woufs.

The twins felt disappointed because they were expecting to read about weapons and how to make them. They turned to the eighth, ninth, and tenth page, which were all blank.

On the eleventh page, they read:

The Makash's point of weakness is like their father's, and the azoufas' weakness is in their vision.

They didn't understand what the book meant by that and turned to the other pages to discover that they were all white and empty. They felt extremely disappointed. They opened it again and again, hoping to see something, but the result was the same, so they decided to go out and tell everyone about their findings.

The others were waiting impatiently for them, hoping to find something in the doom book to save their lives. Jamal and Lillian came out with pretentious unconvincing smiles, which made everyone afraid; they approached Medan and asked to meet with him and Filda alone. The commander agreed to that and went back with the kids to the cave. Jamal repeated what he had read in the book, which put Medan in great shock for moments, whereas Filda pondered over the words carefully and thought them over; then she smiled and said to Jamal, "With the new technique you taught to the Shakam and the priceless information in the book, we will for sure win over them."

They wondered what she meant by that and looked at each other with bewilderment, but she looked at them and said, "We have no time to waste. Let's go and prepare ourselves for war."

THE WAR

King Bermuda's army arrived at one of the open spaces, and to their surprise, they found that the runaways' army was there in wait for them. King Bermuda looked at his army proudly and knew that they had much more power than their enemies, especially because they had air force. He realized that it was impossible to be defeated with such a great power by the runaways no matter what they did to them because they were much fewer in number and much more disorganized and had no air force like that of the Shakam.

The king figured out that it was Jamal who warned them, but he wouldn't care about that, as he was confident of victory.

He ordered his army to stop, and when he saw the runaways' glass shields, he smiled sarcastically. They were all carrying glass shields and wearing eyeglasses, which were something weird and new in Scaban norms and nature. The king laughed because he knew how fragile glass was, and he laughed more when he saw that there were many weak Mobacks in the fugitives' army, which was supposedly good at nothing but chatting and singing. When he saw the three enars, he looked at General Falca and said, "It seems that these idiots have built an army from the weakest creatures of Scaba to face us."

The Moback were all wearing tiny sharp wooden spears on their foreheads, which looked like horns. They were headed by Sisami in the right side of the army and Kilsha in the left side, whereas the five palace kids were centered in the middle.

The fugitives' army was less than half of Bermuda's, but that didn't discourage them or frighten them.

The two armies stood against each other for a while, and then Bermuda sent his orders to his soldiers to shoot the fugitives with woufs. The knights' group started shooting their rays, but when they hit the glass shields, they bounced back to their shooters and injured them badly. The fugitives' army remained motionless at their places. King Bermuda couldn't believe what had happened to his army, so he ordered another group to shoot their woufs, and the same thing happened with them, making the king lose his temper.

He ordered soldiers to prepare the azoufa to throw stones at the other army, so the soldiers in charge brought one to the middle of the army and left the two others at either side of the army, and the three started throwing huge stones when the soldiers pulled their ropes backward forcefully. Stones fell on the runaways' army and broke the glass that covered the wooden shields. Many Shakams were killed because of that. The king then ordered the azoufa to stop and ordered the carpet troops to begin their attack. At that moment, King Medan looked at Jamal and gave him a signal to start his role. Jamal ordered the three enars to fly at the back of their the army while the carpet troops were heading toward the front and started shooting the runaways with the woufs from above and wounded a lot of them. The enars came from behind the runaways' army; some were carrying city children and some the disappeared children, and one of them was carrying Shishar. Some enars were also carrying very huge tree leaves with their teeth. The kids on the enars' backs attacked the carpet force whereas the enars that were carrying the leaves flew with them above the azoufa, which grew very tense and restless when they saw the enars dropping the leaves on the Makash army. They started to run here and there randomly chasing the leaves and crushing the Makash in their way. Chaos spread through the Makash army, and the army started fleeing from the huge azoufa. The enars competed the mission by blowing fire into the azoufas' eyes, which screamed of pain and fell to the ground.

Nearby, the kids started shooting the flying Makash with their woufs and dropping them from their carpets one by one; some other carpets were burned by the enar.

The Shakam soldiers took the fallen carpets and flew them in attack against Bermuda's army. Shishar got down from the enar's back and took one of the fallen carpets and flew it, managing to kill much of Bermuda's army.

Bermuda couldn't believe his eyes because he himself didn't know that the azoufa loved to eat leaves of untamed trees and that the enars could defeat them with blowing fire into their eyes. He didn't want to believe what he saw and shouted at Sikwel, ordering him to try the azoufa once again; but nothing could be done to them as they were in a terrible state, turning round and round and crushing soldiers each time they moved.

Medan ordered the Moback to attack. They were great in number, almost the same as the king's army and double the Medan army, but since they were small beautiful animals, nobody cared for them. Despite the chaos in the army, the king said to Falca, "When these Mobacks start their singing, I want you to attack the scoundrels and terminate them."

They thought that the Moback would sing, but to their surprise, they saw them going through the army's rows toward the army's rear. General Falca laughed seeing the Moback going in between his zebra's legs. The king's snake leaped gracefully and aggressively to chase the Moback. The king smiled for what his snake did. The king raised his hand to give the attack signal, but no sooner had he lowered his hand than he heard lots of screaming from behind. When he looked back, he saw his soldiers falling one by one. He was shocked to see that as there was nothing there to do such harm to them. He couldn't understand what was going on but later discovered that the Moback were the ones killing his soldiers by stabbing their heels with the small spears fixed on their heads. The king at that moment realized that the children, with the help of Kameel, had managed to capture the real book and read it. "Damn these children. I will destroy them," he said to himself.

Then he shouted at the top of his voice, "Crush these Mobacks and attack the fugitives."

The elephants tried to crush the Moback, but thanks to their agility and speed, they managed to evade them. They even succeeded in climbing to the top of the elephants and killing soldiers on their backs. At the same time, many of them were crushed under the elephant's feet.

The king's snake attacked Sisami and tried to sting him. She leaped here and there to evade it but was suddenly kicked by one of the Makash and fell down with severe pain. The snake approached him to kill him while one of the elephants was about to crush another Moback. Kilsha came quickly and pushed it from under the elephant's foot and took her place to seduce the snake to come to her. The snake saw her and jumped to attack her, but Kilsha jumped away, and the elephant crushed the snake instead. Sisami thanked Kilsha for saving her life.

The king got mad for the death of his snake and shouted at his soldiers to attack the other army. The two armies entangled with each other; Sikwel faced Filda and shot her with the Makashan wouf, but she protected herself with a small glass shield and reflected it to him. Samar then got closer to Sikwel and paralyzed him, whereas Wang blinded him, and Shaun made him fall down from his zebra; they all helped the princess, who shot him with a wouf and made him lose consciousness.

Falca, meanwhile, attacked Jamal and shot him with a wouf. Jamal surrounded himself with the aura. Medan was near him, and he threw a ray at Falca that dropped him down, but he didn't faint, and Medan had to face a number of Makashan soldiers. At that moment, Falca rose to his feet determined to kill Medan, but Dana noticed that from above the enar, so she went down fast with the enar and shot Falca with a wouf that hit his neck and made him faint. '

Bermuda was watching all this from afar and noticed that his army was losing, so he ordered the rest to withdraw.

All members of Medan's army rejoiced over the defeat of Bermuda and the withdrawal of his soldiers. The kids and the Shakam celebrated their victory and congratulated each other for it.

Medan, along with his wife and the children, went down to the battlefield to check the casualties. He ordered the arrest of the injured Makashans, and they all went back to their hideout.

Bermuda couldn't accept the defeat, and he met with what was left of his army to plan for the next step. They were a group of twenty Makash. He said to them, "The zero hour is tonight. We have no time to waste."

That evening, the Shakam and the children celebrated their victory; the Moback sang, and the kids danced and taught the Shakam how to dance in a joyful atmosphere. Lillian asked her brother, Jamal, "Do you think Bermuda ran away back to his palace?"

Jamal told her that he didn't know about it, but things would become clearer the next morning as Commander Medan had decided to attack the palace to retrieve rule for the Shakam and terminate Bermuda's tyranny.

While they were busy celebrating their victory, King Bermuda launched an attack with his small troop on the fugitives. He attacked the Shakam guards first and defeated them, and then they went inside the hideout unnoticed. Bermuda was disguised as a Shakam guard, and he went inside without being recognized by anyone. He planned to capture the other dazar, so he tried to locate the attendants and capture the nearest one to him. It was the unfortunate Filda, who was passing by, that fell in the hands of Bermuda. He controlled her with his sturdy hands and took the dazar out of his pocket, threatening to kill her if they didn't give him the other dazar. They were all taken by surprise, and his followers joined him for protection. The Shakams and the children stood perplexed and frightened, unsure of what to do. They all knew that the capture of the other dazar meant the end of the two worlds, so Filda shouted, "Don't listen to him! Don't give him the weapon. He will kill all of us if he gets it."

King Bermuda swore that he would kill her if they didn't give him the other dazar. Medan tried to attack him, but he pointed the dazar at him and forced him to freeze in his place. Dushan ran to help his mother, but Medan caught him in the right moment. When Wang released his mental power to blind the king, he simply said, "Your weak energy will not affect me."

He warned them of any attempts to rescue the princess and started laughing gloatingly when he saw their confusion.

"You thought you could defeat me. I don't care how many Makash you have killed; all I care for is to control Scaba and human land by getting the other dazar." Then he added, "Come on! Give it to me, or I will kill you all."

Kameel, meantime, was outside responding to the call of nature. When he returned inside from behind the king and saw what was happening, he came closer and pushed the king, saying, "This is for what you did to all the children."

The king fell down, but he shot Kameel with the dazar, and for a moment nobody could tell if Kameel was dead or just injured. At that moment, Medan attacked Bermuda with a lethal ray, but Bermuda retaliated with a ray from the dazar that neutralized Medan's ray. Medan had to block it with his glass-covered shield, which couldn't withstand the hard shot and broke down; and Medan fell to the ground, heavily injured.

Princess Filda went back and stood beside Jamal and the other children who formed a ring Commander Medan to protect him. The city children and the others started shooting the king's small followers with woufs. Princess Filda and Dushan shot at the king with their woufs, but he blocked their rays with the powerful dazar, which made the rays bounce back toward their shooters. At that moment, Jamal intervened very quickly and released his mental power and formed an aura to protect them. Jamal then took out the dazar that he had and tried to shoot with it, but the power released from it was very week and didn't hurt the surprised king at all. He shot back at Jamal who protected himself with the aura again but couldn't keep it up for a long time, and the dazar rays penetrated through to hit Jamal and throw him away, and the weapon fell out of his hand. Bermuda was about to run to take the dazar, but Sisami was faster, and he took it and gave it to Lillian who took it in turn and shot at the king with it, but again the power was very weak. Bermuda moved toward her to take the dazar. At the same time, Jamal, despite his injury, stood up and moved toward his sister, and they grabbed the dazar and pointed it with concentration. When they shot this time, it was so powerful that it threw Bermuda up in the air. Despite that, he stood up again and shot at Jamal and Lillian, who shot back at the same time. The two powers met for a short period of time, but the twins' power conquered Bermuda's. He dropped his dazar after his hand got burned, and Shaun picked it up.

Bermuda fell down in agony and pain, so they captured him and tied him up with ropes amid the kids and the Makash's rejoice and delight. They gave one dazar to Lillian and the other to Jamal, and when they all went to see Kameel, they found that he wasn't responding. They tried to wake him up but in vain.

Wajdbeer went closer to check him, and then he asked to transfer him to another place.

When Bermuda fell in the hands of the group, he felt very humiliated and weak. He lowered his head in shame, and Princess Filda said to him, "How do you betray the one who helped you? I told you that one day someone will come and defeat you."

"At last you fell in my hands, Bermuda, and soon your assistant Solar will too," Commander Medan said to him.

Jamal interrupted, saying, "Bermuda is not a Shakam."

They all were astonished to hear this from Jamal who explained by saying, "Bermuda, unfortunately, is a human being."

They couldn't believe him, but Jamal came closer to the king, who was trying at that moment to cover his face with his hands, and peeled off the Shakam mask off his face amid the attendants' surprise and astonishment.

"Bermuda is Solar," Jamal said.

Medan was taken by compete surprise and shouted, "You, I will kill you."

He was about to attack Solar, but Filda stopped him and said it was not the right time to do that. Then she asked Jamal, "How did you discover that, Jamal?"

Jamal explained to them that he suspected this matter when he noticed that Solar and the king never appeared at the same time or in the same place, and Bermuda was the only one among the Shakams and Makashans who was able to touch the iron without being hurt or burned. Also, he wasn't hurt at all by the power released from the kids and couldn't fly the carpet by himself, and his tail was immobile, unlike other Shakams'.

"Solar discovered the secret of Nafarit's hormone, which was intended to make humans shoot woufs, and he used it to have that power."

Filda praised Jamal and said to him, "We will postpone the trial of Bermuda—I mean, Solar—and the dishonest ones with him until we reach the palace."

CELEBRATIONS

D ecorations were fixed in the palace and in the city to celebrate the great victory and announce the end of tyranny. All pictures of Bermuda were taken off the street posts and buildings in the city. Also, fires were lit in the craters spread around the city using wood instead of enars.

Inhabitants of Scaba gathered at the palace to hear the declaration of independence and the end of tyranny.

Senior officials gathered at the royal hall; Princess Filda sat on the throne next to Medan; and their son, Dushan, sat on a smaller throne; and next to him sat Sisami and Kilsha. The city children and the palace children were standing in the middle of the hall with their elegant dresses and suits. Kameel was there with them, with his head bandaged and his hand carried in a splint. Shishar was also there in his stately army uniform along with his wife and children. Even the three enars attended the ceremony and stood next to their friend Jamal.

Jamal carried dazar's box with the two dazars in them, whereas his sister had the *Doom Book*. The twins approached the throne, and Jamal gave the box to the princess, and Lillian gave the book to Medan.

"We will keep this in a very safe place that nobody can reach," Filda said after she received the box.

Jamal got permission from the princess to say something, and when the princess allowed, he said, "I would like to thank you for understanding and helping us and to tell you that you are not to blame for the torture and slavery that we went through. You were enslaved just as we were, and I would like to apologize to you for any harm that our human race might have caused to you."

The princess thanked him for what he said, and at that moment Wajdbeer came in with his colorful grand clothes along with two Shakam children who were carrying two crowns put on two pillows. Filda and Medan stood up, and Wajdbeer took one of the two crowns and put it on the princess's head amid the applause and ovation of the attending crowd. Then he took the other crown and put it on Medan's head with the crowd's exciting shouting and clapping of hands.

"I present to you Queen Filda and King Medan," Wajdbeer said, and the crowd responded with warmer applause and shouting.

Wajdbeer then whispered something in Shishar's ears. Shishar smiled happily and proceeded to where the queen was standing and kneeled down and bowed his head. A Shakam boy went into the place carrying a flying carpet on a pillow. Queen Filda took the carpet and gave it to him.

"Take your carpet, General Shishar," she said.

The crowd clapped their hands and shouted slogans. His wife started weeping because of happiness and excitement.

The queen, king, and Prince Dushan then moved to the terrace that overlooked the big city square where the public was waiting impatiently for them. Adam stood close to Dana and hesitantly grabbed her hand; she grew confused for a moment, but then she looked back at him and put both of her hands into his.

The queen welcomed the crowd, which responded with a warmer welcome, and then she said, "My dear people, I want to convey to you the happy news of the victory of good over evil and the end of tyranny forever."

A chill of excitement rippled through the crowds, which started to move around, clap hands, and shout hysterically.

"We wouldn't have won without the help of these honest and loyal children," she added.

The crowds clapped their hands, and the queen said to the kids, "I want to personally apologize to them for the tyranny and enslavement they had been through, and I wish they can forgive us for that."

The kids rejoiced over that, and the children in the musical band started playing music. The Moback, headed by Sisami and Kilsha who were looking at each other in admiration, sang happily, and the children in the dancing band danced with the elephants. While on the royal terrace, King Medan danced with Queen Filda, Dana with Adam, Sara with Steven, Shaun with Samar, and Kameel with Lillian.

"Come on, intelligent man, let's dance together," Nora said to Jamal.

Jamal danced with Nora, Wang danced with Monika, and Wajdbeer with Nadia.

Steven said to Sara, "Do you know what I desire more than anything else in the world?" Sara lowered her head shyly because she thought she could guess the answer.

"What?" she asked.

"To know how the Moback can speak like human beings. I wish I can dissect them and discover their secret," he replied.

"What?" she asked angrily.

He smiled to her stupidly. Clowns moved around between crowds of Shakams and children, spreading an atmosphere of happiness everywhere in the place. Scaba celebrated its independence and victory for a week. Then all children went back to their world and families without losing their minds. Even those who had turned eighteen and were thrown in remote places retained their mental powers and went back to their families, who couldn't believe that their children were back to them after that long time of absence.

———∘◦⊶❁⊷◦∘———

THE TWINS' BIRTHDAY

A year had passed since the kids returned to their world. The twins' eleventh birthday was attended by their friends who were with them in Scaba, including Dany. They came from different parts of the world. Even Dushan attended the party and justified his unearthly appearance before the twins' parents by saying he was wearing a suit of an alien, as in masquerades. He brought Sisami and Kilsha over, who were constantly chased by Steven, desperate to know the secret behind their ability to talk like human beings.

They all watched the scene and laughed a lot. The kids enjoyed the party, and when the time came to extinguish the candles, the kids told the twins to wish for something special. The attendants stopped talking to give chance for the twins to wish, but instead all the children heard a voice that was repeated many times. They heard it clearly, but the elders attending the party didn't.

Come to the party . . . come to the party.

The kids looked at each other in amazement.